PATH OF EVIL
Concho Book Three

A.W. Hart

WOLFPACK
PUBLISHING
— EST 2013 —

WOLFPACK
PUBLISHING
— EST 2013 —

Text copyright © 2021 A.W. Hart
Special thanks to Charles Gramlich for his contribution to this novel.

Published by Wolfpack Publishing
5130 S. Fort Apache Road, 215-380
Las Vegas, NV 89148

Paperback IBSN 978-1-64734-794-9
eBook ISBN 978-1-64734-795-6
LCCN: 2021941740

PATH OF EVIL

CHAPTER 1

Someone banging on his back door snapped Texas Rang-
er Concho Ten-Wolves out of sleep. He sat up, fully alert. The lumi-
nescent numbers of his bedside clock revealed the time—3:49 AM.
People didn't visit this late at night unless something was wrong.

Dressed only in the loose gray boxers he slept in, Concho
rolled out of bed, his hand snatching up the loaded Colt Double
Eagle .45 lying next to the clock. He padded quickly through his
darkened trailer, which sat on the arid lands of the Texas Kickapoo tribal reservation, just on the Texas side of the Rio Grande
border with Mexico.

The banging stopped as the Ranger stepped into his small den.
He glanced out the narrow windows to either side of the back
door. Moonlight the color of cider painted the glass. Nothing
moved on his back steps.

"Who's there?" he called.

No answer.

"Who's there!" he called again, much louder.

No response came but he wasn't going to simply walk up to
the door to investigate. The door itself was fairly sturdy but the
walls and windows weren't. They wouldn't stop high-velocity
bullets if someone had an ambush in mind. Concho had plenty

of enemies. They'd sent killers after him before. He hadn't survived by being foolish.

As he was deciding what to do, more banging came. This time it was at his front door. Concho spun. Curiosity and caution turned to irritation. He didn't like games. At least not of this kind. The hammering continued as he stalked toward the sound. But now he heard a voice accompanying the banging—a loud, intoxicated murmuring. He recognized it. Flipping on the outside light, he yanked the door open with his left hand.

"Bearfoot!" he said. "What's going on?"

The Kickapoo man called Bearfoot stood at about five feet seven and weighed less than a hundred and fifty pounds. His long dark greasy hair hung to his shoulders. His stained yellow t-shirt stank of sweat. A pair of dirty black jeans encased his skinny legs and were emanating a faint hint of urine.

Bearfoot was an addict and a drunk and Concho didn't much like him. But he'd married Estrella Deer-Run, the daughter of a recently murdered Ben Deer-Run. Ben had once been chief of the Kickapoo tribal police here on the reservation. Concho had respected him and he respected Estrella.

"Help me!" Bearfoot said. His eyes glittered with fear and Concho automatically stepped aside so the man could enter.

"What's wrong?"

"Somethin'…" The man's breathing came fast. He belched, spilling the stale scent of whiskey and cigarettes into the air. "Somethin' after me."

Concho frowned. He studied his front yard under the outside light. Bearfoot's worn ten-speed bicycle rested awkwardly on its side at the base of the steps leading up to the trailer's door. Thirty feet beyond the steps sat the Dodge Ram 1500 pickup the Ranger was driving these days.

The moon cast enough light to reveal the truck and most of the yard. To the left stood a huge mesquite tree and a firepit bracketed by nylon lawn chairs. To the right grew a low row of bushes bordering the dirt road leading from the heart of the reservation out to Concho's trailer. He saw nothing unusual in the yard. He heard nothing, smelled nothing.

"What are you talking about?" he demanded.

Bearfoot turned to look out the door and would have fallen if Concho hadn't caught his arm to steady him.

"Somethin'," Bearfoot said, his voice slurring. "Heard it. Followin'. I was goin' home. But it…too close. Came here. Betta, betta lock the door. Please!"

Concho ignored the request. "Something or someone?" he asked.

Bearfoot wagged his head back and forth. "Not…not person. Off in the bushes 'long the road. Way too big, too fast, I don'….."

The drunkard moaned. He seemed close to panic.

"All right," Concho said to calm him.

He pushed the door shut and locked it, though most likely the skinny Kickapoo had imagined the whole thing. He and Estrella lived closer to the main reservation village than Concho. What he'd been doing out this far on the Rez wasn't clear but he'd obviously found a place to drink.

"Why did you knock on my back door first?" the lawman asked.

Bearfoot looked confused. He tried to focus but his left eye kept wandering. "I don'… I didn't. Too scared."

"I heard you."

"Not me," Bearfoot replied. He appeared to sober a touch as he realized what that meant.

Concho frowned again. It was improbable that two people would knock on his doors so close together in the middle of the night but he believed Bearfoot. About the knocking at least. He didn't know what to make of the "something big" chasing the man through the bushes along the road but it was barely possible a panther might have been stalking him. Sightings had been reported on the Rez.

"Okay," he said. "Stay inside! I'm going to have a look around."

"No! Don't go out there. It'll…get you."

"Stay inside and it won't get *you*! I'll be fine."

Bearfoot backed away, rubbing at his mouth. Concho turned into his bedroom. He tied back his long black hair, which was his most obvious Kickapoo feature. He'd gotten it and his facial structure from his mother; his father had been black and his skin reflected that ancestry. His father had also given him his broad shoulders and height. He stood four inches over six feet.

Pulling on jeans and a gray t-shirt, he slipped into his moccasins and stuffed his pockets with a couple of extra magazines for his Colt. *Someone* had banged on his back door and if it wasn't Bearfoot then their motives were suspicious. He wanted to be armed appropriately for whatever motives an enemy might have.

Plucking the keys to his Dodge off the ring by the door, he stepped outside and went quickly down the steps to his truck. The extended cab area of the pickup was loaded with gear, both police issue and other, non-standard materials. One such piece was a set of night-vision goggles like the ones he'd used in Afghanistan as an Army Ranger. He slipped them on.

The moonlit night grew texture, turned into a cold inferno of yellow-green. He scanned his surroundings. A wide-eared rabbit nibbled tender grass next to the prickly pear at the corner of his trailer. Something startled it away. A mouse darted a blazing streak from beside his firepit to under his house. Perhaps a hunting owl had scared the small creatures. But it made Concho uneasy.

It was October, and cool. A breeze tickled Concho's nostrils. He smelled the fresh green droppings of the rabbit. He smelled mesquite and juniper, and other natural scents. He couldn't hear anything except sounds birthed by the breeze.

Yet, gooseflesh from no normal chill rose suddenly across his body. Just a few nights ago, on one much like this, he'd stood in this yard next to Maria Morales, the woman he loved. She'd gone out to her car for some papers and had called to him in a frightened voice. He'd found her shaking from what she'd seen, though the thing she described made no rational sense—tall, vaguely human-shaped, with purple eyes.

Maria hadn't been the first to report such a sighting on the reservation. At least two other people had seen something similar in just the past week, specifically mentioning the purple eyes. And there'd been other odd events recently. He'd found an arrow on his doorstep, one of his own arrows he'd thought lost. Someone had brought it back to him—broken. And tonight, the mysterious knocking. It all added up to what his Kickapoo grandmother would have called "bad magic."

Concho had been telling himself since he was a teenager that he didn't believe in magic. He'd *never* been completely sure he was telling himself the truth and he'd become less sure with the events of recent days.

Neither on the night Maria had reported the "thing," nor the one where he'd found the broken arrow, had he seen, heard, or felt anything. Tonight was different. He still hadn't seen or heard it. Or smelled it. But he *felt* it.

Nearby. In the darkness. Someone or something watched him with strange eyes.

He'd had this feeling once before.

CHAPTER 2

The Hindu Kush, Afghanistan, 2010:
An hour before dawn.

Concho had been in position on this ridge for twenty min-
utes, crouched in a nest of boulders behind an M2HB heavy ma-
chine gun. Through his night-vision goggles, the dark sky flickered
green. Below the ridge, maybe a hundred yards ahead, half a dozen
mud hovels clung to the earth like ticks on a hound.

Years ago, a village had squatted here, filled with women and
children, with old men and their sons, with goats and chickens.
Now, only Afghan rebels occupied the place, the same ones who'd
attacked a convoy of American supply trucks yesterday. Concho's
Army Ranger unit had been taken up the trail. They hoped to
capture and interrogate but were prepared for violence.

To Concho's right ran a ravine and a stony path leading
directly into the throat of the enemy stronghold. Most of his
twelve-man ODA, Operation Detachment Alpha, crept along
that trail. On the ridge across the ravine, another Army machine
gunner waited along with Concho for any signal from their com-
mander to open fire.

These actions weren't unusual but something unusual interrupted them. From the mouth of the ravine, within spitting distance of the first hovel, a growl arose. It rose, and rose, like a monstrous steam kettle with the pressure building—until it became something else, a scream, a shriek, an echoing, hollow cry like a demon giving birth.

Gooseflesh stippled Concho's whole body. His finger tightened on the trigger of his .50 cal. He held his fire. He had no target, nothing he could see. Nothing he could smell.

Every dog in the Afghan encampment erupted in howls and barks. Men's voices lifted from among the hovels, shouting in Dari. Concho recognized a few words—"God, Devil, beast."

A dozen raiders poured out of the buildings below, waving torches and spotlights. These shone like pillars of flame under the light enhancement from his goggles. Many among the Afghans started shooting into the ravine. Whether they'd seen something threatening or just been spooked, Concho couldn't know. His ODA was in danger, though, pinned down in the narrow shooting gallery. Signal enough for him to open fire if he wanted to save their lives.

Concho pulled the trigger on his machine gun, held it down. The big .50 began to sputter. Hot brass sprayed away from the gun's ejection port, each one a winking jewel in the corner of his goggle-enhanced vision. A whirlwind of dust roiled in front of the barrel as the jacketed shells burned away into the night.

Bullets hammered into the clustered rebels, reaping them like a scythe on wheat. Another kind of scream sounded now, human screams. But not all the Afghans went down. Many dove for cover. Bullets began to ping and ricochet off the rocks near Concho. He ignored them. His friends were taking fire. He kept up his own barrage.

The second Army Ranger machine gunner opened up, too, and the men in the ravine began to return fire as well. Automatic weapons rattled like a hailstorm, interspersed with the pock, pock,

pock of small arms. Tracer rounds followed, floating through the night like lost souls.

Concho concentrated his fire on a window where muzzle flashes showed. The heavy slugs from his machine gun ate through the mud blocks making up the structure, crumbling them inward to open a hole in the side of the building. The window gunner fell silent but there must have been a fuel cache inside.

A breath of dragon fire puffed through the hole. An explosion followed, driving a piston of flame up through the roof. Darkness became incandescence. Concho closed his eyes against the brightness. When he opened them, two men were running from the building, screaming and engulfed in flame. The special forces Ranger swung the barrel of the M2HB after them and mercifully cut them down.

With no targets left, Concho released the trigger. A rattle of rocks sounded; a single brave raider came charging up the ridge toward his position. The man had a grenade in his hand and must have thought the Ranger's machine gun was empty. Concho showed him it wasn't. Half a dozen .50-caliber slugs turned the man into a sieve. He dropped his grenade as he fell; it went off, sending up a geyser of dirt and torn flesh.

Now, the machine gun finally rattled to empty. Light from the burning fuel cache began to dim; a cone of darker smoke twisted above it into the sky, like the face of Baal. The Ranger swung up the top cover of his gun, snapped in the first shell of the next ammo belt. After racking the slide twice, he was ready to resume shooting. But silence had fallen from the enemy stronghold.

A voice bellowed, "Hold your fire!" Concho recognized Russ Adelaide, his commander. He slid his hand away from the machine gun's trigger, flexed his fingers to loosen them.

Without much to burn in the desert, the flames died away among the hovels. Movement came from the ravine as Adelaide and the rest of the soldiers there worked forward. Cautiously, they entered the Afghan base. Concho watched, tracking with his gun barrel in case supporting fire was needed. It wasn't.

Then, a fresh wave of goosebumps lifted the skin on Concho's arms. The hair stood up at his nape. He shivered and spun around to face a presence at his back. His hands grasped the M4A1 carbine slung over his shoulder and brought it to bear.

Despite his night-vision goggles, he could see nothing but gravels and dirt and a few low bushes. He could hear nothing, smell nothing. But the darkness wasn't empty. The speed of his heartbeat and the brass taste of adrenaline in his mouth told him so.

He rose to a crouch, his gaze darting everywhere. From the direction of the Afghan encampment, Russ Adelaide called his name. He dared not respond, dared not tear any shred of attention away from the hidden thing watching him.

In the next instant, the presence disappeared, like a soap bubble popping. He stared a moment longer, while his heart calmed. He called out to Adelaide to say he was fine. Only then did he rise to his feet and re-shoulder his carbine. Hefting his machine gun, he went down the ridge to join his fellow troopers among the ruins and the dead.

***

Standing in his yard now on the Kickapoo reservation, Concho remembered speaking to his companions in the ODA about the strange cry they'd all heard just before the firefight. No one knew exactly what it was; no one had seen anything that could have made the sound.

One soldier claimed it was an injured dog. Others suggested it might have been a big cat, such as a caracal or a leopard. Such had been sighted in the Hindu Kush mountains which extended some five hundred miles across Afghanistan and included a vast area full of snow-capped peaks and deep hidden valleys.

Concho never believed it was a dog or a big cat. He didn't know what it had been but it was here again—tonight. Or, rather, something *very much like it* was here. In Afghanistan, faced with the unknown, he'd come close to freezing. He wouldn't this time.

Closing the door to his pickup, he began a systematic search of his yard for anything unusual, starting in the front. He kept his gun handy. The moon rode high above him, a sharp crescent in a sky full of the icicle points of stars.

His goggles amplified available light, turning the darkness into a green seascape, as if he were underwater. Nothing out of the ordinary swam by. Other than the scuffs in the dirt left by the passing of Bearfoot's bicycle, he found *no* sign of any invaders. He moved around to the back of the house. His body tensed, his fingers tightened on his Colt. Someone had crossed this yard to knock on his back door, someone who wanted to remain unknown.

Another thought began working in his mind. A few days ago, while seated around Concho's firepit, one of the tribal elders, Meskwaa, had told him a "power" had come to live on the reservation that should not be here and to stop it he'd have to remake a ceremonial wood and hide shield he'd been given at his naming ceremony at age sixteen. The shield had burned a month ago when some of his enemies set fire to his old trailer.

Admittedly, weird things had been happening on the Rez since the fire—the thing with the purple eyes being an outstanding example—but he couldn't believe the lost shield had anything to do with it. At least, he didn't want to believe it. He did intend to remake the shield, though. And he intended to use boar hide, just as Meskwaa had told him he should.

The question now was whether the knock at his back door tonight was merely someone messing with him or whether the action had a more mysterious and, perhaps, sinister origin.

At first, the backyard seemed as empty of a sign as the front. Behind the southern end of the trailer, a copse of mixed mesquite and juniper grew. The grove wasn't very thick, though, and he had practice studying it. He could have detected anything hiding among the trees. The rest of the yard mixed dirt with clumps of dry brown grass stretching down to the edge of an old arroyo running past the rear of his place.

As he moved over to the short set of stairs leading up to his back door, he spotted a thin smear of something on the bottom step. He took off his goggles and squatted down. Running a finger through the smear revealed it to be fresh mud. An oddity. It hadn't rained in three weeks. He knew of no mud anywhere nearby.

Putting his goggles back on, he walked over to the crumbled edge of the arroyo. The drop-off was about four feet, with no easy way to climb back out. He couldn't see any marks in the dirt wall where anyone or anything had tried climbing but an animal trail about fifteen yards down to his right could be used to access the arroyo by anyone who knew about it.

He stepped off the edge, dropped the few feet into the bottom of the arroyo. The ground where he landed was dry and flaky but a few weeds had sprouted since the last rain tore through. Their leaves would be yellow-green under normal light, indicating water in the earth beneath them.

He began searching along the bottom, working his way toward the animal trail he knew of, and soon discovered the likely source of the mud on his back steps. A low trough of dug out soil glistened wetly under the moon. No visible water filled it but he could smell the damp. Tracks covered the area around—deer and wild pig and coyote. The pigs had likely scooped the small wallow out with their snouts and tusks.

Wishing he'd brought a flashlight, he bent close to search for any human tracks. A low, huffing grunt from the darkness in front of him stabbed into his awareness. He jerked upright, every muscle thrumming with tension.

CHAPTER 3

A wild boar stood in the middle of the arroyo, glaring at Concho. The bristles covering its body were solid white. In his goggles, the beady eyes shone a pinkish color, suggesting it was an albino, unusual for such a beast. It was less than fifteen feet away. How had it gotten so close without him hearing it?

This wasn't the biggest boar he'd seen on the Rez but still probably weighed a good two hundred pounds. Its shovel-shaped snout was lowered; the four-inch tusks to either side of its mouth looked as sharp as scalpels.

Concho tried not to move. Feral hogs were notoriously foul-tempered, boars especially. Almost like a big cat, this boar picked up one front foot, pushed it forward and placed it down. It shook its head and snorted, sending spittle flying.

"Get out of here!" Concho snarled.

He lifted his gun, showed it to the creature. Many animals understood the threat of guns and pigs were very smart. This boar didn't care. It shook its head again and took another step forward.

If he'd faced a wolf, or even a mountain lion, he wouldn't have been overly worried with a .45 in his hands. But wild hogs had incredibly thick skulls in the front and the slope of their head could deflect bullets striking from an angle.

Ten-Wolves considered whether to risk a warning shot. Before he could, the boar ended the standoff. It charged, squealing with rage while its feet dug up the dry dirt of the arroyo and sent it spraying.

Concho swung his Colt to bear, took a two-handed grip and fired. The beast's head wove back and forth as it charged; the bullet struck the snout but only cut a slash through the flesh at one side. The animal squealed louder but kept coming.

Ten feet away. Five.

Concho raised his aim slightly, fired twice more. Both bullets struck, one almost straight between the eyes. The big boar squealed and staggered. It went down but in the next instant thrust back to its feet and lunged toward its foe, slashing at him with its saber-like teeth.

The lawman threw himself to the side, narrowly avoiding the swinging tusks, and emptied the rest of his clip into the beast just behind the shoulder—where the heart would be. The pig tried to swing back toward him but lost its balance and fell. Its legs thrashed and it lifted its head for a moment before it thumped dead back to earth.

Concho climbed to his feet, breathing hard. Slipping the emptied magazine out of his Colt, he reloaded, then said a quick prayer in Kickapoo for the boar's spirit. He would have preferred to avoid shooting it, but he knew several reservation families who could benefit from the meat it would provide once he'd dressed it. And he'd have the hide to make his shield. It was almost too fortuitous.

He'd need help getting the thing out of the arroyo, though. Bearfoot could be useful there. He turned back toward his house, taking the game trail up to the edge of his yard. He still moved cautiously, though he could no longer sense the strange presence he'd felt before. It had not been the boar. Of that, he was sure. Whatever it was, it had withdrawn for now.

As Concho opened the front door of his trailer and stepped inside, Bearfoot let out a hoot of fear. The skinny Kickapoo was hiding behind the couch. He'd sobered quite a bit.

"You're safe," the lawman said, pulling off his goggles.

"Was that you shooting? What at?"

"A feral boar. Had to kill it."

"Is that…what chased me?"

"Might have been. I need your help getting it out of the arroyo out back. I'll dress it, give the meat to some who can use it. Afterward, I'll give you and your bike a ride home in my truck."

Bearfoot stood up slowly. He panted for breath. "You sure you wanna go back out there?"

"Not going to let the meat go to waste. It's not our way."

Walking past the other man into his den, Concho laid his goggles on a table and took down the dual gun belt hanging from a weapon's rack on the wall. The belt already carried one Colt Double Eagle. He holstered the second one and buckled them on, then grabbed a flashlight. Bearfoot remained in the living room.

"Come on!" Concho called, exasperated.

He opened the back door and Bearfoot came reluctantly into the room. Only after the lawman beckoned demandingly with the flashlight did the other man follow him outside. They walked to the edge of the arroyo with Bearfoot jumping at every shadow. Concho flipped on the light, flashed it toward the spot where he'd killed the boar.

The hog's body had vanished.

***

Knowing he'd need daylight to properly track whoever or whatever had taken the dead boar, Concho drove Bearfoot and his bicycle home. They didn't talk. Bearfoot climbed out of the pickup in front of his darkened house. He glanced back at Concho as if hoping for a volunteer to stay and run interference with the skinny Kickapoo's wife, Estrella. Concho had no intention of doing so. Estrella had a very sharp tongue and it tended to cut bystanders about as much as it cut perpetrators.

A light came on in the house. Bearfoot sighed, then reluctantly pulled his bike out of the Dodge's bed and pushed it toward his front door. Concho quickly backed out of the driveway and hit the road for home. It was dawn by the time he arrived.

Since he couldn't be sure how long he might be on the trail, he fixed himself a hearty bacon and egg sandwich first. Next, he made up a small backpack with camping gear, jerky, and other travel foods. He drank his fill and added a canteen to his supplies, then dressed in heavy canvas trousers and replaced his moccasins with boots. The outside temperature hovered around fifty so he slipped on a long-sleeved blue cotton shirt.

Finally, he returned to his truck. He radioed Texas Ranger headquarters to say he wanted to take a couple of personal days after the conclusion of the bank robbery and kidnapping case he'd just finished. Next, he took out two weapons to carry in addition to his Colt Double Eagles and the big Bowie knife hanging with them on his belt. The first was a Remington .30-06 hunting rifle with a Leupold VX scope. It had enough punch to stop a bear and would surely do better against another boar than his .45.

The second weapon was a private one, a bow he'd carved from an Osage orange tree growing on the reservation. Buffalo horn and deer hide strengthened the bow. Many Kickapoo sacred symbols lay incised along its length.

With the bow came a deer-hide quiver of arrows made from ash and fletched with wild turkey feathers. He'd knapped the flint heads himself. The quiver was supposed to carry twelve arrows but currently held only ten. He'd used two recently in foiling the kidnapping and hadn't had a chance to make new ones.

The morning sun gleamed like a vast orange spotlight in a quickly clouding sky by the time Concho dropped down into the arroyo and approached the site where he'd killed the boar. He'd had a quick look around last night before taking Bearfoot home, just to make sure the animal hadn't crawled off a ways from where he'd shot it. It hadn't.

Now, he could see drag marks and thick black smears of dried, stinking blood in the dirt where something had pulled the carcass across the arroyo and up onto the far bank. Even this late in the year, a few flies buzzed around. A search for prints proved a waste, making it look as if they'd been deliberately obscured.

A mountain lion would have had the strength to drag the dead boar but they straddled their prey when they did so and he would have seen the tracks. A bear would also have such strength and might have pulled the boar behind it as it backed away from the scene but surely there would have been a few traces of its paw prints. Besides, he'd not seen a bear around in a long time.

This thief had to be human. But what was the purpose? Someone from the tribe might have heard his gunshots and come to investigate. If they found the boar, they wouldn't want it to go to waste. But he couldn't imagine any of them simply taking it. His house was right there. They would have come to ask if they could have the meat. And if they'd intended it for food, they would have likely gutted it where it lay, not carried the whole thing off.

The far bank of the arroyo wasn't as high as the one next to his trailer. Concho pulled himself up on it and went back to studying the ground. He frowned. The dead hog was no longer being dragged here. The Ranger could see droplets of its blood spattered across the ground but someone had to be carrying it. He still saw no footprints, only long, broad scuffs in the dirt.

Whoever had left this trail must have wrapped their shoes to keep from leaving clear prints. Why? He could still follow the trail easily enough, perhaps more easily than if he had to pick out the individual marks of feet. The only answer he could think of was that the perpetrator figured Concho would recognize something about his or her prints.

The trail ran clear and he began to trot along it, holding the 30-06 in his hands and leaving the bow slung across his back. His target had a several-hour lead on him but carrying a two-hundred-pound animal would slow them down.

Mid-morning came. The sun disappeared behind steadily

thickening clouds. The trail continued straight into the most unin-habited area of the reservation, through a rolling landscape of low hills and dells. A roadrunner paced him for a while. A few lizards scattered as he jogged past through an arid landscape of mesquite, juniper, prickly pear, and various dried grasses.

He found no sign that his target had stopped to rest and put the carcass down. His admiration rose for the man he tracked. He was a strong man himself but could not have carried such a weight this far without rest.

A wind began to prowl around him. It rushed like phantom horses across the land. A rumble in the distance brought his head up to see thick clouds building high in the west. Violet streaks of lightning tore them. This area of Texas had gone weeks without rain but it looked like it might come today. Just what he didn't need.

He reached the top of a small hill. Past winds had scoured it free of soil, leaving only a layer of scratched rock. The trail disappeared.

CHAPTER 4

Rain began to fall, only a patter at first but intensifying quickly. Concho crossed the area of bare stone to look for tracks beyond. He found none. This meant that the man he pursued had taken the opportunity to change direction. He located signs on both the east and west sides of the hill. One set had to be a fake trail, meant to throw off any pursuit. There'd be no time to find out before the rain washed the real trail away.

Reaching over a shoulder into his backpack, Concho drew out a tan poncho from his camping gear and pulled it on, draping it over his rifle as best he could. He had a decision to make: go home or pick a direction. To the west of the hill, the ground dipped and rose, and rose some more. To the east, the trend was downhill into a valley full of mesquite and acacia trees.

Concho had explored every inch of the reservation in his lifetime but he'd not been through this area since he was a kid. Traveling to the west would take him off the Rez and eventually onto the land of local ranchers. It was usually a long dry walk, much of it uphill. The eastern track would keep him on the Rez for a ways and take him across at least two creeks before he hit the distant highway. He turned east and begin trudging downhill.

Rain pelted him; thunder and lightning crashed all around.

Rivulets of water twisted past like snakes racing down a slope. With such little groundcover to soak up and slow the deluge, every step soon clogged his boots with runny mud. Any semblance of a trail to follow quickly became lost.

Keeping to a straight easterly line, Concho soon came to a bluff with a stand of juniper clustered at its base. Bending down, he crept under the sticky green limbs of the junipers, seeking some little relief from the soaking. Right up against the bluff, he found a semi-dry spot covered in a thick blanket of browned juniper needles. He pulled off his pack and sat, stoically bearing the discomfort of wet clothes.

A dull glint from the rock face of the bluff caught his attention. He scooted a little closer. An image about the size of a man's hand had been carefully scratched into the rock, in this place where no one would notice unless they crawled under the trees. It was the likeness of a wild pig with a spear piercing its neck. But this was no ancient petroglyph. The shine of the scraping indicated that it was new work. Maybe a few years old, maybe a little more or less.

The edges of the piece were beautifully outlined. The image's creator had taken their time and even used pigments to enhance their creation. The body of the pig had been blackened, perhaps by charcoal, with red ocher marking the point where the spear supposedly stabbed. The tusks were not pigmented but existed as scrapings themselves.

No teenager had defaced this stone on a lark. A mature artist had created the image. And they must have had a purpose. Was it sympathetic magic, meant to draw prey to the hunt? Or did it have some other meaning?

Concho scooted back from the bluff face to get a better look. His boots scraped away the covering of dried juniper needles, revealing a gleam of white buried in the sandy loam beneath.

Frowning, Ten-Wolves brushed more dirt away from the white material. *Bone!* He grasped it with his fingers and tugged it loose. A whole length of it came up out of the ground, long and pale and not very old. He held a humerus, what would be the upper arm bone in a human. But *was* it human? All four-legged animals had the same basic bone connected to their shoulder.

Setting the humerus aside, Concho pushed through the ground litter with his hands. More bones turned up. It looked like he'd uncovered a full skeleton. He found the skull; it stared at him with the dark pits of empty eyes.

So, the skeleton was human and, judging by the dented area above the left eye socket, a victim of murder.

***

The rain had stopped temporarily. The land remained drenched. A row of four-wheelers sat parked in the mud near the bluff where Concho Ten-Wolves had uncovered the skeleton. It was a little after three in the afternoon and growing colder under the gray sky.

As soon as he'd found the bones, Concho had postponed his search for whoever had stolen the boar from the arroyo out back of his house. With no cell phone service in the area, he'd returned home as quickly as he could to report his find to Roberto Echabarri, the head of the Kickapoo Traditional Tribe of Texas (KTTT) police force.

Several men and women of the KTTT worked in an organized fashion around the area of the bluff, sifting for clues. Concho and Echabarri stood over an unzipped body bag where the recovered skeleton had been laid out. As far as Concho could tell, every bone was there, including the humerus he'd first pulled up.

"What do you think?" Echabarri asked. "Man or woman?"

"Woman, I figure," Concho said. "Looks like they were only about 5'2".

"Probably," Echabarri agreed. "Could be a child, though."

"Possible. I imagine the coroner will be able to tell us more."

"You reckon they're Kickapoo?"

"Out here?" Concho replied, gesturing around at the reservation, "I'd say so. You know of anyone who's gone missing? I don't think these bones are all that old. Could be a few months. Maybe a few years."

Echabarri took off the gray Stetson he'd taken to wearing and wiped his forehead with the back of a hand. He was only twenty-seven, very young to be a Chief of Police, but Concho thought he was doing an excellent job.

"No reports since I've taken over," he said. "But it's only been a handful of months. I've been slowly going through Ben Deer-Run's files, too. Nothing about any missing person so far, but there are a lot more files to look at. The problem is, many members of the tribe also have homes down in Nacimiento, Mexico. People come and go across the border all the time. Sometimes they go and stay. No one keeps any records as far as I know."

"The elders might know," Concho said. "Or talk to Melissa Nolan at the Lucky Eagle. Our casino manager has a mind for remembering people."

Echabarri nodded. "I'll do that." He glanced up at the sky which looked to be building toward a resumption of the rain. "But maybe we should head back."

Concho was about to agree when a voice called out excitedly. "Sheriff! Ten-Wolves!"

A KTTT deputy named Arturo Ramon stood near the stand of juniper where Concho had taken shelter before finding the skeleton. He'd been cutting some of it back with a machete, and now he gestured wildly for his chief and the Texas Ranger to join him. They did so.

Arturo's face was gray, his lips reddened by rain and emotion. He pulled back some tree limbs where he'd been hacking, revealing the deepest, darkest heart of the small grove. A second skeleton revealed itself. It had been lifted a few inches up off the ground by the growth of the juniper shoots piercing its rib cage.

It was tiny, no more than an infant. The miniature skull, smaller than Concho's fist, seemed to accuse the world. Who could blame it?

CHAPTER 5

Further searching around the rocky bluff and the stand of juniper revealed no other bodies. The two skeletons were loaded onto a four-wheeler and driven off by one of the deputies. The Kickapoo reservation sat some eight miles southeast of the town of Eagle Pass, Texas. Both were part of Maverick County. The bones would be taken to the county coroner.

Concho and Roberto Echabarri remained behind as his deputies left the scene. The rain had not returned yet, but the clouds hung on and the already dark sky began to darken further toward evening.

"One thing I wonder about," Echabarri said. "Those skeletons don't look very old to me either, so how come they're *just* bones. In a generally dry area like this, you'd think at least some of the skin and hair and ligaments would be left. This is the kind of place you find desert mummies."

Concho nodded. "Agreed. Which is why I think the flesh was actually removed from those skeletons before they were placed here."

"On purpose?"

"Yeah. I don't see any other explanation."

"But why?"

Concho shrugged. He explained to the Kickapoo police chief

why he'd been out in this area in the first place. He'd let the other deputies think he'd been hunting which was true, in a way, but certainly not the complete story.

"So, you trailed this mystery pig thief to here?" Echabarri asked. "You think he had something to do with the bodies?"

"I lost the trail before I found the bodies. No way to connect the man I followed with them. It's suspicious, though. I guess I'm working around a hunch that the pig thief, the thing with purple eyes, and the skeletons are all connected in some fashion I can't yet see. By the way, what's the latest on missing animals here on the Rez?"

Echabarri had relayed the first sighting of the purple-eyed mystery creature to the Ranger and he'd also indicated several tribal members who'd reported missing cats and cattle and other animals. A man named George Night-Run had lost a cow and, during the search for it, he'd discovered a slaughtered feral hog hanging up in his barn. Concho had seen the hog himself and noted how some of the internal organs had been removed. George and his son had also seen the thing with the purple eyes near the barn.

"Actually had another missing animal report just this morning," the police chief answered. "Sam Whiteheart came in. Said his wolfhound, Mahkwa, had been gone a couple of days. He was pretty angry about it. Wants me to put it at the top of my list of things to do."

"Sounds like Sam. He lives over near George Night-Run, doesn't he?"

"Yeah."

Sam and George were both farmers. Sam sold vegetables directly out of his gardens to many, both on the reservation and off. George raised cattle and grew his own hay to feed them. Sam's wolfhound, Mahkwa, was big and black-furred which had probably earned him his name, a word meaning "bear" in the Kickapoo tongue.

"Does George still think he and his son saw a Chupacabra over by his barn?" Concho asked.

"He does. And he's telling others about it. I'm hearing talk about 'dark magic,' too. It's beginning to worry me."

"I understand. Rumors like that spread fast. Next thing you know, someone is getting blamed for being a witch."

"And maybe getting shot!"

"We'll have to make sure it doesn't happen here." Concho slapped Echabarri on the shoulder. "Since we've found these skeletons and it looks like murder, I'll be officially assigned to the case. You and I are going to be working closely together for the foreseeable future."

"Good. I'll appreciate the help. So, what do we do first?"

"Ben Deer-Run's old files, I guess. You see if he had any reports of missing people. I've got some things to do too before we hear from the coroner. Let's get home before it rains again. I'm wet enough from the previous downpour to last me."

***

Because every arroyo, stream, and rivulet on the Rez ran brimful from the rain, Echabarri and Concho took a roundabout route back to Ten-Wolves' trailer. The expedition to retrieve the skeletons had been mounted from there but by the time the two officers arrived, the only vehicles remaining were Concho's Dodge Ram and Echabarri's white SUV with the emblem of the Kickapoo Tribal Police emblazoned on the side.

Concho helped Echabarri load the four-wheeler onto the trailer behind the SUV, then watched the chief pull out of his yard on the way back to his office. A deep dusk had fallen with the light rapidly fading. The clouds meant very little moon tonight.

Concho stepped into his trailer. It was cold and dark and felt strange and lonely to him after the events of the day. He flipped on more lights than he needed and turned on the heater for the first time this fall.

Pulling out his phone, he thought about giving Maria Morales a call. But she'd gone into Dallas for some mall managers' convention. He didn't want to bother her. Setting the phone on his counter, he was taking the makings of a late evening breakfast out of his fridge when Maria called him.

"Hey!" he said as he answered. "Was just thinking of you. It's great to hear your voice."

"Yours too," Maria said. "Wish I was home. I'd like to see you."

"Same here. More than you know. How's the convention going?"

"Doesn't really start till tomorrow. I'm just settling into the hotel. How are you doing?"

"Looks like I've got another case. A weird one this time." He told her about the skeletons, though he didn't give her all the details about finding them.

Maria verbally winced when he mentioned the infant. "Always so hard to hear about things like that."

"Yeah."

Maria hesitated, then said, "Harder to actually see them. Are you OK?"

"I will be. When will you be home?"

"Not till Sunday evening. Probably late. But I'll let you know."

"Good."

"Guess I better go," Maria said. "The hotel restaurant closes pretty soon. I need to grab a bite to eat."

"OK. I'm just getting ready to eat here, too."

Maria's voice sank an octave as she whispered over the phone line. "Make sure you do. I want you to have plenty of energy when I get home."

Concho felt his face grow hot. "Pretty cruel to tease me when you're out of reach."

Maria chuckled. "Wouldn't want you to forget me."

"That seems unlikely."

They shared a few more words before Maria disconnected.

Neither said anything about "love" but the feeling hung in the air between them.

The Ranger was exhausted. He'd gotten up before dawn and lived through a strenuous day. He ate and tried to read for a while but soon gave it up and went to bed. His dreams were full of disturbing visions he couldn't recall in the morning.

CHAPTER 6

Concho awoke at his usual 6:00 AM. He'd slept ten hours, though it didn't feel like it. Something seemed off. He realized the problem when he stepped outside for a breath of the crisp morning air. He found his gaze drawn to his firepit, to the lawn chairs clustered there beneath the big mesquite. All three chairs sat empty.

Meskwaa, he thought.

Meskwaa, whose name meant "Red" in the Kickapoo tongue, was a tribal elder, one of Concho's oldest supporters on the reservation, both in age and in time served as a friend. He was also a medicine man, a Naataineniiha. He had visions, sometimes confusing but often helpful. Lately, every time the lawman felt troubled, Meskwaa had shown up sitting in one of his lawn chairs to help him get perspective. After yesterday's unpleasant experiences, the medicine man's absence this morning left the Ranger feeling discomfited.

His restless mood drove him back inside to get dressed in his typical work uniform: boots, new jeans, and a long-sleeved white cotton shirt over a sleeveless black tee. After grabbing some jerky for the road and buckling on his twin Colts, he headed to his truck. A radio call to Texas Ranger headquarters let them know about the skeletons and that he was investigating. He then took the road to Meskwaa's place.

Like Concho, Meskwaa lived along a dirt road outside and isolated from the primary cluster of buildings known as Kickapoo
Village, which was where the reservation police station, daycare,
and most of the stores and homes were located. The elder had a
small trailer, shabby and worn, but spent much of his time in a
wickiup, the traditional lodge of the Kickapoo people.

Wickiups were built from posts of juniper or desert willow covered with walls of sotol stalks and cut saplings bound together with
"pita" twine, which was made with fibers drawn from the maguey
plant. The roofs were constructed from mats of river cane and
cattails, and the floor of tamped down dirt was kept neatly swept.

Traditionally, the Kickapoo built four types of huts, summer,
winter, cook, and menstrual. The summer house was the largest
and. in the Texas climate, Meskwaa kept the summer house all year
round. Inside was a space of about two hundred and forty square
feet which reached to about six feet high along the centerline.

Wickiups had no windows and didn't need a smoke hole because they got plenty of ventilation due to the loose construction
of the sotol stalks. Most had a porch, called a "ramada," at the
front, which was open on three sides and had a long bench or two
for sitting, or for sleeping on in good weather. Meskwaa always
spent a lot of time on his ramada.

Concho tried the wickiup first. A dead gnat floated in the water
bucket sitting on the porch. Not a good sign. The colorful blanket over the doorway hung stiff and cold. No response came to
a shout. Though it would be a grievous breach of politeness under normal circumstances, Concho pulled back the blanket and
slipped inside the wickiup without an invite. The single-room
dwelling stood empty, the fire pit dark. He checked the ashes in
the pit; they looked to be at least a couple of days old.

Leaving the wickiup, the Ranger walked over to the trailer
and knocked on the door. The windows showed no light and
only hollow echoes responded to his knocking. He tried the

doorknob, found it unlocked.

Yesterday's rain had passed and the day was warmer and full of sun. Meskwaa might well just be away from home, perhaps hunting or fishing, or gathering plants, or merely wandering—as he did sometimes. He kept to no one's timeline. But, all the odd happenings lately had Concho on edge and he was worried. Breaking tradition again, he stepped into the trailer. He trusted the old medicine man would forgive his trespass if he were wrong.

Meskwaa's trailer was much smaller than Concho's. It mainly consisted of three rooms, the living room/workroom—where Concho stood—a bedroom with a small closed-off bathroom at the other end, and a tiny kitchen/dining area in the middle.

The living area was cluttered, but clean and organized. The linoleum floor had been recently swept. Piles of books and clothing and various medicine items such as feathers and stones and herbs each had their place. A few motes of dust spun in the light from the windows. In one corner, a spider had spun a web. Not unusual. Concho had never seen Meskwaa kill an insect other than mosquitoes or biting flies. He rather liked having spiders in the house. He said they kept down the actual pests.

The air made a stew of smells—leather and grease, freshly cut antlers and cured hides, wood polish and juniper and sawdust, the scent of various flowers and plants. Only one smell seemed out of place, something very faint but acrid and unpleasant. It *wasn't* the smell of death which brought a sense of relief. Nor was it the smell of cigarettes. Though Meskwaa chain-smoked, he didn't light up in his trailer.

Concho started through the living room in search of the out-of-place scent, weaving around a book pile that threatened to topple at a heavy step. A soft rustle came from the bedroom area.

Concho paused. "Meskwaa!" he called.

Footsteps exploded from the other room. Concho heard the rattle of the back door and rushed toward the sound. A wide, door-less opening connected the living area with the kitchen and dining room. As Concho crossed that threshold, he glimpsed a dark-clad figure jerking open the back door and hurtling through. It wasn't Meskwaa.

The Ranger got the impression of youth, and of long, dark hair flying. A package lay tucked under one arm; a ski mask had been pulled over the head. Concho lunged in pursuit. The door slammed almost in his face. Footsteps banged down the trailer's back steps into the yard. Concho jerked the door open and leaped out. The thief, or whatever he was, had a lead of only a few steps. Concho thought he could catch him.

Splinters of fragmented oak railing sprayed suddenly over Concho's hand. The high-pitched crack of a gunshot followed. Meskwaa's place was well watered by a nearby spring. A grove of hardwoods grew only forty yards from his back door and someone had shot at him from that grove.

Concho ducked automatically, then threw himself back through the door into Meskwaa's trailer. A second gunshot smacked the door frame over his head. He rolled to one side, drawing his right-hand Colt. By the time he had a chance to glance out into the yard, the dark-haired thief had disappeared into the trees.

Concho's main concern was for Meskwaa. Had the thief been something more than a thief? Was Meskwaa lying hurt or dead somewhere in the house? Pushing to his feet, he rushed the few steps into his friend's bedroom. The old medicine man wasn't there, nor in the bathroom or closet. The rank smell he'd detected still lingered and he realized it was probably some kind of hair grease. The thief must have worn it.

A quick examination of the whole house revealed no sign of the older man. Concho called KTTT police headquarters to request backup, then slipped cautiously out the front of the trailer and went to his truck. After throwing on his body armor, he started the Dodge. Swinging the vehicle around the wickiup, he plowed into the backyard toward the trees.

No shots flew his way and he pulled to a stop as he reached the tree line and leaped out with one pistol drawn. Sirens wailed in the distance—help coming—but a quick circuit through the trees led him to the point where the shooter had hidden.

Leaf clutter had been trampled into mud. Four-wheeler tracks led away from the site. He found two sets of tennis shoe tracks. These were distorted in the mucky ground but he got a few photos with his phone.

A wink of brass led him to a shell casing for a .22 rifle. Such guns were common on the Rez, although you wouldn't think anyone who expected to shoot at a human being would bring along such a small-caliber weapon.

The same odor of hair grease he'd detected in the house hung in the air here. But more striking was the scent lingering on the leaves near where the shooter had stood—jasmine and rose. Somebody's perfume.

CHAPTER 7

After briefing Echabarri and two of his deputies on the situation and pointing out the shell casing and footprints of the perpetrators, Concho headed back into Kickapoo village. He drove to John Gray-Dove's auto repair shop, barely a hundred yards down the road from the police station.

The big Kickapoo lawman parked next to the Ford F-150 he would normally be driving and which he actually owned. The Dodge Ram he currently drove was only a loaner from the Maverick County Sheriff's office. The Ford had been shot halfway to shreds in a recent ambush on the road by rogue bikers. Gray-Dove worked to repair it.

John Gray-Dove's shop was a metal and tin building open at the front. He had three stalls for automobiles, only one of which was in use at present. A rust bucket El Camino stood up on jacks in one stall. The sound of tinkering came from under the vehicle and Gray-Dove's booted feet poked out.

The mechanic heard footsteps approaching and called out, "Who needs me?"

"It's Ten-Wolves," Concho replied. "I was over this way and thought I might check on my truck."

Gray-Dove lay on a creeper seat under the El Camino. He

pushed his way out and glanced up at Concho. The man's short hair still gleamed a glossy black, despite approaching forty. His eyes, though, were almost a gray color, a family trait that had contributed to their name.

Gray-Dove stretched out his hand and the Ranger grasped it and pulled him to his feet. John tucked the wrench he held into a pocket of his grease-stained army-green coveralls and wiped his hands on a rag dirtier than himself.

"Ordered a part," the mechanic said. "Take a couple of days. Ready no later than Monday!"

"Gotcha. You mind if I use your workshop this morning?"

"Just don't hurt it."

"I promise."

Gray-Dove's face creased into a frown as he studied Concho. "You OK?"

"Drove over to Meskwaa's this morning. He's not there but someone had broken into his house. I'm a little worried."

Gray-Dove nodded, but said, "Meskwaa may be old but he's the most dangerous man on the Rez. Present company *not* excluded."

"You're right," Concho said. "He's probably just off on a wander. But I'll feel better when I see him again."

"Course," the mechanic said. "Help yourself to the workshop. Unless," he gestured at the El Camino, "you want to help get this wreck of a car running again."

Concho grinned. "I'll leave the miracle work to you."

***

John Gray-Dove was good with his hands. In addition to his auto repair work, he also built furniture and had a woodworking shop loaded with the tools of the trade, from belt sanders, lathes, and drills, to hammers and wood files. Concho borrowed his shop whenever he needed to make more arrows. And he'd use it now to start on the shield he'd promised Meskwaa he'd make. Maybe that would help ease his worry about his friend.

Gray-Dove had provided Concho with his own shelf in the shop. The Ranger pulled out a big plastic bin and opened it. Inside rested a dozen arrow shafts made from ash, each twenty-nine inches long. He'd already polished and balanced them, which required close work with a piece of sandstone to take off any knots or smooth out any bends.

He'd also cut a notch in the front of the shafts for setting arrow points. Originally, he'd made all his arrowheads from flint, a common material and one used by his ancestors. Recently, though, Meskwaa had provided him with some chunks of obsidian given to the medicine man by a Mexican Kickapoo tribesman. Concho had already knapped several obsidian heads and thought he'd use these on the two arrows he planned to make today.

Knapping arrowheads was a time-consuming process and took considerable effort to master. Concho had learned it from Meskwaa as a child. A year ago, he'd taught it to John Gray-Dove, who'd proven a quick study and was at least as good as the Ranger now, if not better. Part of it might have had to do with Gray-Dove's smaller hands and thinner fingers.

To knap an arrowhead, one used various bone or wooden tools to break off a suitable flake from a lump of flint or obsidian and then one carefully shaped the piece to keep it sharp and balanced. The base of the arrowhead was notched to fit into the tip of the arrow and set using glue.

Early Native American tribes had typically made the glue from rendering the hooves of buffalo or horses but many stronger adhesives were available today and Concho used one he'd purchased specifically for arrow work. He first filled the notch in the arrow shaft with glue, then seated the head firmly. Pulling a thin roll of copper wire out of his storage container, he made several tight turns with it around the notch to hold everything steady.

Setting the arrows aside to dry, he went to work on the fletching. Eagle and hawk feathers made the traditional fletching for arrows but both were illegal to hunt these days. Concho didn't mind. He'd rather see such birds in wild flight than adhere to that tradition. Wild turkey flight feathers worked just as well, although he'd also used goose and buzzard feathers. For the best balance on the fletching, he'd found it necessary to use three feathers from the same wing of the bird.

Stripping the fletching feathers down involved using an extremely sharp blade—he used a scalpel—to trim the rib of the feather to razor thinness. He often had to shave the feathers themselves slightly to get them even, but once he had them down to the desired shape and length—about six inches—he used a wooden fletching jig Gray-Dove had made for him to attach the feathers to the arrow shafts. The jig acted much like a vice grip to hold the glue-coated bottom strip of the feather to the wood until a bond formed.

While the arrows continued to dry and set, Concho opened a second bin on his shelf and took out some willow reeds. Such reeds were great for making baskets but his fingers were a little thick for such delicate weaving. Instead, he began to work the flexible willow into a wooden base over which he'd stretch hide to form the shield he wanted to create.

Originally, two kinds of shields had been commonly made—war shields and medicine shields. War shields needed a much stronger base than willow reeds and would be constructed from several layers of hide. Certainly, such shields would not stop high-velocity modern bullets but they'd been used in history to successfully block arrows and musket balls. The medicine shield was much lighter, meant for protection against spiritual attacks rather than physical ones. Both types would be painted with appropriate symbols.

Meskwaa had told Concho he should use boar hide for the face of the shield and he'd planned to use the hide from the boar he'd been forced to kill in the arroyo out back of his house. That was no longer possible but he'd figure out something.

Morning fled away while Concho worked. He'd just finished gluing the base pieces of the shield together when his phone rang. He took it out, saw Echabarri calling, and immediately answered.

"Any sign of Meskwaa?" he asked.

"Afraid not. I hope he's all right. But I just got a call from the coroner. He's got a report for us on the skeletons and wants to see us. I'm on my way to my office. Can you swing by and pick me up?"

"Will do. See you in about ten."

After hanging up, Concho put his shield work away and cleaned up any mess he'd left. Taking the two new arrows, he carried them with him to his truck and headed for KTTT police headquarters.

CHAPTER 8

A little after two in the afternoon, Concho pulled into the parking lot of the Maverick County Coroner's office. Roberto Echabarri rode in the passenger seat. Only a few vehicles sat parked in front of the one-story, L-shaped building at 1995 Williams Street in Eagle Pass.

The current coroner was Earl Blake. Neither Concho nor Echabarri had ever met him, though they'd seen photographs. Rumors claimed Blake was a bit of a curmudgeon. Concho generally got along with such types; he'd probably be called the same when older.

Blake himself greeted them as they came through the door. He was a heavy-set man, mostly bald, in his late fifties. He stood near a counter to the right of the entrance, filling a glass beaker from a coffeepot. He raised it to acknowledge them but took a long sip before speaking.

"Sheriff and Texas Ranger," Blake finally said. "My cup runneth over."

Echabarri introduced himself and Concho, then added, "I talked to you earlier about the skeletons brought in yesterday afternoon."

"Yes," Blake said. "I know perfectly well who you are. Come

on back to my office and I'll give you what I've got so far. Grab yourself a cup of coffee if you want. It's godawful but it'll keep your arteries from closing up."

"Thanks, but we're good," Echabarri said.

Blake shrugged. He turned down a hallway toward the back of the building. No one else seemed to be around. Blake entered the first door on the right and moved around to sit behind a desk cluttered with papers, various writing instruments, and a few weighty reference tomes. Shelves on the wall behind him held many more books while the wall to his right stood lined with rows of tan filing cabinets.

Two chairs sat in front of Blake's desk. Both looked…unsturdy. At six feet four and better than two hundred and sixty pounds, Concho needed sturdy. He chose the soundest looking of the chairs and eased his way into it. Echabarri took the other.

Blake studied them, then picked up a sheet of paper off his desk. He didn't appear to need it, since he didn't bother to glance at it as he spoke.

"The larger skeleton is definitely female. Probably around eighteen. Maybe a year younger or older. About five-two in height. The smaller skeleton is not an infant."

"What?" Echabarri asked.

"Not an infant," Blake repeated. "It's a fetus. About six months. Toward the end of the second trimester. That's why it's so small."

"Could it have been born prematurely?"

"I don't think so," Blake said. "The female's pelvis shows no sign of her having given birth."

"So, the dead woman is definitely the mother?" Echabarri asked.

Blake shrugged. "Almost certainly. But I'm running DNA tests on the bone marrow that'll prove one way or the other."

"You think the woman is Kickapoo?" Echabarri asked.

"I'm leaning that way. The bones show evidence of malnutrition in childhood. The DNA will give us more certain knowledge, although," he glanced at Concho and away, "many tribal members have some mixed heritage."

"How long you think they've been dead?" Concho asked.

"Harder to tell. At least three or four years. Maybe as much as a decade."

"Older than I thought," Concho said.

Blake shrugged.

"They were just bones," Echabarri said.

Blake appeared to understand what the police chief meant. "Yes. Both skeletons had been denuded."

"You mean the flesh was taken off," Concho commented.

"That's what I said."

"How would someone do that?" Echabarri asked.

"Various ways. Depending on finances and time and situation. First thing is the…corpse needs to decompose. With something the size of a human, that could take months. Especially in our dry climate here. Of course, if it were outside the body would have to be protected from scavengers like buzzards and coyotes who might carry off the bones. You *can* speed the decomposition process with maceration."

"Which is?" Concho asked.

Blake shifted into what could only be called "lecture" mode. "You let the body decompose inside a closed chamber which is regulated for temperature and humidity. It's generally done by teaching hospitals, to create articulated skeletons for educational purposes. Or sometimes by coroners for investigations. I've got access to a maceration chamber but I've never used it.

"Beetles can also be employed. People often call them carrion beetles but there are actually many different species that feed on dead things. Carrion beetles typically eat the flesh itself. Then there's Dermestid beetles, which can digest keratin and eat skin and hair. But both maceration and the beetles are expensive and require high-tech equipment.

"Of course, if you found an already decomposed body. Say

a deer in the woods. You'd wash it off with a safe detergent. Not bleach, which will eat away bone. You'd soak it in a hydrogen peroxide solution until any remaining bits of flesh softened and could be scraped away with a brush. People who want to display bones usually use a toothbrush at that point to avoid damaging them."

"Any idea what technique was used with these skeletons?" Concho asked.

"There are abrasions on the bones of both. They were scraped with a wire brush. But I can't rule out other techniques being used as well."

Echabarri asked another question. "Will the DNA tests help us identify the bodies? The woman, at least?"

Blake shook his head. "Not unless she had a DNA test while she was alive and the sample is still available. It'll give us a good idea of whether she's Kickapoo. That's about it."

"What about the indentation over the left eye socket?" Concho asked. "Is that what killed her?"

"It's possible but I doubt it. It certainly would have given her a concussion and rendered her unconscious. But the neck vertebrae are damaged. I believe she was strangled to death."

Both lawmen winced.

"Any idea what kind of weapon might have made the indentation?" Concho asked.

"It was smooth, not jagged. That likely leaves out a rock or brick. It wasn't very large so that leaves out tools like a shovel. It could have been a hammer. Or a heavy wrench. Could even have been something like a rolling pin."

"And the baby…the fetus was cut out after?" Echabarri asked. The Tribal police chief looked both angry and horrified.

"Yes."

Concho shook his head, primarily to himself. He wanted to get up and walk outside for a breath of fresh air. That wouldn't help much. "Anything else you can think of to tell us?" he finally asked.

"Just a thought," Blake said. "Very speculative, of course.

And you may have already arrived at the idea. But, the combination of rage to strangle someone and the cutting out of the fetus, makes me consider a spurned lover. Someone, perhaps, who'd been cheated on, or felt cheated on. The fetal DNA may help us identify the father. If he's still around and I have samples to compare."

"A useful thought," Concho said.

Echabarri sat nodding his head. "If she *is* Kickapoo, I'll see what I can do about getting you some comparison samples. I'm not sure where to start but it's a small Rez."

Blake offered him a thumbs up.

"All right," Concho said as he rose to his feet. "We'll get out of your hair."

Blake looked up sharply at the Ranger's words, his bald pate shining. "That supposed to be a joke?"

Concho held his thumb and index finger up about an inch apart. "A little one," he said, grinning.

Blake stared at the Ranger, then laughed as he waved them out.

Echabarri didn't speak until they were back in the truck and halfway home to the reservation. "I'll never understand that kind of evil," he said.

"Be glad you can't," Concho replied. "But right now, you need to be concerned with the fact we're being followed."

CHAPTER 9

Echabarri knew better than to look around to see who was following them. "Tell me," he said.

"A white Durango has been with us for over a mile. I even took a side road to test them and they're still hanging. Though they've dropped back."

"Could it have anything to do with the Mason French kidnapping case you just closed?"

"Maybe. French might still have some friends who want payback for his death. And I never did figure out who was feeding him information and manipulating for him behind the scenes. That's someone I'll have to deal with eventually."

"Well, at least they won't follow us onto the Rez."

"No fun in that," Concho said. "I want to know who it is." He glanced over at Roberto. "Feel like a beer? I feel like a beer. There's a little bar I know, just ahead."

"I'm game."

Concho switched lanes and turned off into the sparsely-populated parking lot of a small bar. The sign read, "*Camino del mal.*"

"Evil ways?" Echabarri asked as he translated the Spanish phrase.

"Title of a song," Concho said. "From a musician named Blues

Saraceno. He's part of a movement called 'Dark Country.'"

"Which is…?"

"Southern gothic country blues."

"Hmm," Echabarri said as he climbed out of the truck. "That clarifies it all for me."

The bar was a long, one-story cinder block building painted black with no windows and a bloodred door. Concho stepped inside with Roberto behind him. A slow, guitar-heavy blues tune played on the juke. The lyric repetition suggested it might be called "Wicked Gonna Come."

Concho pointed toward the jukebox. "Dark country," he said to his companion by way of explanation.

The drinking area measured smaller than the building's outside suggested. Almost a third of the structure remained sealed off behind a blue brick wall to the left. A single pool table and about twenty tables filled the rest with a black bar stretching along half the back wall.

Three or four of the tables were occupied. The clientele appeared mostly Hispanic and no one smiled at the newcomers. Although smoking was illegal inside bars and restaurants in Eagle Pass, just about everyone in the room had a haze of smoke hovering around. No one seemed overly concerned about two law officers walking in.

Concho didn't approach the bar, though his gaze met the bartender's. Instead, he led Echabarri to an empty table away from the worst of the smoke and seated himself. The drink slinger walked over to a blue door in the sealed-off portion of the building and knocked. Someone opened it and the bartender spoke to him a moment, pointing across the room toward Concho's table.

The man who came walking toward the lawmen then was about an inch under six feet and built compactly, with just the beginnings of a small gut. His hair and eyes were dark. Three scars lent his face a sinister appearance. A white hairless streak cut through his right eyebrow. A rough, X-shaped cicatrix showed on his chin. The deep, sickle-shaped wound on his right cheek glistened pinkly as it curved from just below the eye to his jawline.

"Concho Ten-Wolves!" the scarred one said. "Why you think you can come here?"

"It's a bar, isn't it? I thought I might find a beer. But it smells like you only serve orina and mierda."

"To you, that is just what I serve. Your friend may have a beer, of course."

Concho glanced over at Echabarri, who looked distinctly uncomfortable. The Ranger grinned. "Roberto," he said. "Meet Piero Almanza. Owner of *Evil Ways*. He's about half Italian, half Mexican, and half Cherokee, with a whole lot of asshole mixed in. He comes from a family of pirates so watch your money and your honor."

Almanza grinned too. "A man such as yourself speaking of honor. That is indeed rich." The bar owner glanced over at Echabarri to say, "And by pirates, this big, ugly black Kickapoo means scions of the noblest blood."

"Isn't that what I said?" Concho asked.

Almanza chuckled. He pulled up a chair and sat, then gestured toward the bartender and called, "Tres Dos Equis, Miguel. Por favor."

Miguel carried three opened dark beers to the table and placed one in front of each man. The chilled glass bottles wept as they warmed.

"Imported from Mexico," Almanza said. "Still the old dark, dark brew. Not like the stuff made these days for weak American taste buds."

Concho took a sip. "Mmmm, I remember it. Some things were better in the old days."

"Sometimes one can still find the old days. If you look hard enough."

Concho glanced at Echabarri again. "Piero served with me in the Amy Rangers. We grew up about a dozen miles from each other but never met until the Army. Of course, he's a whole lot older than I am. Well past his prime."

Almanza snorted. "Three years older, if that. Past my prime, true. Yet still the better man. This big Kickapoo is a sad statement on our young folk today." He pointed a finger at Echabarri. "You excepted, of course."

Having no idea how to respond to the banter, the young chief of police only sipped his beer.

"So," Almanza said to Concho, "why you stop by? Not just for a visit."

"No. Pretty sure we're being followed. I'd like to find out who."

"Ahh," Almanza replied. "I am happy to help. Give whoever it is a few moments to settle. After that, I'll go out for a smoke and have a look. What do I watch for?"

"A white Dodge Durango. New model. Tinted windows. I couldn't see the passengers."

Almanza filled the next ten minutes with small talk, then rose and went outside, pulling a cigarette from a pack in his pocket as he left. He returned five minutes later with information.

"You are right. They're parked across the street in front of an old video store. Vacant now. From the movement of shadows inside, I'd say two men."

"This place still have a back door?" Concho asked.

"Si," Almanza said. "And I have car waiting there. I can drive you around behind their building. Drop you off. Of course, I would be happy to help personally to confront them."

Concho drained his bottle of beer and rose. "Appreciate it," he said. "But Roberto and I better do that part on our own. We'll take the ride, though."

Almanza nodded, rose as well. The three men moved toward the bar. Almanza spoke with his bartender, then led the way through the blue door into a cluttered room that seemed undecided as to whether it was a bedroom or a gun shop. Weapons lay everywhere, many in various stages of being stripped down on tables and desks and chairs.

"You need more firepower, I got it," the bar owner said, gesturing around.

"My guns will be enough," Concho said, patting the twin Colts at his belt. "But maybe you could give Roberto a shotgun. Body armor would be good, too. If it's who I suspect it might be, they've shown a propensity to shoot first and shoot second."

Almanza chuckled. He pulled two bulletproof vests out of a pile and quickly helped the other men don them. Concho's vest made a tight fit. The bar owner handed a loaded Mossberg 12-gauge pump-action shotgun to Echabarri, with extra shells for his pockets.

Leading the small group out through a back door to his room, Almanza took them down a short hallway and out into a loading dock area behind the bar. A green garbage bin sat next to a massive gray Toyota Highlander by the dock. Concho lay down in the back seat of the vehicle while Echabarri hunched low in the front passenger side.

Almanza pulled out on the highway. Two roads converged at a sharp angle here. The bar owner made a U-turn and went down the second road until he pulled into the parking lot of a Chinese restaurant which butted up against the empty building where the men in the Dodge Durango sat watching his bar.

Concho and Roberto bailed and Almanza waited with the engine running. A narrow alley, less full of trash than one might expect in a relatively rough area of Eagle Pass, ran down the side of the Chinese diner, leading the two officers directly to the back of the Durango. The Ranger crept close and pressed his eyes to the back window to peer through. Music thumped inside the vehicle. Two men sat in the front seats, seemingly oblivious to the world around.

Concho held up two fingers to Roberto, who nodded. Crouched low and moving slowly and deliberately, the Ranger worked his way around the back of the SUV and down to the driver's side door. Reaching up, he grasped the latch, then jerked the door open as he surged to his full height next to the Durango.

The man inside, with short, bristle-cut red hair, startled violently. The thirty-two-ounce drink he was sipping sprayed all down his front. Concho grabbed the man's right arm to keep him away from the pistol holstered at his belt. He stuck the barrel of his own pistol into the man's neck as he bellowed, "Freeze or die!"

The man in the other seat twisted toward his partner, dropping his own drink as he clawed for his gun. Glass shattered inward all around the fellow as Roberto bashed the passenger-side window out with the butt of his Mossberg.

"Hands up!" Echabarri shouted, his voice pitched high with tension.

"Don't shoot! Don't shoot!" the driver shouted. "We're FBI!"

CHAPTER 10

Concho's shoulders stiffened at the man's unexpected words. "What?" he demanded.

"We're FBI," the driver said again. "We were just…following you. Don't shoot."

Concho glanced the man up and down. He wore jeans and a black Hawaiian shirt. Only the pistol, a Glock 40, appeared official. The passenger was dressed similarly and wore the same gun.

"You don't look it," the Ranger snapped.

"I can show you my badge," the driver said. "Just let me get it out of my pocket."

"Don't move except when I tell you!" Concho ordered. He tugged on the man's arm. "Get out of the vehicle."

The fellow obeyed, but blustered, "You're going to be in big trouble for this."

"Maybe later," Concho said. "Right now, it's you and your buddy who are in big trouble." He shoved the man back against the SUV and the fellow lifted his hands.

Concho pulled the Glock out of the man's holster and gave it a quick glance over before sticking it through his belt. He gestured toward the second man, who was still in the SUV. "Use two fingers and hand your gun to my compadre there. Then slide out on this side."

Again he was obeyed and, in a moment, the two men stood with their backs against the Durango while Concho's pistol covered them. Echabarri came around the vehicle and handed his shotgun to Concho while he patted the two down. The driver was clean; the passenger had a small hideout pistol in a holster sewn into his boot. Echabarri slid it into his pocket.

"I'm gonna want that back," the passenger said.

"If we get the answers we want," Concho replied. "Now, one at a time, show me your IDs. But move like your life depends on it. Because it does."

The driver lowered his hand very slowly to the right front pocket of his jeans and drew out a billfold. He flipped it open to an apparently authentic FBI badge and an identity card giving his name as "Special Agent Brian Duke." The second man, who had dark skin, revealed a badge and a card claiming his name as "Cameron Voight."

"Satisfied?" Duke asked snidely.

"Not nearly," Concho replied. "I want to talk to your handler. Take out your phone and call them. Put it on speaker."

"I don't think that's going to happen," Duke said.

Concho took a step closer to the man. He was three inches taller, forty pounds heavier. He let his shark smile emerge. "Either you do it, or I do it while you're in cuffs. Make your choice."

Duke's brown eyes flashed with furious anger but grudgingly he took the phone from the other pocket of his jeans and punched up a number. It started to ring and he pressed the button to activate the speaker. A woman's voice came through the line, sounding impatient.

"Yes!"

"We've got a problem," Duke said.

"How could that be?" the woman's voice answered. "You had a very simple job."

"The problem is, I don't like being tailed," Concho said, loudly enough for the woman to hear.

"Who is that?" the woman's voice demanded. "What's going on?"

"It's Concho Ten-Wolves. Texas Ranger. The same man your unleashed hounds have been trailing. Badly, I might add."

"He's holding us at gunpoint," Duke added.

"Ten-Wolves," the woman said. "You need to listen to me. Put away your gun and back off. Or else you're going to spend some time in jail."

"Oh, I think someone's gonna see some jail time. Not sure who, though. Who are *you*, by the way?"

"Special Agent Della Rice."

"Well, Special Agent Rice, I've got two witnesses to your men acting suspicious while tailing me. Without cause. So what's it all about?"

"Nothing I care to discuss with you."

"All right," Concho said. "Then we're going to hang up here and you'll find your men in jail on the Kickapoo Tribal reservation. Going to be a jurisdictional nightmare for you to get them out, but I promise they'll be well treated for however long it takes. Of course, I'll be in touch with my own commanding officer in the meantime. I'm sure that'll shake some trees."

"Ma'am!" Duke said into his phone. "He ain't joking."

A moment passed. "All right," Agent Rice said. "I can talk to you. But not over the phone."

"Not at your office either," Concho said.

"Where?"

Concho considered. "The Lucky Eagle Casino. Tomorrow noon. There's a grill called 'The Red Sky.'"

"Why not tonight?"

"Didn't figure you were in town."

"I am."

"Tonight then. 7:00."

"Done."

The woman disconnected without bothering to speak further with Brian Duke. The FBI agent shrugged and pocketed his phone. Concho pulled Duke's Glock out of his belt and handed it over. Roberto gave Voight's weapons back to him.

"This ain't over," Duke said.

Concho smiled. "Better hope it is." He walked away with Echabarri following.

They returned to Piero Almanza in his Highlander and the bar owner drove them back to *Evil Ways*.

"Didn't hear any shooting?" Almanza said.

"Not worth the bullets," Concho replied. He glanced over at Piero. "Appreciate the help. If you could drop us off by my truck, we've got to be running."

"Anytime," Almanza said as he pulled up beside the Ranger's Dodge in the parking lot.

Both lawmen shook hands with Almanza as they got out. Soon, the two were on their way back to the reservation.

"You did good," Concho said to Echabarri.

Echabarri sighed. "I was scared shitless."

Concho grinned. "Lets you know you're alive, don't it?"

The Kickapoo police chief nodded. He sighed again. "The FBI! What the hell's going on, Ten-Wolves?"

"Maybe I'll find out tonight. From Special Agent Della Rice."

"I don't envy you. She sounds like she eats razor blades for snacks."

"I'll just turn on the old charm."

"Spirit forbid," Echabarri said, chuckling.

Concho's grin subsided. "In truth, I'm a little scared myself. Too many things going on I don't understand."

***

Only after dark did the tall figure rise from a bed of dried grasses and leave the cave where he slept. Though no moon had yet risen and only a few stars winked in the night sky, he had little trouble seeing through the blackness as he loped across the desert landscape.

A few minutes led him to a bluff and a cluster of junipers torn up by searchers during the day. He stood for a long time looking down at the empty grave where *she* had been buried.

At last, a single lonely howl broke across the night. No one was near to hear it.

CHAPTER 11

At 6:45 in the evening, Concho pulled into the parking lot of the reservation casino for his meeting with FBI Special Agent Della Rice. The Kickapoo Lucky Eagle Casino and Hotel was a six-story structure with the gaming hall on the bottom floor. It provided substantial funds for the tribe and its members, although no gambling enterprise came without attendant problems. Concho had dealt with his share of those.

A black sky crowned the parking lot with only a faint glow in the west from the setting sun but the lot itself and the casino blazed like electric jewels. Concho entered through the gaming area, hearing it well before he saw it. The cacophony of the slot machines mixed in a heady stew with the background murmur of customers and an occasional shout from a winner or a loser. Most of the gamblers were white and middle class, a little above average in age. Tourists and locals rubbed shoulders.

Concho didn't much like the gaming floor. It reminded him of psychological experiments he'd read about in college where rats pressed leavers for food rewards in small cages called Skinner Boxes. But the gambling hall wasn't far from the Red Sky Grill which was one of six restaurants in the casino/hotel complex and the one Concho tended to favor.

The Red Sky offered Texas barbecue and various other southern comfort foods, often accompanied by jalapenos. They had good steaks, as well, which Ten-Wolves liked. He ordered a sirloin and paired it with a cold bottle of Shiner Bock beer as he waited for Della Rice.

When she arrived, almost perfectly punctual at 7:01, the FBI agent wasn't what he expected. She was thin, but tall for a woman, almost six feet. Her skin and hair were dark, with the hair wavy and cut to shoulder-length. Her features were sharply defined, though her nose had a faint crook to the right that suggested it might once have been broken. She wore a striped suit over a dark purple blouse, paired with flat-heeled shoes.

Concho rose. Della Rice shook his hand, without smiling, then waved him back to his seat and sat down herself. The waiter arrived, bringing her a water and a menu. She thanked him, sent him off with a "I'll have what the gentleman is having. Separate checks."

"I might be ordering calves' livers for all you know," Concho said.

"Then I'd eat calves' livers," Della Rice said. "But I imagine you've ordered some kind of steak and that will be fine with me."

"Sirloin," Concho agreed.

Rice picked up her water and turned it around in her long, slender hands. *Piano player hands*, Concho thought. She took a sip and put the glass down.

"Let's be clear," she said. "We're not going to become friends here tonight."

Concho nodded. "Because I'm under investigation. For reasons unknown."

"For reasons *I* know," she corrected.

Concho did not reply. She'd either tell him or she wouldn't. Neither assertiveness nor compliance would move this woman to give anyone anything she didn't want to give.

"I've learned quite a lot about you in the last couple of days,

Officer Ten-Wolves," Rice continued. "Born on the reservation. Raised by your grandmother who was murdered when you were fifteen. Some interesting things happened around that time but we don't need to go into those here.

"You attended Haskell Indian Nations University, where you excelled in both football and academics. Majored in languages. You joined the Army and served with distinction in Afghanistan. In fact, you received a commendation for actions that have been...redacted."

Concho grinned. "I was a really good cook. Wouldn't want those recipes to become common knowledge."

The faintest of smiles, a purely perfunctory expression, curved Della Rice's lips. She continued:

"Given your knowledge of languages and your commendation, you could have stayed in the Army and written your own ticket to officer training and a lifetime career. Instead, you left the Army abruptly and returned here. A few years of apprenticeship in the Highway Patrol, and you transitioned into the Texas Rangers. One wonders why."

"Maybe I just got homesick."

"Then, after a relatively unremarkable year in the Rangers, you suddenly became a hero a little over a month ago, stopping, almost single-handedly, a terrorist attack by the Neo-Nazi Aryan Brotherhood on the Eagle Pass Mall."

"Not even close to single-handedly," Concho said.

She went on as if she hadn't heard him. "I don't believe in heroes. Never met one who didn't have feet of clay."

The waiter returned with bread and salads. Concho waited until the man was gone and he'd eaten a bite of salad before saying, "A little cynical of you. But I generally agree. I'm not sure I know what a hero is. I did what I thought best in the situation and I got lucky."

"And now, not so much."

"Tell me what I'm supposed to have done."

The waiter interrupted them momentarily again with plates full of Texas-sized steaks. Agent Rice cut a few slices of hers and ate one before speaking.

"I'm going to tell you some things I probably shouldn't. Given the circumstances, though, there doesn't seem much choice. A few days ago, we received a tip that you were protecting local drug dealers *and* facilitating the movement of drugs from Mexico into the US by way of the Kickapoo reservation."

Concho made a valiant attempt to arch an eyebrow and failed. "Was this an anonymous tip?"

"Yes."

"And on the strength of that you launched a full investigation? Did you consider it might be someone deliberately trying to discredit me?"

"The border is a problem area," Rice said. "You know this. Truckloads of cash and the opportunities provided by power often breed corruption. The FBI always takes such possibilities seriously. But there was more than just a tip. The informant provided evidence."

"Don't see how that's possible."

Rice's responding smile came perilously close to a smirk. Concho took a deep breath to hold back the flush of anger surging up inside.

"Well, let me share," Rice said. "We received photos of you meeting with Lucio Zapatero, a known drug dealer. One photo showed you and Zapatero having a face-to-face in the parking lot of the Eagle Pass Mall. A second identified your vehicle and a man who certainly appears to be you entering Zapatero's compound in Eagle Pass."

"Seems like someone's been very busy following me around. And doing a better job of hiding it than your two…agents."

"So, you don't deny the meetings?"

"Why should I?"

"You don't think it looks suspicious?"

"Not to anyone who knows the whole story. First, Zapatero is not a 'known' drug dealer. You probably got that idea from your informant. I do believe Zapatero has skirted a few laws here and there regarding transportation of materials across the border but I don't have any evidence of him actually dealing drugs."

Rice started to speak and Concho held up a finger to indicate he wasn't done.

"And," he continued, "you apparently aren't aware that Zapatero's wife, Emily, was a witness to a bank robbery I recently investigated. I went to the Zapatero residence to interview *her*. Later, her husband and some of his men followed me into the mall parking lot. He was upset that I hadn't cleared my visit with his wife through him first."

Agent Rice blinked. "I knew about the robbery investigation. I didn't know Emily Zapatero was a witness."

"Guess you didn't have time to look into every detail during your rush to judgment," the Texas Ranger said. He took another bite of his steak and leaned back in his chair to chew, even though he'd lost his appetite for food.

"There is more," Rice said. "And not so conveniently ex-plained."

Concho felt a retort forming and swallowed it down. He needed information and, for now, Della Rice was talking.

"What?" he asked.

"You recently investigated the murder of a man named Donnell Blackthorne. I doubt you can deny he was both a drug user and a dealer."

Despite his attempt to control it, the Ranger felt himself stiffen at Agent Rice's words. This was not going to be good.

"No," Concho said. "He was certainly both."

"And, I believe he was your father!"

CHAPTER 12

Concho fought to stifle his growing anger at the accusa-tory tone in Della Rice's voice. He was pleased when his own voice came out calm and controlled as he said,

"I wouldn't call Donnell Blackthorne my father. He impregnated my mother."

"Also a drug user, I believe."

"I'm trying *not* to get angry," the Ranger said, "but the idea that because my mother may have used drugs I've betrayed my oath as a law officer is ridiculous. I wonder what we'd find if we went through *your* entire family history."

For an instant, the FBI agent looked guilty for the swipe at Concho's mother but any such emotion quickly disappeared as she continued.

"What we have is Donnell Blackthorne, a drug dealer and drug addict *and* your father, found murdered on *your* reservation. Just from the little bit of investigating we've done so far, Mister Blackthorne was here at least a week before his death. Spending time at this very casino. Tell me, if you were an independent authority, wouldn't you find that suspicious?"

"Suspicious. Yes. Not damning. I didn't know he was here. I didn't speak to him or know his name. I certainly didn't know he was my…father. Not until after he got killed, when the DNA tests came back and identified him. Only then did I realize who he was. You can speak to Isaac Parkland of the Maverick County Sheriff's Office. He's the one who invited me in on that murder investigation."

"We already know about Parkland. I'll speak to him and I'm sure he'll corroborate your story. Of course, he would only be able to verify what *you* told him about Mister Blackthorne."

Concho gripped the edge of the table tight with both hands. He'd given up on his meal. "Is there any part of you that wants to find the truth instead of proving a case against me?"

Rice took a deep breath. "It's nothing personal. My job is to be suspicious. Your job is the same. But, of course, I want to find the truth."

Concho shook his head. "No, my job isn't to be suspicious. My *job* is to speak for the ones who can't speak for themselves and to protect those who need it."

Rice studied him as she sipped her beer. "You sound sincere."

Ten-Wolves felt his teeth grinding and forced his jaws to relax. He sipped his own beer until it was empty. But he didn't want another. He wanted only for this farce to be done. He had too much to take care of—finding Meskwaa, finding out who had murdered a woman and her unborn infant and buried their skeletons in the dirt, finding out why strange things were happening on the reservation.

"I don't like you very much, Agent Rice," he said.

"Now *that* I certainly believe," the woman replied. She lifted her hands in a kind of shrug. "But you see my dilemma. You expect me to believe your father was here on this reservation for reasons having nothing to do with you. That he didn't seek you out during his week here. That you didn't even know he was here. I'm afraid I don't find such 'coincidences' credible."

Concho pushed his plate away with almost half his steak left uneaten. "If you think about the usual relationships between fathers and sons, I can see your doubts. But I never met Donnell Blackthorne alive. I had nothing to do with him and never wanted to. Because it's too much of a coincidence, I suspect, as you do, that he chose this reservation in part because I was here. Maybe he *intended* to reach out to me. If so, it was probably because he thought I'd help him. But he didn't reach out. Maybe he ran out of time. Maybe he changed his mind. But he never approached me. And you won't find any photos suggesting he did."

Rice's mouth opened slightly, then closed. Concho realized there were still more shoes to drop but he'd had all he could take for the night. And Della Rice appeared to be of the same mind.

Concho had eaten the exact same meal at the Red Sky Grill before. He knew what it cost and took enough cash out of his billfold to cover it, along with a tip for the waiter. He stuck the money under his empty beer bottle.

"All right," he said, rising to his feet. "I have a friend to check on and another murder investigation to get underway. I'm sure we'll be seeing each other again."

Della Rice took a pocketbook out of her purse and left the same amount of money by her plate. She rose to join him. "I'll walk out with you."

"No need to sully yourself," the Ranger said and realized he sounded just a touch petulant.

"I told you, it wasn't personal."

"Afraid it is for me," he replied.

They'd reached the gambling area. Rice seemed about to say something but, before she could speak, a huge gasp of collective surprise swept the casino floor.

"He's got a knife!" someone yelled.

A woman came racing out of the crowd which swayed away from her like reeds parted by a wind. She was young, with black hair flying, wearing the uniform of the casino servers—maroon skirt, white shirt, maroon vest and black heels. Her face made a study in fear and concentration.

A young man thundered in the woman's wake; a Bowie knife with a ten-inch blade glittered in his right hand. He was close to her and closing. His left hand reached, snagged the collar of the woman's vest.

"I'll kill you!" the man screamed as his grip jerked the woman up short.

The knife lifted; Concho hit the man from the side, his shoulder smashing into the fellow's chest. His left arm struck the man's knife hand and flung it back. The woman twisted free and fled as Concho wrapped his right arm around the knife wielder's waist and slammed him back into the wall of the casino. The room shook.

The woman's attacker was several inches shorter than Ten-Wolves and not nearly as heavy but he was immensely strong. His left arm slammed into the side of the Ranger's head with brutal force. The blow loosened Concho's grip and the man jerked his knife hand free and plunged the blade down.

Concho twisted to one side, throwing an arm up and out to block the descending blade. The knife's sharp tip caught in his white shirt, tearing through and scoring a narrow line of red down his arm.

Concho rocked an uppercut into the man's chin. The punch would have put most men on their backs but this one merely grunted and shook his head. His pupils were widely dilated, the whites of them bloodshot. He was on something.

The knife slashed across at Concho's belly. It missed narrowly as he dodged backward. The shouts of casino security guards could be heard as they pushed through the crowd.

The knife slashed at the Ranger again. He grabbed the wrist behind it, let his fingers close down hard. The man grunted, slung his other fist at the lawman's face. The punch smacked into Concho's palm as he blocked it. He locked his fingers around the man's fist. The two men strained. Concho's strength began to tell as he forced his foe's arms down.

A keening cry bled from the attacker's mouth. He began to

pant and grunt like a beast. Suddenly, he let his arms be driven down as he lunged forward with his upper body, his mouth open and teeth gnashing.

Concho jerked his head aside as the man's teeth snapped shut half an inch from his ear. He snapped his knee up between the man's legs, getting in a solid shot to the groin. The pain of that blow got through.

The man cried out. His fingers loosened on the knife and it clattered to the floor. A bystander kicked it away. Concho shoved the fellow backward, followed quickly with his fists striking. The Ranger hit the man twice in the face; his head rocked backward but he bellowed and came charging back at the lawman.

One of the security guards had gotten close. He thrust a taser into the fellow's back at the level of the kidneys. The man screamed but still didn't go down. He swung an elbow that pulped the guard's nose.

But now, the man was half turned to one side and the Ranger pounced. He flung one arm around the attacker's bull neck and noosed it tight. His free hand rabbit punched into the fellow's side.

The fellow's hands flailed over his shoulders, trying to hit, trying to grab. Concho tucked his face in between the man's shoulder blades and tightened his arm further. Another security guard arrived; he slammed a nightstick into the drug-crazed fellow's right leg and it folded under him.

They went down with Ten-Wolves on top, exerting his strength as he tried to choke off the windpipe. The man flailed and bellowed. He got his arms under him and tried to push up against Concho's weight. The lawman tightened his grip further. A gurgle trickled from the man's mouth and he suddenly collapsed onto his face.

Concho held on a moment longer before loosening his grip and sagging back with his chest heaving like a bellows. That didn't stop him from yanking the cuffs off his belt and locking the unconscious man's wrists together behind him.

The Ranger climbed ponderously to his feet. Sweat coated his face. The two guards stared at him. One had a hand cupped over his bleeding nose.

"What the hell?" the injured guard asked.

"PCP, I think," Concho said. "If you've got cuffs or zip ties, better get a set around his ankles. He may wake up again at any second."

Both guards fumbled zip ties out of their pockets and went to work. Soon, the man on the floor was trussed up beyond any capability of escape.

"Better call the KTTT police," Concho said.

"Already done," one of the guards replied.

Concho turned toward where he'd left Della Rice standing. She had a gun in her hand but slipped it back into her purse as he walked up to her.

"No chance to use it in here," the agent said. "Does this kind of thing happen often?"

"No. Very rare."

"You know them?"

"The woman works here but doesn't live on the Rez. She's got some relatives here, I think. Not sure of her name. Someone will know. Haven't seen the guy before but he definitely looks like he's got some Kickapoo in him. Not very old either. Twenty-three maybe."

"Drugs?"

"Judging from the dilated pupils and the crazed strength, I'd guess Phencyclidine."

"Angel dust! Is that much of a problem on the reservation?"

"So now we're openly sharing information?"

Della Rice's mouth pursed into a moue of irritation. "I shared quite a lot."

Concho stared at the agent. "PCP has never been a serious problem here as long as I've been around. And I'll find out why this happened. Without the help of the FBI."

He stomped away.

CHAPTER 13

After a pleasantly uneventful night's sleep, Concho awoke
Friday morning to a cold house. The thermostat read 52 °F so he
kicked on the heater and dressed in jeans, boots, and a long-sleeved
blue cotton shirt over a long-sleeved black tee. Ravenous after the
unusual experience of not being able to finish his supper the night
before, he fixed himself a big breakfast of four eggs, two slices of
toast, and plenty of bacon. The heat of the stove felt nice in the
chilly room.

As soon as he'd eaten, Concho slung on his guns and headed
to his truck. The sky hung gray and thick with clouds above him.
A fitful wind carried icy knives in its fingers. The Dodge's ther-
mometer reported the outside temp as 39 °F, unseasonably cold
for this time of year.

Concho thought about Meskwaa and thought led to deed. He
drove quickly over to his friend's house, hoping to find the old man
finally home. No such luck. Both Meskwaa's wickiup and trailer
sat empty and cold.

Concho walked back to his truck through the scattered needles
of a passing drizzle. What should he do? What *could* he do? Meskwaa had never owned a cell phone and was used to coming and
going as he pleased. As a medicine man, he picked up and went

whenever he felt called. This wasn't the first time he'd disappeared for days without telling anyone.

But, Meskwaa *was* getting old. He joked about being over a hundred; it was more likely his late seventies. Still, pretty old to be out in weather like this. Meskwaa was tough but age takes its toll on the toughest. And, after the break-in at his friend's house and all the weird happenings on the reservation lately, Concho worried and felt largely helpless to do anything to alleviate his worry.

Starting the Dodge, Concho drove toward the casino. It was only 7:30 AM. The gambling area would be closed but the hotel was open and Meskwaa typically bought his cigarettes from the vending machines there. Maybe he'd find the old man there. He knew he was grasping at straws.

As he drove along the road past the KTTT police station, he saw lights blazing and turned into the station parking lot out of curiosity. Echabarri should have been home but his SUV sat in the lot and much of the light emanated from his office. Concho went in.

Arturo Ramon sat at the dispatcher's desk and lifted a hand in acknowledgment.

"Gonna talk to your chief," Concho said.

Arturo nodded.

Concho crossed the waiting area to tap a knuckle on Echabarri's open door. The chief of the Tribal police looked up from the papers he studied, then motioned his friend over.

Echabarri put down the folder he held and leaned back in his chair. "Morning," he said. He picked up the coffee cup near his hand and frowned at finding it empty. "Guess I don't need any more anyway."

Concho studied his friend's drawn face and bloodshot dark eyes. The normally dapper chief looked disheveled and frazzled.

"You sleep at all last night?" he asked.

Echabarri shook his head and sighed. "I keep thinking about those skeletons. Lying there in the dirt. For years. With no one knowing. No one to speak for them." He brushed his hands through the pile of folders on his desk. "I've been going through more of Ben Deer-Run's old files. Hoping to find something."

"Any luck?"

"Not yet."

Echabarri picked up his coffee cup again as if it might have magically filled itself. When he saw it hadn't, he swiveled his chair only to find the coffee pot he often kept percolating on a shelf behind his desk empty as well. He returned his cup to his desk with a click.

Concho rose and scooped up the cup. "I'll get you some more coffee," he said. "You just take a few minutes to relax."

"I can get it," the man protested.

"I'm already up," Concho said, smiling. He left Echabarri's office and went down the hall to the officer's lounge in the station building. After filling the chief's cup with a fragrant blend of black coffee with chicory, he went back to Echabarri, only to find him leaning excitedly over a slender folder spread open on his desk.

"What is it?" Concho asked, setting the cup near Echabarri's hand. The man picked it up and took a long sip without looking away from the folder. Then he glanced up at the other lawman. His eyes had a shine to them they'd lacked moments before.

"You're coming in to visit may have brought me luck," he said. "I think we might have something here."

Concho slid down into the chair across from Echabarri. "Tell me," he said.

Echabarri picked up a single sheet of typed paper from the folder. "Agustina Cardenas," he said. "Age listed as eighteen. Looks like she disappeared about eight years ago. Before you left the Army and came back to the Rez. Report made by her mother, Juana Cardenas."

"Any resolution?"

Echabarri turned the paper over and back. He shook his head. "Nothing listed. The time is right, though. The age is right. No mention of any pregnancy."

"I don't know the name," Concho said. "Nor the mother either."

"The girl would have been quite a bit younger than you," Echabarri said. He put the sheet of paper down and frowned. "About my age actually. I'm trying to remember…"

Concho let the younger man work it out and was rewarded with a snap of Echabarri's fingers.

"Aggie. Aggie is what everyone called her. I never really knew her last name but I bet it's her. We went to school together. In Eagle Pass. She dropped out. Around fifteen or so, I think. I don't remember anything about her after that. She was about a year younger than me."

"What was she like?"

Echabarri winced. "Not popular. Probably why she dropped out. Her family must have been very poor. She wore old clothes. Patches upon patches. Out of style. And she was kind of dirty, I remember. Riding the bus, she…smelled. Only looked at people through her hair. She got teased a lot. No," he shook his head. "Not teased. Bullied." He sighed.

"Sorry to hear."

"I should have done something. I remember…feeling bad for her. A couple of times I started to speak up for her but I…didn't."

"You were only a kid," Concho said.

Echabarri looked up and met his friend's gaze. His eyes revealed his pain but he didn't say anything else.

"What about her mother?" Concho asked. "I don't recognize the name. Did she leave the Rez? Is she still alive?"

"The name's not very common. She must not be around now or I would have heard it and remembered it."

"The tribal rolls will list her if she's getting any money from the casino."

"Yeah, yeah, they would. But there may be a quicker way to find out." The police chief glanced at his watch.

"Oh?"

"I'll call my mother. Encyclopedia Yolanda. She's always up

by this time."

Concho gave Echabarri the thumbs up.

The chief took out his cell and placed a call, then set the phone on his desk and pressed the speaker option so they could both hear the conversation.

"Roberto!" a woman's voice said. "Are you all right? What's wrong?"

"I'm fine, mom. I just wanted to ask you a question."

"But it's so early. Are you sure you're all right?"

"Yes, mom. I'm sure."

"Your bed wasn't slept in. Where are you? You aren't hurt or sick, are you? Have you had anything to eat? I hope you're not just drinking that coffee like you do. It'll eat your belly out if you don't put food in there. Come home and I'll make you something."

Like many folks on the reservation, Roberto lived in a multi-generational home with his family. His mother, Yolanda, was nearing sixty, and sometimes acted more like a white suburban mother than a traditional Kickapoo woman. His father had been killed in a construction accident just after Roberto turned seventeen. The young chief of police also had two younger sisters, one of them living at home as well, with her husband and a new baby. Concho wondered if his sister's recent pregnancy had heightened Roberto's emotional response to the skeletons they'd found.

Echabarri's gaze crossed with Concho's and he blushed slightly at his mom's overprotectiveness. He didn't put down the coffee cup he was still sipping from, though. "I'm at work, mom. I'm not starving. Everything's fine. But I *really* want to ask you a question."

"What kind of question?"

"Do you know a woman named Juana Cardenas?"

"Why do you want to know? Is there some kind of trouble?"

"Mom!" Echabarri said. Exasperation rattled in the young chief's voice even though he tried to hide it. "I'm looking through some old records," he continued. "I need to learn more about the people I'm serving. Do you know Ms. Cardenas?"

After a brief pause, Echabarri's mom spoke. "Yes, of course, I knew Juana Cardenas. It is a small reservation, after all."

"Knew?" Echabarri asked.

Yolanda cleared her throat. "She died a few years back. When you were away in college."

"Do you know what she died from?"

"It's not for me to say."

"It could be important," Roberto said.

Again, Yolanda cleared her throat. She was fond of gossip, though she always pretended to be above it. Sometimes, she needed a little coaxing to share or at least acted as if she needed it.

"I don't know if I should," Yolanda said.

"Mom, you know I won't tell anyone except in the line of duty."

A sigh came across the line, the sound of reluctantly giving in.

"She did not take care of herself. And had no husband. She drank and drank. Her liver blew out. At least that is what I heard."

Roberto nodded to himself, then asked: "She had a daughter, didn't she? A girl named Agustina?"

"She did. Just the one child. They were very poor."

"Was she called Aggie? I think I went to school with her."

"I don't know about the 'Aggie.' Juana never called her anything but Agustina. But you did go to school with her." A clear note of disapproval entered Yolanda's voice as she finished with, "Until she dropped out."

"From what I'm reading in Ben Deer-Run's files, the daughter disappeared about eight years ago. You remember anything about that?"

A snort of derision came clearly through the phone. "She didn't…disappear. She ran off with that man."

"What man?" Echabarri asked.

"Who knows his name? I didn't. I don't know anyone who did. He never spoke to give it. Or to say anything else. Some claimed he was mute. I thought he was probably like what people say now…retarded!"

Concho watched Echabarri wince and couldn't stop a small smile at his friend's discomfort.

"That's *not* what people say now," Echabarri explained. "But what else do you know about him?"

"Not much. He only stayed on the reservation for half a year. Right at the time Agustina 'disappeared.' He came from Mexico, I heard. Maybe he had a little Kickapoo in him but he was mostly something else. A huge square face. Skin kind of dark and dirty looking."

"And this man and Agustina Cardenas ran off together? Did they go to Mexico?"

"Everyone said so. Of course, I don't pay attention to that sort of thing. Anyway, Agustina was a bit of a...well, you know."

Echabarri frowned. "You mean, she had a lot of lovers?"

"Roberto! That is not nice language. I did not teach you to speak that way."

Echabarri bit his lip and Concho quickly put his hand to his mouth to keep from laughing.

"I'm sorry, mom, but is that what you mean?"

"Yes."

Echabarri glanced at Concho, then asked into the phone. "Would you happen to know the names of any of the men she... may have been with?"

"I know Daniel Alvarado was one of them. He was always into that kind of trouble as a teenager."

Again, the two lawmen's gazes crossed.

"There are rumors of others," Yolanda continued, somewhat snidely. "Some of our prominent tribal families of today maybe weren't always so upstanding."

"Like who?"

"I couldn't say."

Echabarri paused, then said, "OK, thanks, mom. I appreciate it. I'll be home for supper."

"You sound tired," Yolanda said. "You should—"

"I will, mom. Gotta go. Thanks again."

Echabarri swiped the end-call button and leaned back in his chair, shaking his head. "'Prominent tribal families!' She's probably just blowing hot air but I'll corner her about it when I get home."

"And Daniel Alvarado," Concho added.

"Should have known he would be involved," Echabarri said.

"Too bad he's dead and can't answer any of our questions," Concho replied.

CHAPTER 14

Up until a little over a month ago, Daniel Alvarado had served as a member of the KTTT tribal police. He'd even acted as chief of police for a few days after his predecessor, Ben Deer-Run, was murdered, until he, too, fell victim to homicide.

For a while, Alvarado had been Roberto's boss. Concho had a much longer history with the man. They'd fought each other since childhood. Concho had long considered Alvarado a bully and he'd suspected him of involvement with criminal activities. That suspicion had proved true. Alvarado's connection to one specific criminal had gotten him killed.

"Eight years ago, Daniel Alvarado wouldn't have been a teenager," Concho said. "Mid-twenties at least. That also would have been about the time he was courting his wife. Or maybe already married. He should have known better than to mess with Agustina Cardenas."

"When did you ever know Alvarado to do anything not to his convenience?"

"Right. Is it possible he got the girl pregnant and killed her to protect himself?"

Echabarri's eyes flashed wide. "A little early to jump to that. We've got another suspect, too. The square-faced mute guy with no name."

"And members of the 'prominent tribal families.'"

"Plus, we don't even know for sure the skeleton *is* Agustina. Or that the fetus was hers. I know some of the Mexican Kickapoo down in the Múzquiz area. I'll call around today. See if anyone knows anything about her or the mute fellow. Maybe they're living all happy as a cow in corn."

"I'm not giving up hope but I doubt it."

Echabarri nodded and sighed. "I know. I think Aggie Cardenas is in a body bag over at the coroner's office."

"To start with," Concho said, "Alvarado has lots of relatives still on the Rez. One thing we could do is get some DNA samples from his relatives to give to Earl Blake. For comparison to the fetus's DNA."

Echabarri groaned. "By 'we' you mean 'me.' I'm not looking forward to asking any of those folks to swab up some spit."

Concho grinned. "Well, I certainly don't have favored Kickapoo status among the Alvarados. They might just shoot me if they saw me coming."

"Might mean fewer problems for me in the long run," the chief of police replied dryly.

The Ranger grinned again. "But you wouldn't have the benefit of my scintillating company." He rose from his chair. "Sounds like you've got a busy day. But to echo your mother, I strongly suggest you take a lie down on the couch back in your lounge. You need a little sleep. Let's touch base this afternoon to see what we've got."

"OK," Echabarri said, nodding. He went to take another sip of coffee and found his cup empty again.

This time, Concho decided to let him fill his own cup. And maybe notice the couch next to the coffee pot in the officer's lounge.

***

The man known by certain parties as "Scout," turned into the Kickapoo reservation and drove up to the Lucky Eagle Casino. He didn't like coming here. It was risky for him but some things needed to be done in person. He doubted he'd run into Concho Ten-Wolves and he'd already prepared a story in case it happened.

Becoming abruptly conscious of the gun holstered under his coat, he felt again the urge to just shoot the Texas Ranger and be done with it. But that wasn't the plan he'd been given. And the people who'd provided him with the plan were not the kind one wanted to thwart, even though—he considered—their ideas sometimes contradicted each other and so far had borne no significant fruit.

***

After leaving the police station, Concho resumed his journey to the casino to look for Meskwaa, though he felt pretty sure it was a fool's errand. The game room had opened by now and, judging from the number of cars in the parking lot, it must be bustling with activity. Concho parked well back in the lot and headed for the entrance.

Off to his right in the parking area, he spotted Selena Garcia, a young woman of fifteen or so who was the niece of the recently deceased and recently discussed Daniel Alvarado. Selena stood talking with a man who had his back turned. Both wore hats and were bundled up against the chill.

Something about the man seemed familiar, however. Trusting to impulse, Concho pivoted and started in that direction. Selena saw him coming and gave him a sour glare. Then someone stepped into the Ranger's path and he halted to avoid running them over.

"Tamara!" Concho said, frowning. "Why are you over here at the casino? I doubt your mother would be happy."

Tamara Redvine was sixteen and the polar opposite of Selena Garcia. Selena was already something of a bully, like her uncle had been. She was loud and brash. Tamara was generally shy and bookish. But Tamara's dark eyes flashed fiercely now. She wore no cap and her long dark hair twisted around her face in the cold wind.

Tamara didn't answer the question she'd been asked. Instead, she fired one of her own. "Well, are you going to do anything about it?"

"Do anything about what?" Concho asked. He glanced over Tamara's shoulder to see that Selena and the man she'd been talking to had disappeared, probably into the car with tinted windows backing out of a nearby parking space.

With his frown growing, Concho started to step past Tamara to go after the car. Selena was streetwise and tough but if she was in that car she might be in trouble. Tamara shocked him by grabbing his arm and pulling him around with surprising strength to face her.

"Something has to be done!" Tamara said.

"About what?" Concho demanded again.

"My cousin," she said. "He does not use drugs. He wouldn't. And he would never attack anyone with a knife."

A memory flashed through the Ranger's head—the man in the casino the other night who'd been chasing one of the casino employees with a knife, the man who'd seemingly been high on PCP.

"I'll talk to you about it," Concho said. "But right now, I want to make sure Selena is all right. If she got into that car with a stranger—"

"It's her boyfriend," Tamara interrupted, with a smirk.

"Boyfriend! She's fifteen!"

Tamara shrugged. "I've seen her with him several times. He hasn't hurt her before."

Concho glanced back toward the car pulling out of the lot. A gray Chevy Malibu. Nondescript. He memorized the license plate. Shaking his head, he turned back to Tamara.

"You're sure about that boyfriend thing? Who is he?"

Tamara shrugged her shoulders. "I don't know him. A white man. But I've seen her with him before and they just seem friendly. *Real* friendly. If you know what I mean."

Concho couldn't help the look of distaste that crossed his mouth. "All right. Give me a moment."

Taking out his cell phone, he called KTTT police headquarters and got the dispatcher—Arturo Ramon. He recited the plate number of the Malibu to Ramon and asked him to run it before hanging up.

"Now," he said to Tamara, "tell me everything about what's going on with your cousin."

CHAPTER 15

After talking with Tamara Redvine about her cousin and promising he'd look into it, Concho made a sweep of the casino and hotel to search for any sign of Meskwaa. No such luck. He spoke to a few people, asking about Meskwaa. No one had seen him. Finally, he grabbed an early lunch at the Red Sky Grill before heading home. The morning had gotten away from him and it was nearly 11:00.

The world had warmed a little as the clouds broke up and the sun began to make itself known but it was still a cold day in Texas. Concho kept his heater on and his windows up, something he seldom did. He normally loved the feel and smell of fresh air.

As he drove, the Ranger went over in his head what Tamara had told him and what he'd found out afterward from the Kickapoo police office. Randall Wilford turned out to be Tamara's cousin through his Kickapoo mother. Randall's father was white. The parents were divorced and the father had taken the boy off the reservation soon after birth to live with him in Dallas. Only recently had the twenty-two-year-old begun trying to discover some things about his native heritage. He'd spent the last week living with Tamara's family.

According to Tamara, Randall did not use drugs or alcohol

and was very much nonviolent. However, the blood tests done on Randall at the sheriff's office had confirmed PCP in his system. And many witnesses had seen him brandishing a knife. It wasn't clear when or how he'd taken the drug and the knife had not yet been traced to its source.

The young woman Randall attacked bore the name Isabella "Bella" Mora. She was twenty-one and had worked for the casino for almost a year with an undistinguished but satisfactory record. In her interview with the police, she said she'd brought a drink to Randall while he played the slots. She said he'd been nearly incoherent and she'd decided not to serve him, thinking he'd had too many. He'd grabbed her arm, spilling the drink on himself, and drawn the knife from inside his shirt. She'd thrown the empty drink glass in his face to break free and run. Other than serving him an earlier drink, she said she'd had no contact with Randall before.

Tamara Redvine had suggested that Randall might have been drugged without his knowledge. However, Echabarri's people had already reviewed the footage from the casino's surveillance cameras, which appeared to confirm Bella's story. If Randall's drink had been drugged, it had happened off camera.

The most disturbing part of Tamara's story involved her claim that the NATV Bloods were behind the drugging, though she couldn't give any reason why Randall had been selected for a target. The Bloods were an Indian gang. They'd been in existence for many years, at various levels of activity across the country. They'd spread to many different reservations.

The Bloods had tried to recruit Concho as a teenager. He'd turned them down flat. A car bomb, probably meant for him, had killed his grandmother instead. He'd taken his revenge and the Bloods had disappeared for a time from the Texas Kickapoo reservation. Only a month ago, the adult Concho had squashed—or thought he'd squashed—a local resurgence of the Bloods. Now, Tamara was telling him he'd failed, though she claimed not to know the names of any current members.

Concho pulled into the driveway of his trailer home and got out. His thoughts were still on the Bloods and, for a moment, he failed to notice a figure dressed in an oversized red shirt and floppy hat sitting in one of the lawn chairs by his firepit, just under the big mesquite tree. His heart leaped in his chest when he did notice.

"Meskwaa!" he called happily as he strode quickly toward the figure.

Almost instantly, joy turned to fear. The figure had its back to him and didn't move. Its head hung down with its arms folded in its lap. Meskwaa was thin but this figure looked deflated, almost empty.

No! Concho's thoughts shouted. *He's not dead!*

He rushed forward, reached the figure, closed a big hand on its shoulder and pulled it around to face him. A scarecrow dressed in Meskwaa's clothes slowly folded up and slid from the chair to the ground.

Concho stepped back abruptly. *The sound!* When the scarecrow's head struck the earth, it made a thunk—as if something besides straw stuffed the cloth head. Concho's pupils dilated. He turned and ran.

***

Scout came out of the car rental place on foot and started up the sidewalk toward the heart of Eagle Pass. He began to relax as he approached his actual car, which he'd parked up the road from the rental agency so no one there would see it.

This morning had been a close call. He'd never expected to run into Ten-Wolves during the short time he was over at the Casino. The Texas Ranger had an uncanny way of appearing in the wrong place at exactly the wrong time. Though not ideal, it wouldn't have been a problem if he'd run into him in the casino itself. Gambling was legal, after all. But for the Ranger to have seen him talking to Selena Garcia was not good.

Fortunately, he'd had his hat and coat on and didn't believe

Ten-Wolves had recognized him. He'd gotten out of there quickly and, even if the man had memorized his license plate, the car was a rental—under an assumed name—and he'd altered the plate number anyway. While he was thinking of it, he pulled two small strips of black electrical tape out of his coat pocket, wadded them up, and tossed them in the gutter.

A smile crossed his face as he reached his vehicle and slid in behind the wheel. *Safe!* And maybe. Just maybe. If things went right, no one would have to worry about Concho Ten-Wolves much longer.

***

As Concho raced away from the fallen scarecrow, he heard behind him a soft whirr and a snick. He made a flying dive toward his truck, struck the ground and rolled trying to get behind the vehicle. He didn't make it before the morning ignited. A gush of flame rippled out from the center of the explosion, blackening grass, turning leaves on the big mesquite to ash. The boom hammered like steel on an anvil.

Concho closed his eyes and threw his hands over his head as he tried to push himself into the ground. A rage of heat swept over him, blistering but then gone. The concussive shock rattled his teeth. Debris began to rain down around him.

Melted dirt and rock struck his legs and back. A piece of lawn chair banged on the hood of his Dodge and slid off. He huddled close to the earth, only gradually relaxing as the sound died away.

Rolling over, he sat up. Two of the three lawn chairs that normally sat around his firepit were torn wrecks, one of them reduced to a few strips of metal and charred plastic. The third chair had been knocked over and blackened.

Twigs on the nearby mesquite smoldered and ashes continued to drift down from the sky. Fortunately, the ground and its plant cover were still damp from the recent rain. The fires would not spread far. The scarecrow dressed in Meskwaa's clothes had virtually disintegrated. No evidence would be found there as to who had planted the bomb.

After checking himself over and finding nothing broken or seriously burned, he climbed to his feet. His experience in Afghanistan with mines and other explosives had served him well but he'd still been lucky to recognize the danger and run when he did.

He hadn't escaped completely unscathed. His ears rang. He could smell burned keratin and brushing his hand over the back of his head revealed numerous small beads of charred hair. Other scents made themselves known too: melted plastic, superheated mesquite sap, and something vaguely like phosphor.

Drawing a Colt into his hand, the Ranger inspected the area near the fire pit. He could see where some tracks had been brushed away. He'd follow those in a moment but, first, he had to check around his house for more explosives.

Both the front and back doors of his trailer remained locked, with no sign of any trespass or any more bombs. He returned to the scuff marks by his fire pit and began to follow them. Two hundred yards along, the trail led him to a partially overgrown oil well road. Crushed brown grass revealed where a four-wheeler had parked. Any footprints of a rider or riders had been brushed away but he used his phone to take pictures of the tire tracks.

The tracks led to the main dirt road where they joined others, including the much wider tracks of his truck, which overlay them. Whoever it was, they'd headed for Kickapoo Village and he didn't bother to follow any farther. As soon as they reached town and hit paved roads, he'd lose them anyway.

Taking out his cell phone, he called Tribal police headquarters to report the attempt to kill him.

CHAPTER 16

Arturo Ramon answered Concho's call at the police station.

"Is Chief Echabarri awake?" Concho asked.

"He fell asleep a little while ago on the couch in the lounge," Ramon replied. "You want me to wake him?"

"No, just have him call me when he gets up. Did you get anything on that license plate I asked you about, the guy who picked up Selena Garcia?"

"Afraid not. No such plate exists according to the database."

Concho frowned. "I thought I had it right."

"Maybe you did. I've seen criminals alter plate numbers with strips of black electrical tape. If it's done well, you can't tell at a distance."

"Yeah, I've seen such too. Maybe if I give it some thought I can guess as to how it was altered. I'll let you know."

"Sure. And I'll have the chief call you."

"Thanks," Concho said, as he hung up. After sticking the phone back in his pocket, he struck a fist into a palm.

Another dead end. Far too many of them in this case. The frustration was starting to get to him. He wanted someone or something to push back against. He didn't have it.

***

Concho had barely gotten back to his trailer before his phone rang. Caller ID identified it as Roberto Echabarri.

"Hey," the Ranger said. "You didn't get much sleep."

"About an hour. I'm OK. The coroner's call woke me."

"Oh. What did he have to say?"

"DNA tests were conclusive. The dead woman was Kickapoo. The fetus was hers."

"What we figured," Concho said.

"Yep. But why did you want me to call you?"

Concho told his friend about the scarecrow dressed in Meskwaa's clothes and about the bomb that had nearly taken him out.

After a shocked silence, Echabarri recovered his voice. "Sorry, man! You want me to call the bomb squad to have a look?"

"No. Whatever the device was, it's blown to smithereens. But if anyone reports a missing scarecrow, let me know."

"Do you think…Meskwaa? I mean, do his clothes on the scarecrow indicate they have him? Or…?"

"I've been giving that some thought and I don't believe so. The clothes were definitely Meskwaa's. The hat, too. But it wasn't the hat of many stains. You know what I'm saying?"

"You mean the gray hat with the mustard stain on the crown?"

"Yeah. Meskwaa's favorite hat. The one he always wears. If whoever set the bomb had the old fellow, they would have used the clothes he was wearing. And it's the wrong hat."

"I see. So how did they get *any* of his clothes?"

"From whoever broke into Meskwaa's house the other day. I saw them with a package under their arm. Must have been the clothes."

"Makes sense," Echabarri said. "If we knew who *that* was."

"I've got an idea."

"Oh?"

"I'm thinking there are at least three groups who want me dead."

"Only three? I think you underestimate yourself."

"Ha, ha."

"So what three?"

"First, the local Neo-Nazis. For taking down their leader, Darrel Fallon. Second, Jacob Drake's co-conspirators. For busting their boss and putting him in jail. And...."

"And who?"

"The NATV Bloods."

Concho could almost hear his friend's frown. "We took those out during the Jacob Drake affair," he said.

"We thought we did. We hurt 'em anyway. But Tamara Redvine told me this morning they were still dealing drugs on the Rez. And since I've gotten in their way more than once, I can imagine them wanting me dead and having local access to try it."

"Interesting. Tamara give you any leads?"

"No, but I've got one anyway. And I'm headed out to shake some trees."

"What trees you talking about?"

"Daniel Alvarado's relatives," Concho replied.

"Whoa, whoa, whoa! Didn't you tell me just a while ago that you were *persona non grata* around the Alvarado family? In fact, I believe you said they might shoot you on sight."

"They might. But Alvarado was involved in the original NATV Blood rising on the reservation. And also, with the recent resurgence. Maybe this last time he started his recruiting efforts close to home."

"Makes sense but it's still dangerous. Want me to go along? Or at least send a deputy with you?"

"No. I think it's important for the Tribal police to remain neutral in whatever I'm caught up in. Or at least appear neutral. But if I call for backup, I hope I'll get it."

"You will," the police chief said. "I'll make sure."

"Thanks!"

"Good luck. Call me whatever happens."

"Will do," Concho said as he hung up. He headed for his truck with every intention of starting a ruckus.

***

Daniel Alvarado was survived by his wife and two young children, all of whom had relocated to the Oklahoma Kickapoo reservation, and by two older sisters who still lived on the Eagle Pass Rez. The sisters were Leticia and Francisca. Both had children.

Leticia, sometimes called Letty, was the older of the two and had married a man named Henry Garcia, who was three-quarters Kickapoo. Their daughter was fifteen-year-old Selena, and they also had a son named Francisco, who called himself Cisco. He was seventeen. Alvarado's father had been knifed to death in a barroom brawl when Daniel was twenty-two. His mother, Rosa, was still alive and lived with Henry and Leticia. Ten-Wolves had never been on good terms with any of them.

As he pulled up the driveway of Henry and Leticia Garcia's red brick house on the outskirts of Kickapoo Village, a young man stepped onto the porch carrying a shotgun. He was tall, maybe 5'11", and thin, with nearly waist-length black hair flowing freely. Concho recognized Cisco and something else he thought he'd remembered—and had. This youth had the same apparent build and hair as the person he'd seen robbing Meskwaa's place.

As Concho's truck rolled to a stop, Cisco racked the slide on the shotgun to chamber a shell. The sound broke loudly across the late morning, but Concho didn't let it stop him from opening the door of his vehicle and stepping out into the cold air.

A woman came out of the house behind Cisco. She snapped something at the youth, then grasped the barrel of the shotgun and pulled it away. The woman was Leticia Garcia, nee Alvarado. She pushed Cisco toward the house but he only took a few steps back to lean insolently against the wall.

Leticia stood nearly as tall as her son and the resemblance between the two was clear. People always said the Alvarado genes "bred true," and this certainly seemed evidence of it. Leticia's daughter, Selena, had the same general look.

Concho shut his truck door and took a step toward the house. Leticia held up her palm to stop him.

"You are not welcome here, Ten-Wolves. Not with the blood of my brother on your hands."

"You know I didn't kill your brother," Concho said. "In fact, the man who did is dead in large part because of me."

"Not pulling a trigger is not the same thing as being innocent," Leticia retorted.

The screen door on the house opened and Leticia's husband, Henry, came outside to stand at his wife's shoulder. He was the same height as his wife but much heavier. His short, brownish-black hair had thinned a lot in the past few years. The scraggly growth of whiskers on his face was salted with gray. An unkind thought crossed Concho's mind: living with Leticia had to be stressful.

"Henry," Concho acknowledged.

Henry said nothing, though he gave a little jerk of his chin to match the Ranger's greeting.

"Why are you here, Ten-Wolves?" Leticia asked.

"I came to make sure Selena was all right."

Both Leticia and Henry frowned. Cisco looked sullen and angry but that wasn't any different from the face he normally wore.

"What is your concern with my fifteen-year-old daughter?" Leticia demanded.

"I saw her over at the casino this morning. Getting in a car with an older man, someone I didn't recognize. I wanted to make sure she'd gotten home safe."

"Since when do you care about anyone with Alvarado blood?" Leticia retorted.

Henry made a face behind his wife's back at the "Alvarado blood," and Concho almost smiled. To cover it, he said, "I'm no enemy of the Alvarados. Despite what you believe. Is Selena at home?"

"That is none—" Leticia started to say before Henry interrupted:

"She ate here a little while ago but is gone again. What man did you say she was with?"

Leticia focused a laser glare on Henry but he stared past her. It had to be deliberate; Leticia was not easy to ignore. Henry often seemed to lack backbone where his wife was concerned but it seemed his feelings for his children had brought a little strength out in him.

"I believe he was a white man," Concho said. He decided to keep Tamara Redvine's name out of it; she'd told him the man was white. "But I didn't see him clearly. He wore a coat and hat against the cold. I didn't recognize his car either. A gray Chevy."

"What time was this?" Henry asked.

"Around 8:00."

The man relaxed a little. "She's been home since then," he said. "Good."

Leticia's anger at being bypassed in the conversation had been growing. She blurted, "If that's all, Ten-Wolves, you can go. You needn't concern yourself with how I raise my daughter."

"There's one more thing. A question for Cisco there. I'd like to know what he can tell me about the NATV Bloods on the Rez."

Leticia's son had seemingly lost interest in the conversation. Outside of maintaining his well-practiced "you're lame" expression, he wasn't paying any attention to Concho—until the mention of "Bloods." Then the boy jerked upright and a quick flash of excitement combined with fear crossed his features.

Henry gazed at his son with curiosity. Leticia sputtered with rage. "You do not question my son," she snapped loudly. "He is not of age."

"It's not supposed to be incriminating," Concho said. "I figure he can answer on his own."

Cisco's fearful excitement had quickly given way to caution. "I don't know what you're talking about, black man," he said.

"A couple of days ago," Concho continued, ignoring Cisco's taunt, "someone burglarized old Meskwaa's trailer. Stole some clothes—"

"What do you accuse my son of?" snapped Leticia. "He is no thief!"

"I'm not accusing him of anything," Concho said patiently. "But Cisco probably hears much more about the actions of young people on the Rez than I do. I'm only wondering if he's heard anything about such an incident. Someone said it was the NATV Bloods. Frankly, I need help and I hoped Cisco might be able to provide it."

"Why do you say it was young people?" Henry asked.

"Because I saw one of 'em. He had a ski mask on but was definitely young. He had the long black hair of a Kickapoo. Also had a friend with him. Someone who shot at me. They escaped on a four-wheeler."

Briefly, Cisco's eyes flashed in the direction of the family garage. Concho noted it but didn't let on.

"I don't know anything about such," Cisco said. "I don't trust your word. I doubt the house was even robbed."

Concho smiled. "All right," he said. "I was just hoping for a break in the case. I'll head on." He tipped an imaginary hat toward the Garcia family and tromped back to his truck.

Not one of the three took their eyes off him as he backed down their driveway and turned away up the road. He figured there'd be some yelling and accusations made between the three after he was gone.

"Ruckus raised," he muttered to himself. "Hornet's nest stirred."

Now to see what crop his plantings would bring. He hoped it wouldn't be a more successful bombing attempt.

CHAPTER 17

Before heading home, Concho drove by Meskwaa's place one more time. There was something he wanted to check on. The last time he'd visited, he'd brought along a roll of transparent tape and he'd cut two thin strips and stuck them across the bases of both the front and back doorways.

He hadn't wanted to lock Meskwaa's trailer in the aftermath of the robbery. He didn't know when the old man might come home and Meskwaa didn't normally carry any kind of key. But, he *had* wanted to know if anyone else had come and gone. A check of the tape showed it still in place, so no fresh intrusions had occurred.

Walking over to Meskwaa's wickiup, he picked up the bucket of water sitting on the dirt floor of the ramada, the front porch. The dead gnat still floated in the water and he dumped it, refilling the bucket from the nearby pump. Putting in the dipper, he scooped up some of the fresh *agua* and drank. The cold of it hurt his teeth and numbed his throat.

He grabbed a coat out of his truck and slipped it on, then sat down on the sleeping bench on the ramada where the chill wind was at least partially blocked. He leaned back against the wickiup and closed his eyes, trying to imagine himself as Meskwaa, trying to get a feel for where the old man might be. Despite the chill, he dozed. A dream visited.

He stood beneath the oak tree where all the sacred deer were born. The tree existed on the Rez. He'd been there many times. The deer part of the story wasn't true although Concho had always thought it should be. The tale had been created by Estrella Deer-Run for a high school English class. It had won a contest and been published in the Eagle Pass paper—a moment of pride on the reservation.

The oak tree stood on the edge of an old arroyo. In his dream, Concho could see something coming down the arroyo, something very big and white. It smelled rank. It was a feral boar, a monstrous one that must have weighed nearly a thousand pounds. Its flanks brushed the arroyo banks to either side of it. Its tusks curved like sabers. The pig was an albino, with its blood-red eyes glowing under the moonlight.

A black wolf faced the boar, a snarl of defiance creasing its muzzle. The wolf could not match the greater beast and slowly retreated as the monster drew closer. Now, a man appeared in the arroyo as well, a large man dressed in skins with a head almost square, with long dark brown hair tangled and matted like half a dozen birds' nests. The wolf backed up until it stopped next to the man. Together, they stood facing the boar. For what purpose, he did not know.

"You must make the shield," a voice next to Concho said.

The Ranger turned. Meskwaa stood there, not dressed in his normal clothes but wearing a ceremonial outfit of moccasins, deer-hide trousers, and a deer-hide vest that left much of his bony chest bare. A crow perched on his head like a living hat.

"You're alive!" Concho exclaimed.

The crow answered rather than the man. "That is of little matter," it said.

Concho's eyes snapped open and he sat bolt upright on the bench where he'd fallen asleep. His breathing came fast; his heart pounded.

"Just a dream," he muttered.

But was it? Meskwaa…saw things. He knew things he could not know about through normal means. Concho had seen it with his own eyes, heard it with his own ears. He believed.

The Texas Ranger, college educated and knowledgeable of the world, did not like to call such events magic, though most of his fellow tribal members had no problem doing so. But whatever the true explanation, Meskwaa's power was undeniable. And now, here on the bench where the old medicine man, the Kickapoo Naataineniiha, spent so much of his time, the Kickapoo lawman had experienced…something.

The wind had died here in the early afternoon. It was nice in the sun. Concho took off his coat as he climbed into his Dodge. He started it up and headed for the tree where all the sacred deer were born.

***

Half an hour later, Concho turned onto a rutted old hunt-ing road leading deep into the southwest corner of the reservation. He drove between stands of mesquite and juniper peppered with a few hardwoods—mostly oak. A small meadow rose in front of him and he pulled to a stop. Though the temperature was still cool, only a rare wind ever entered this small vale and, even now, a few white and yellow blooms nestled amid the green and brown grasses.

Some fifty yards across the meadow stood the oak tree which Estrella Deer-Run's story had named as the place where the sacred deer were born. An arroyo ran beside it, partially under the old tree so that blackened, skeletal roots stabbed through the bank and out into the open air.

Concho walked slowly toward the tree, listening to bird song all around. The afternoon seemed peaceful, though his own internal state remained agitated. He had no idea what he expected to happen here; he was acting purely on instinct.

Despite the recent rains, the ground of the arroyo was dry. But here and there a little greenery poked through the soil, hinting of water below. As he moved around the tree, he discovered a deep set of scrapings along the ground, indicating the presence of feral pigs in the meadow, probably in search of acorns from the oak. Hog tracks were clear in places but none as big as the monster boar from his dream. He laughed at his own imagination which helped him relax.

Grasping one of the tree's roots, Concho dropped down into the arroyo itself. His boots sank almost an inch into the soft soil of the ravine bed. Anything moving along here would leave clear prints and he could see more pig tracks as well as the three-toed dinosaur-looking marks left by a big egret or heron.

The bank beneath the oak had been partially eaten away by rushing water, leaving a shallow dark hole. The sun was at the wrong angle and he couldn't see the back of the hole. But something out of place lay in front of the hole. He bent over and picked up a chunk of flint.

Rushing water could move pretty heavy stones but this one probably weighed four or five pounds. It had also clearly been worked by someone. The Ranger noted where several large flakes had been knapped away from the stone core, possibly to make arrowheads or spearheads. And this was no old core; the fracture lines were clean and fresh.

Concho took a step closer to the hollow under the oak, peering intently to try and make out the depths. A low, rumbling growl froze him in his boots while it sped his heart. A glow of yellow eyes blinked open. A shadow stirred in the hole. The smell of wild animal filled the man's nostrils. He took a step back, drawing his left-hand Colt.

The growl segued into a snarl. Concho took two more steps backward. The shadow within the dark stepped into the light. A wolf. A black wolf. Though, on closer examination, the muzzle was too short. Maybe it was some hybrid of a wolf and dog. The beast's lips curled upward in threat, showing reddish gums and ivory-colored teeth. Concho took one more step backward.

"Easy," he said. "I'm not your enemy."

The wolf-dog closed its mouth. It took another step out of its lair but did not move directly toward the lawman. It shifted its gaze away from his for a moment, looking around to see what other dangers might lurk. Finally, it skirted wide around him and loped off down the arroyo until it disappeared around a curve in the waterway.

Concho watched the animal go, thinking how closely it resembled the black wolf of his recent dream. He wasn't particularly surprised. Finally, he let out the heavy breath he'd been holding and holstered his pistol.

His phone had a flashlight app. He turned it on and pointed the light into the hollow where the wolf-dog had lain. The glow wasn't bright but it revealed a thick pile of dried grass, a few bones of what must have been prey, and something else never constructed by any animal. A small, circular pit of stones held the burnt ashes of a recent fire.

Something human had been living here.

CHAPTER 18

It was nearly dark by the time Concho got home and growing colder again with the coming blackness. He sat in his truck for a moment, with the heater going while he studied his house under the headlights. Everything appeared normal except for an object resting on his top step, just in front of his door. It didn't look like a bomb but he wasn't going to take chances.

Opening the door on the Dodge and leaving the lights on, he slid out and cautiously approached the steps. His right hand rested on the butt of one of his Double Eagles but he didn't draw it. To his right lay his destroyed fire pit with its ruined lawn chairs. About thirty yards to his left stood bushes empty of any sound or movement.

The object on his step was a rolled-up hide, a boar's hide he realized. It was pure white, which told him where it had come from. This was the hide off the albino boar he'd killed just the other day in the arroyo out back of his trailer, the boar someone had stolen. It seemed they'd brought a piece of it back to him. It still smelled of meat and blood.

Concho picked up the hide. It had been tied with two lengths of deer sinew. He untied it, unrolled it. It had not been cured but all the residual tissue had been scraped away in preparation for tanning. He couldn't help but think of this as a gift from whoever had taken the boar in the first place.

But why? They surely couldn't know he'd planned to use this hide to make a Kickapoo shield. *Unless.* Unless it was Meskwaa who'd brought this hide to him? He shook his head. Not possible. Meskwaa would not have left it for him like this, not without some note or message.

Returning to his truck, he killed the lights and engine and set the car alarm. He seldom did so but it made sense now. Anyone trying to put a tracker on his vehicle or rig it to blow would set off the alarm.

Taking the hide and a couple of items from the extended cab area of the Dodge, he headed inside his house, and after a complete search of the premises decided to start the process of salting the hide for preservation. He already had a tanning board, made to fit over his bathtub. He attached the hide to it with clips, skin side up, then fetched an unopened one-pound container of iodized salt.

For the next forty-five minutes, he worked the salt into the hide, making sure to cover every inch of it. At the same time, he scraped away the bristly hair covering the outside of the hide, letting this fall into the tub to later discard. He'd need more salt to complete the process but things had to sit overnight anyway and he could pick up more in the morning. Finally, he cleaned himself up and sank onto his couch to rest. It had been a long day.

His phone rang.

"Yes," Concho said as he answered.

"Ten-Wolves."

"Special Agent Della Rice," Concho said. "What can I do for you?"

"It's more what I can do for you," Rice replied.

"I'm listening."

"I'm hearing rumors there may be an attempt on your life."

"Who from?"

"Darrel Fallon and his Neo-Nazi friends in the Aryan Brotherhood."

"Since they've made no secret of wanting me dead in the general sense, I'm assuming you're talking about some specific incident they have planned?"

"Something specific in the next few days," Rice replied. "Thought you should know."

Concho considered telling the FBI agent about the bomb he'd recently survived but decided against it. She hadn't exactly earned his trust. "I appreciate the warning," he replied instead.

"There's something else," Rice said.

"Oh?"

"Seems like most people who aren't criminals around Eagle Pass think you're a pretty decent sort."

"Glad to hear it. Even more glad for *you* to hear it."

"I told you when we met that I wanted the truth. All of it. I'm working to get it."

"That's all I can ask," Concho said. "Have a good night. And thanks for the tip." He hung up.

So, he thought. *Some enemy plans to kill me. And more immediately than the general run of enemies who've threatened to murder me.*

The first question was, had the attempt already been made and failed—the bomb in the scarecrow? Or, was that a separate attempt from the one supposedly being planned? Had the Aryan Brotherhood planted the bomb he'd survived? Or had it been the actions of another party? Was there any connection?

He'd been leaning toward the NATV Bloods as responsible for the scarecrow attack and, because of Meskwaa's clothes, he suspected Francisco Garcia of being involved. The Bloods wouldn't normally be expected to ally with white supremacists but hatred can pull together strange bedfellows. As he'd seen before.

The second question was what to do now? Continue as normal? Go into hiding? Something in between? His first impulse was to dare them to come after him. That had been part of the reason he'd gone to the Garcias', to let them know—if any of them were involved—that he'd not only survived the bomb but had them on his radar.

He made a decision. The hallway between the bathroom and his utility room had no windows and several walls between it and the thin, non-bulletproof outside skin of the trailer. He set up a camping cot in the hallway. He put guns, extra ammunition, his police issue body armor, his bow and quiver, the keys to his Dodge, and his night-vision goggles beside the cot. After making himself a supper of pork chops and microwave rice, he dressed in black BDUs over long johns and went to an early bed. He slept soundly. For a while.

***

The helicopter flew in from Corpus Christi and landed at a private ranch outside Eagle Pass, Texas at about 2:00 in the morning. It wasn't a military craft. Its normal duties involved ferrying work crews from the coast out to oil drilling platforms in the Gulf of Mexico, which meant it had a long range. After refueling, it picked up a different kind of crew tonight, three men dressed in military-style BDUs and carrying M4 carbines, fully automatic rifles that civilians shouldn't normally have access to.

The battledress uniforms of the three would certainly have raised the eyebrows on any police officer who happened to see them. The rifles were flat-out illegal and did not have special licenses. The men had such licenses though they wouldn't stand close scrutiny. It wasn't yet deer season in Texas either but the three had a cover story, one about serving as a feral pig eradication unit. Various parts of the state had established such units.

After the three men loaded aboard the copter with their gear, the machine took them up and headed almost straight west toward the Texas Kickapoo reservation. The leader of the three was a crew-cut ex-soldier named Curt Godwin. With the stub of a lit cigar clenched between his teeth, he was the living stereotype of an American mercenary. He gave his two companions a grin.

"Reservation's full of pigs," he said. "Time to trim the herd a little."

CHAPTER 19

A low vibration filtered into Concho's sleeping mind. As it brought him toward wakefulness, it first triggered a memory of Afghanistan and his days as an Army Ranger.

The Hindu Kush, Afghanistan, 2010:

Distorted by the moonlight and the night-vision goggles that Concho Ten-Wolves and the rest of his twelve-man ODA wore, the choppers looked like monstrous alien dragonflies as they swept over. A few soldiers cheered. Their commander, Russ Adelaide, had other things on his mind.

"Take off your goggles!" he snapped. "Now!"

Concho had just pulled his off. The others followed suit. And none too soon. Almost as one, the choppers fired a barrage of rockets into the stony hill overlooking the Army Ranger position.

The world reversed, from night to incandescent day. A hundred fire-roses bloomed across the hill, bloomed and merged into one vast and fatal flower. Behind the boulder where he squatted, Concho ducked even lower and closed his naked eyes against the brightness.

Smoke blacker than the night roiled up as the choppers' crews opened up with .50 caliber machine guns. Even rocks splintered under that hail. And the enemy screamed as flames and lead tore into them.

For four hours, Concho and his team had been pinned down by a well-hidden and determined foe. Now, half a dozen choppers from the 75th Ranger Regiment strafed back and forth across those deadly hills. Afghan fighters fired at the choppers and were cut down. They ran and were cut down.

As the rocket's glare died away, Concho slipped his goggles back on. A soldier named David Lanoue squirmed up to his boulder. Concho glanced at his friend, who offered him a wry grin.

"I love the smell of rockets in the morning," Lanoue said, channeling the movie Apocalypse Now.

"They don't," Concho replied, gesturing toward the dark hill where the last gunfire from the Afghans had faded to nothing.

***

Concho came to full wakefulness with the sound of a distant helicopter thrumming through his head. He didn't need to check the time; his sense of its passage was good. It had to be around 3:00 in the morning.

Rolling out of bed, he strapped his pistols on. Body armor and night-vision goggles followed. He slung his bow over his shoulder and plucked up a Remington .30-06 deer rifle from where it leaned against the wall. He pushed his car keys and a flare gun into a pocket of his army-issue BDUs.

Rushing into his home office at the end of the trailer, which he'd converted from a small bedroom, he unlocked the window and pushed it up, then snapped the screen out of its grooves and slid through to drop to the ground outside. A small grove of mixed juniper and mesquite surrounded him and hid him from any watching eyes.

The helicopter sounded like it was hovering off to the east. He figured it must be a mile away and, apparently, not coming any closer. A copter on the Rez at this time of the morning might be innocent but he doubted it. And given what FBI agent Della Rice had told him, he suspected the vehicle was unloading men who were coming after him. He didn't know how many. If he were wrong, he'd lose a little sleep. It wasn't anything he hadn't lost before.

Going to his belly just in case any enemies had already arrived at his house, he squirmed out of the grove and worked his way around to the bushes on the south side of his place. The darkness of the night clung everywhere but the goggles let him see.

Concho still had plenty of army training in him. Almost as soon as he'd moved into his home here, he'd prepared a few defensible bolt holes. The small depression he crawled into now looked natural to the casual glance. It was far from it.

Ten-Wolves had physically moved and replanted the three mesquite bushes around the depression. He'd also piled up a short, circular wall of rocks around the hole and covered that with dirt and grass. He nestled down in comfort and sighted the .30-06 in on his front door. The wait began and, with the cold of the early morning, he was glad he'd put on long johns beneath his BDUs.

About forty-five minutes passed by his reckoning before Concho heard the first sound indicating he was indeed being hunted. A tiny clicking sound came from along the dirt road leading to his trailer. *A boot*, he thought, striking a rock.

Very slowly, he turned his head in that direction. Three men, spread out and wearing night-vision goggles much like his own, came creeping into his yard. All were dressed in military fashion and carried automatic or semi-automatic rifles. He could even make out grenades hanging from their vests. The bulkiness of their fatigues indicated that they wore battle armor over their clothes. It would make this night's work more difficult.

The three spread farther apart. Their focus rested on his trailer; their intent was clear. Unfortunately, two went around the passenger side of his truck where he couldn't see them. The third moved along the Dodge on Concho's side, though he was careful not to touch it and set off any alarm.

The one Concho could see paused. Very slowly, he reached into a pack on his back and drew out a brick-sized object. Concho recognized the shape. He'd seen plenty of claymore mines. These were anti-personnel weapons loaded with ball bearings and usually detonated remotely. They'd mow through just about anything within a hundred yards in front of the device.

Very slowly, Concho set down his rifle and picked up his bow instead. The assassin had his back to the Ranger and was focused on the object in his hand. The Kickapoo lawman rose to a kneeling position, nocked an arrow and drew the string back.

The bow draw made a soft sound, like a sigh. The assassin turned halfway around to locate the sound. Concho released the arrow. The flint arrowhead punched in through the man's left cheek, just below the rim of his goggles, and punched out the other side an instant later, burying itself to the feathers.

The man released a distorted cry as the impact of the arrow knocked him sideways into the door of the Dodge. He dropped the mine, which did not go off. The truck alarm did. A loud siren wail filled the night.

The man was badly hurt but not dead. He threw himself on the ground and grabbed for the rifle he'd lain down when he took out the claymore. He opened fire but he didn't know where the arrow had come from; he shot toward the house. Bullets rattled against the siding. The other two would-be assassins held their fire. They were professionals.

A voice called from the other side of the truck, almost screaming to cut through the blare of the alarm. "J! What's happening?"

Concho dropped the bow and grabbed the .30-06. As fast as he could pull the trigger, he fired four times into the assassin's prone shape. At least one of the slugs found a breach in the man's body armor and punched through. The man gave a strangled cry and collapsed, the rifle falling from his fingers.

Concho left the bow behind momentarily and squirmed out of

his laager with the .30-06 in hand. Ten feet to his right lay a pile of dirt scraped up by the bulldozer that had cleared the area for his trailer. He'd made sure it was never removed. Now, he slid behind it. Though his truck still stood partially in the way, he could see the far side of his yard better from here.

The faint outline of a man's upper body appeared at the rear of the Dodge pickup, the bulky goggles on his face turning him into a mutated insect. Concho didn't have a good shot but he had a memory of rockets in Afghanistan. He drew the flare gun from his pocket and pushed his own goggles up onto his forehead. The night went nearly black for a moment, leaving only the dim glow of the white truck.

He aimed carefully for the ground right at the back of the vehicle, then closed his eyes and fired the flare toward it. The night lit up, blasting white light even through the lawman's closed eyelids.

Both men on the far side of the truck cried out as their eyes were dazzled by the flare. Concho opened his own eyes, brought the rifle to his shoulder. The flare had struck the ground just to the right of where he'd aimed. The light turned night into fluorescent day. A knee, a shoulder, and part of the head of the assassin were visible.

The man had torn his goggles off and was shaking his head, trying to clear his vision. Concho darkened that vision permanently with a .30-06 slug into the left eye socket. Blood, brains, and pieces of skull misted the air as the dead man fell backward with a thud.

The flare began to die out. Concho waited behind his pile of dirt until it was almost gone before putting his goggles back on. He had only two shots left in the Remington's magazine so he switched it for a fresh one.

Pulling his truck keys out of a pocket, he pressed the button to silence the alarm. The sudden quiet felt heavy after the cacophony moments before. He heard nothing to suggest the presence of the third man and was beginning to wonder if the fellow might have fled when a voice cracked through the darkness.

"Just the two of us now!"

From the echo of the voice, the man had moved to the north side of the trailer, probably to give his eyes a chance to recover from the flare. Not much cover there and Ten-Wolves knew every blade of grass and clot of dirt. He also knew the man was hoping he'd respond to the words, to locate him. He decided it might be worth it to give the fellow something extra to consider.

"Better think again about the two!" he called back as he prepared to make a move. "I've still got friends left."

CHAPTER 20

Now began a game of blind man's chess. The would-be assassin was a pro. He'd know that any chance of surprise had fled and he was now fighting on the Ranger's turf. His best bets were to retreat or stay put. Concho didn't know this man but had a feeling retreat was not going to be his choice. At least the assassin had been driven out of the front yard and probably wouldn't come back to the scene where his two companions had died. That gave the Ranger a moment to do what he wanted.

Moving quickly, in a crouch, Concho darted toward his truck and dropped to one knee beside the first man he'd shot. The assassin lay dead and rapidly cooling in the chilly morning. He stank of blood and voided bowels.

Concho ignored the claymore mine. He had eyes for something else, the two grenades hanging on the man's vest. He pulled them free and tucked them into a pocket of his own vest.

Moving back to his first defensive site, he took up his bow again. Sliding the rifle over his shoulder, he squirmed on his belly to the back corner of his trailer. His ears were attuned to every sound but he heard nothing from the last location of his enemy. He considered the possibilities. No way for the man to get on the roof from his current location unless he had some kind of rope and hook, which Concho doubted, and which would also make a lot of noise being used.

Similarly, the underside of his home was blocked off by a metal skirt surrounding the trailer. The skirt was made up of individual panels that allowed access in case of plumbing or other issues but none of those panels could be lifted without sounding like a shrieking covey of ghosts.

On the other hand, stealthy movements along the ground might escape even Concho's sensitive ears. If the man sought to escape, he'd probably go north straight away from the trailer. If he planned to take the offensive, he'd likely head west toward the arroyo. If he'd stayed put…

Slipping along the rear of the trailer, Concho reached the mesquite and juniper grove outside his home office. He came to a crouch there and began to carefully study his backyard and the bank of the arroyo bordering it.

Nothing could be seen.

Putting down his bow and rising to his feet, he took out one of the grenades he'd gotten from the dead assassin and pulled the pin. Holding the safety lever down to keep the grenade from going off, he calculated the distance across his trailer. Just as he drew back his arm to throw, something heavy bounced on the roof above his head, then spun down to the ground a dozen feet away. Instantly, Concho understood what it was. The assassin had the same idea he'd had and had beaten him to the punch.

The Ranger's fight or flight impulse kicked in. Still holding down the lever of the grenade he held, he hurled himself forward into the grove of bushes in front of him. This took him behind the corner of his house and out of the direct line of the grenade's explosion. He hit the ground.

The enemy grenade boomed. Dirt and shrapnel hurtled outward. Concho threw his hands over his head as the side of his trailer took the brunt of the explosion. The tin skirt at the bottom peeled back. Siding shrieked as hot steel cut through it, leaving the air laced with the smells of explosive, melted metal, and smoke.

Shrapnel chopped into the grove of trees where Concho hid, slicing through trunks and clipping off limbs and twigs that rained down on top of him. His ears rang. The odor of burnt tree sap assaulted his nostrils. He smelled flash-fried paint from the side of the house.

Once again, however, he'd escaped the brunt of an explosion. He rolled onto his side, breathing hard. He still held his own grenade with the safety lever down but he'd lost the pin so he couldn't reinsert it.

"A chess game," he muttered to himself. "And I'm close to being checkmated."

He still had a move though. He lifted his voice, cried out, trying to put the sound of agony into his words. "No! No! God. My legs are gone! Help!"

As soon as he'd let out the shout, Concho came to his feet, staying within the trees to break up his outline. Sudden footsteps burst along the back of his house. A man in black raced toward him, risking everything in a run for the finish. He heard a voice mutter:

"Got you, you son of a bitch!"

Concho launched himself out of the grove. In an instant, he and the last assassin stood face to face. Concho had the grenade in his right fist but no other weapon handy. The Colt Double Eagles still hung at his belt.

The assassin had a rifle; he flung it up, preparing to fire at point-blank range. Concho snapped a kick into it. The blow knocked the weapon out of the man's hands, sent it flipping out into the trailer's backyard.

"My legs grew back," Concho said.

"Son of a bitch!" the other man cursed again.

He launched a return kick at Concho. The Ranger swayed aside. A flurry of blows followed, strike, block, strike. The whispers of misses, the thud of hits, the grunts of effort. Concho had to keep his right fist closed around the grenade but that added weight to his punches.

The Ranger couldn't make out much of his enemy's face behind the thick night goggles. He saw a strong chin, shaven, on a man a couple of inches shorter than him. He still had his own goggles on, too, and he wondered for a second if anyone watching this fight would see it as two big alien mantises facing off against each other.

He had no time to wonder at anything for long as the assassin dropped and spun, trying to sweep Concho's legs from under him. The lawman leaped back, then instantly charged in again as the other pushed to his feet. They exchanged blows. A punch to the cheek loosened one of Concho's teeth, but his own heavy blow with his right fist drove the man to his knees.

Concho snapped a kick at the fellow's goggles but only caught a shoulder as the man twisted his head aside. The blow still knocked the fellow off balance and he stumbled up and backward trying to regain it. He tripped over something in the yard and went down.

Ten-Wolves stalked forward. But the assassin had tripped over his own lost rifle and he grabbed it and started to swing it around. Concho dove forward. His shoulder struck the gun again and knocked it free. His weight landed on top of his downed foe. The man grunted but his bulletproof vest protected him from losing his air.

They fought in the dirt then, beating the rain-softened soil to mud. The yard here sloped down toward the arroyo bordering it. The frantic battle took the two of them closer and closer to that edge.

Ten-Wolves slammed an elbow into the man's face, knocking the goggles askew at one side. The shadow of an eye socket shone, and the gleam of bared teeth. The assassin smashed a fist into Concho's side but it did nothing against the Ranger's vest.

Concho tried to drop with his elbow into the man's neck. He got only partial success; his elbow punched into the left side of the man's throat and slid off, driving into the ground. The assassin gagged but got his knee up and levered Concho to one side.

They struggled right on the bank of the arroyo now. Ten-Wolves landed with an "oomph" and punched the ground with his right fist to keep from going over the edge. He heard an awful sound, a sound that instantly drenched him in cold sweat. The safety lever of the grenade he held had snapped under the pressure; in seconds the grenade would blow.

The assassin got both knees under him and swung up a knife that flashed a gleaming shine. He either hadn't heard the snapping sound or didn't know what it meant. He stabbed downward with the steel blade in his hand. Concho blocked the attack with his left arm, locked his own arm around the other's wrist and twisted.

The assassin grunted as his body bent backward from the knees. For an instant, his bulletproof vest rode up, revealing a dirty white patch of belly. Concho stuffed the grenade up under the man's vest, then swept the assassin's legs from under him. With no time left, he kicked the man off the edge of the arroyo.

CHAPTER 21

The assassin realized what had been shoved under his vest. He screamed as he fell backward off the bank of the arroyo. His hands flailed for support. They found none. The man still hung in the air when his last moment ticked away.

Concho threw himself down in his yard and closed his eyes. He had half a second to pray to his ancestors before the grenade went off. A bloom of white seared away the darkness. One thunderous boom cracked the air, followed instantly by another as a second grenade, which the mercenary must have been carrying in a pocket of his BDUs, exploded.

Dissolved blood and tissue sprayed in every direction. Shrapnel whumped into the side of the arroyo. Concho heard the whine and whip of metal fragments pass over his head. His body jarred as the ground jarred. Something ripped like a buzz saw across the back of his vest. He tried to sit up and failed the first time. Finally, he made it to one knee.

A scallop of the ravine's bank had been torn away by the explosion. The yard all around lay littered with debris, some of which had once been part of a living human being. Concho pushed himself upright. He swayed like a tree in a hurricane wind but somehow managed to keep his feet.

A quick examination revealed blood trickling down his left hand from a cut on his wrist. More blood splotched his right arm and shoulder, though much of it wasn't his. His ears thrummed and hummed; he hoped he hadn't ruptured an eardrum.

Something was wrong with his armored vest, and when he unstrapped it at the front and peeled it off, he could see the whole back ripped open. Not an easy thing to do. Sticking a hand behind him, he tried to feel for a wound but couldn't reach high enough to find any. His fingers glistened sticky with blood when he examined them though.

Concho almost took a step closer to the arroyo to gaze in at what remained of the final assassin. He spat instead and turned away. He'd seen enough bodies hit by high explosives in Afghanistan. He didn't need to see more.

Staggering back up the yard toward his house, the Ranger picked up the assassin's M4 carbine. A few steps farther on, he found one of his Colts lying in the dirt. He hadn't even realized it had been torn from its holster. He picked it up and brushed away as much mud as he could before sticking it back where it belonged.

His back door was locked but he had the key in his pocket. He opened it, stumbled inside and clicked on lights. One pocket of his muddy BDUs held his cellphone. He pulled it out and was surprised to see it still worked. The clock read 4:57 AM. A lot had happened in a short time.

Punching up the last number he'd gotten a call from, he hit redial. Four rings later, a voice answered.

"Yes!" Della Rice said.

"Don't you ever sleep?" Concho asked.

"I was asleep. I just wake up quick."

"Hhm. Well, you nailed it about the assassination attempt. Two and a quarter of three killers are lying dead in my yard right now."

"And a quarter?"

"Grenade," Concho replied. "Maybe you better get some of your people over here to look things over. You know where I live?"

"Not exactly."

"Stop by Tribal police headquarters. I'll call ahead and make sure someone is there to guide you."

"Are you OK?" Rice asked.

"Not completely sure yet. But I'm alive. See you when you get here." He hung up.

His next call went to Kickapoo Tribal Police headquarters. Nila Willow, appointed by Roberto Echabarri as the first female officer in the tribe's history, was on duty and picked up the phone.

"Police," she said.

Concho explained the purpose of his call and a little bit about what had happened. Nila normally never said any word that wasn't absolutely required but when she responded to the description of the attack with, "Wow!" Concho felt like he'd won the lottery.

After hanging up, Ten-Wolves stripped off his muddy clothes and checked himself in the mirror. He found half a dozen scratches and gouges, including a long one between his shoulder blades that had bled heavily and was just beginning to clot. Plenty of aches and pains would soon grow into bruises.

He took a quick shower but tried to avoid getting his back wound wet. The sting of soap and water on his other cuts felt strangely good. He wrapped an ace bandage around himself to protect the wound on his upper back, then slipped on a loose shirt and some sweat pants. Examining his other clothes, he found the jeans salvageable but the shirt torn to shreds. The heels of his boots were partially melted from the heat of the last explosion. He'd have to get a new pair.

After flipping on the outside lights, he fetched his bow and his .30-06 from outside. He cleaned all his weapons before going into his home office to see how much damage his enemy's grenade had caused. Over a dozen holes had been chopped through his outside wall, ranging from baseball-sized to penny-sized. Darkness seeped in through the gaps, along with a chill.

One shrapnel fragment had embedded itself in his computer

monitor like a nail in an eyeball, turning it into landfill. Others had churned through bookshelves, tearing reference works into shreds. He could smell singed cloth and paper. Luckily, a fire hadn't started. He'd have to borrow a tarp from someone to cover the side of the trailer until he could get repairs made.

The sound of approaching sirens pulled him away from the destruction and brought him to his front door. Within a few minutes, half a dozen vehicles pulled to the edge of the road leading to his place and stopped in a line. First up was a white SUV with the Kickapoo Tribal police emblem on the side. The rest all had FBI written on them somewhere.

"The cavalry has arrived," Concho murmured to himself. "Late, of course. And let's hope they're on the side of the Indian."

***

Concho Ten-Wolves sat on a stool in his own kitchen, sans shirt, while a paramedic cleaned the gash in his back and put in six stitches. The rear door opened and Special Agent Della Rice came in wearing a blue windbreaker that read "FBI" over the pocket. The jacket hung unzipped, showing the Glock 40 semi-automatic pistol holstered at her right hip.

A bright light stabbed into the room with the agent. It dimmed when she closed the door. Although it was close to dawn, the Federals had brought spotlights with them to help study the scene outside.

Rice strode over to Concho. Her gaze was frank and a little admiring as she studied his bare and muscled upper body, and she didn't seem embarrassed to be seen doing it.

"Guess I need to up my workout regime," she said. "What's your secret?"

"Bacon," Concho replied.

Rice's response included a bare hint of a smile. "You did some damage here tonight," she said, turning completely serious.

"They were uninvited guests."

Rice nodded. "No ID," she said. "To be expected. They read as mercenaries to me, rather than Mafia-style assassins."

"Yeah, that's how I'd call it, too."

"The two who weren't blown to shreds had claymores. They came armed for bear."

"For wolves," Concho corrected, earning him another small smile from Agent Rice.

The medic finished with his stitches and patted Concho on the shoulder to indicate he could dress. Still sitting on his stool, he picked up a shirt from the counter next to him and eased it on. It was yellow cotton, old and worn and faded enough to be soft against his cuts and bruises.

Rice watched him pull the shirt on and start to button it before she continued: "We're looking into the helicopter you reported. No land vehicles anywhere close so I imagine you're right in guessing the copter as transport. If it left from any of the airports around, we'll find out. But I imagine it was private."

"Certainly," Concho agreed. "Looks like all the mercenaries had radios. The chopper was probably supposed to come back to pick them up. But there would have been some signal agreed upon and we don't know it."

"We checked the frequencies the radios were tuned to," Rice said. "Nothing."

"Professionals," Concho said.

"Not professional enough," Rice replied.

"Don't sound so disappointed."

Rice blinked. "If I hadn't wanted you to survive, I wouldn't have bothered to warn you."

Concho grinned. "I was joking."

"Don't quit your day job," Rice replied dryly.

"Ouch. And here I've always prided myself on being a laugh riot."

Rice started to say something else when the front door opened and Roberto Echabarri came through. He must have just arrived to take over for Nila Willow as the KTTT's police representative on the scene. He looked tired and agitated but all that was erased when he saw Concho.

"You all right?" he asked, striding quickly over to his friend.

"Will be. Better than the three who tried to kill me."

"I just heard," Echabarri said. "What can I do?"

"I'm going to check on our team's progress," Della Rice interrupted. "I'll let you two talk." She headed toward the front door, moving with lithe grace.

Roberto's gaze followed her an instant before sliding back to Concho. "That's a…fine looking woman," he said.

"And scary," Concho added.

Echabarri chuckled. "True too. And I'm glad she's gone. I have to tell you something. And it's tribal business I'd rather not share with the F…B…I."

CHAPTER 22

The man called Scout paced restlessly back and forth through his efficiency apartment in Eagle Pass. He checked the time. 6:04 AM. Four minutes after the last time he'd checked. He'd gotten a call late last night informing him of a planned attack on Concho Ten-Wolves. After it was over, he had orders to move in and muddy up the scene but he should have gotten the word to go well before 6:00. The mercenaries were late.

Something had gone wrong.

Maybe they're just delayed, he thought. *Can't expect everything to go smoothly in an operation like this. Be patient.*

He tried patience for fifteen more minutes before the cursing began. He spent ten minutes on that before his phone rang. He snatched it up and hit receive. Hope vied with fear in his mind as he said, "Hello!"

Fear won out as he recognized his caller's voice and the anger surging through it.

"Listen and don't speak," the voice said. "Ten-Wolves survived! I don't know how but he survived. It's your turn. I'll give you five days. If you fail, I doubt I'll have to do anything to you. Ten-Wolves will take care of that. Of course, if he doesn't…"

The caller hung up without finishing his statement.

Scout set the phone on the table and dropped into a chair. He hung his head in his hands. Had he just been thinking the other day how he'd like to kill Ten-Wolves directly himself? What a fool he'd been.

But now he had five days to do it. And no choice to refuse.

He needed help. But, so far, everyone who'd tried for the Texas Ranger had failed. *He* had to succeed. But how? An idea occurred to him but it was far too risky. He put it aside. He had a little time. Surely something better would come along.

***

"So, what do you want to tell me that the FBI shouldn't hear?" Concho asked Roberto after Della Rice left them.

"Well, first, I made those calls to Mexico I told you about. To check on whether our missing woman, Agustina Cardenas, has been living there. Or seen there."

"And she hasn't?"

Echabarri shook his head. "No. There are a few different communities but they're all small. Someone would know."

"You said 'first'. What's second?"

"Remember I was going to grill my mother over her 'prominent tribal families' comment. Those who supposedly might have been involved with Agustina eight years ago?"

"Right," Concho said. "Along with Daniel Alvarado, of course."

"Yeah. Well, I got two names. Disturbing ones. Whiteheart and Night-Run."

Concho felt his mouth actually fall open. "Not Sam and George!"

Echabarri shook his head. "Their sons. Pete and Manuel. Eight years ago, when Agustina disappeared, they would have been teenagers. Pete Whiteheart would have been nineteen, I think, and Manuel only about sixteen. But they both ran with Daniel Alvarado, who was quite a bit older certainly."

Concho nodded, almost to himself. "Alvarado always liked to

hang with a younger crowd. He wanted to be admired. Come to think of it, I recall Pete Whiteheart trailing after him like a puppy even when we were kids. Not Manuel, though. But maybe he was just too young."

"Mom notices those kinds of things," Echabarri said.

"She does," Concho agreed. "I'll take her word for it."

"Could…" Echabarri started, and finished, "Could Pete and Manuel have been in on the NATV Bloods with Alvarado?"

"If they hung around with him, and were close, they probably were. Though it doesn't necessarily mean they still are."

"I happen to know Manuel pulled away from that crowd a long while back. Pete Whiteheart didn't. He was still hanging out with Alvarado before Daniel got killed."

Concho sighed. "It's all a complication we don't need."

"Yeah. We have to talk to them both. But their fathers wield power on the Rez. Sam Whiteheart is even on the Council."

"Maybe I should talk to them alone," Concho said. "The Tribal Council could remove you from office. They have no direct power over me."

Roberto shook his head. "No. This case belongs to both of us. I'll do my part."

"All right. Let me deal with the…" he waved his hand around, "aftermath here and the F…B…I, and then I'll drop by your office this afternoon. We'll go talk to Pete and Manuel."

"Good," Echabarri said. He tipped his gray Stetson before heading out.

Concho rose to his feet with a deep sigh and prepared to face whatever would come from the rest of an awful morning.

***

Pete Whiteheart worked in Eagle Pass and wouldn't be home until later in the afternoon, around 3:00. Concho and Roberto Echabarri drove out to the Night-Run place to speak to Manuel. The Night-Run farmhouse was a two-story frame building built by George Night-Run himself. Other than needing a repaint and having some of the original shingles replaced by nailed-down pieces of tin, the place hadn't changed much since it had been put up.

As Concho pulled up in the yard, with Roberto in the passenger seat, three dogs came to greet them and sniff around the Dodge's tires. All were mutts and friendly. Each got a bit of petting. George Night-Run stepped out of the house in overalls and work boots and stood gazing at them from his porch. He looked wary.

"News on my missing cow?" George asked.

"Afraid not," Roberto said.

"Well, it looks like I've lost another one. Should have a heifer with a new calf but I can't find her."

"She could be hold up someplace for the birthing," Echabarri said.

"Maybe," George agreed. "You better go talk to Sam White-heart, too. He had a whole field of radishes tore up by a sounder of wild hogs. Something needs to be done about those monsters."

"I'll look into it. Maybe we can get the state to put up some money for pig eradication. We hoped to talk to Manuel though. He around?"

"About what?"

Roberto smiled and whenever anyone saw that smile, it felt like everything would be OK. Concho envied such talent and it was why he let the police chief take the lead now.

"I'm looking into some of Ben Deer-Run's old cases," he said. "About eight years ago we had a woman reported as missing on the Rez. Her name was Agustina Cardenas. Did you know her? Or her mother?"

George shook his head. "Not really. Saw 'em about. What do they have to do with my son?"

"Well, I remember riding the school bus some with Agustina," Roberto said. "And Manuel rode the same bus. I wondered if he remembered anything about her. I can't recall much."

George relaxed a touch. "Maybe. Don't know." George jerked

his chin toward a big, slat-sided structure sitting about fifty yards from the house, next to a rusty windmill. "Manuel is workin' down in the barn. You'll find him there."

"Thanks," Roberto said, smiling again.

George turned back into the house and the two lawmen headed for the barn, stepping through the wide-open front door into the sweet smell of hay and the pungent odors of manure and cattle urine. They found Manuel Night-Run forking hay to a couple of cows who'd just had their calves. He was dressed in tennis shoes, jeans, and a faded blue t-shirt reading Dallas Cowboys.

Manuel stood only 5'7". His eyes and hair were dark, with the hair cut short like his father's. Though thin and skinny, Manuel supposedly put food away by the plateful. Or so Concho had heard. Maybe he and the young man had that in common, at least.

Manuel looked his surprise at the visit from the officers. Barely glancing at Concho, he kept his focus on Echabarri. He stuck the tines of the pitchfork in the dirt and leaned awkwardly on the tool as he spoke:

"What can I do for you, Chief Echabarri?"

"Hoping you can give us some information from years back," Roberto said. "You and I rode the bus to school together. For a few years, there was a girl named Agustina Cardenas who rode with us. I think we used to call her Aggie. You remember her at all?"

It was clear from the moment Manuel heard the name that he remembered Agustina. The skin around his eyes whitened and wrinkles appeared on his forehead. His hand tightened on the pitchfork.

"I...I...I...uh yes, I...remember her. A little."

Roberto went on smoothly. "How would you describe her in those days?"

Manuel licked his lips and wiped his mouth with the back of his hand. "She never talked much. I remember that. But it was a long time ago."

"She dropped out of school, I think," Roberto continued.

"You recall?"

Manuel shook his head but then said, "I guess she must have. I don't remember her much when we got older."

"Not 'much', you say?" Roberto asked. "So, I guess you did see her some after she dropped out?"

The young man looked startled. And maybe a little afraid. "I don't... I didn't... You can't put words in my mouth. I never said I saw her after the bus."

Roberto offered the man an easy smile. "Sorry, I misunderstood, I guess. So, you *never* saw her after she stopped riding the bus?"

"Well, I don't...remember. Maybe I did. I just couldn't say."

"We heard she was close for a while with Daniel Alvarado," Roberto said. "You ever hear that? Or see her talking to Daniel?"

The young man glanced quickly around the barn. Concho thought for an instant he might run. He prepared for a chase but the need didn't arrive. Manuel finally just shook his head vigorously back and forth.

"I don't recall that at all."

"Gotcha," Roberto said. "You have any idea where she lived?"

Without looking, Manuel waved his hand toward the west, toward a relatively uninhabited area of the reservation. "Over that way, I think. Her mother was a strange one, I guess. Didn't like being around people."

"I see," Roberto said. "But you don't know exactly where?"

Manuel straightened his back and looked indignant. "How should I know? I didn't go visitin' her."

"All right," Roberto said, clapping his hands together. "We appreciate your help, Manuel. You take care."

"OK," Manuel said. "Guess I better finish feeding these cows."

Roberto flashed a small smile at the young man and left the barn; Concho fell into step beside him. They reached the truck and climbed in. Only after they'd backed out of the farm's driveway and started back toward town did they speak.

"The boy was scared to death of something," Echabarri said.

"Yeah," Concho agreed. "He either knows something he shouldn't about Agustina disappearing. Or he was involved."

"That's gonna break his parents' hearts," Echabarri said.

"Not as bad as someone broke Agustina's," Concho replied.

CHAPTER 23

Sam Whiteheart's vegetable farm lay only half a mile from the Night-Run's place but Pete Whiteheart didn't live at that home. He'd recently moved into Kickapoo Village with his new wife, supposedly a pure-blood Kickapoo woman of the Oklahoma tribe. Concho didn't know for sure. Nor care. He did know she was expecting the couple's first child.

Pete worked in Eagle Pass but was home by the time Concho and Roberto turned into his driveway. Or, at least his blue Chevy pickup sat in front of the house. Pete's job apparently paid well. The pickup was only a year old and the house was one of the newer brick houses going up on the reservation. This one was a kind of yellow brick structure, a single story, but probably over two thousand square feet. The yard looked well-kept and had recently been mowed.

No dogs here, but a shaggy brown tomcat lazed on the front steps. Echabarri stepped over the cat, who didn't move, and rang the doorbell. Pete opened it himself, still wearing his work uniform of slacks, a white shirt, and a loosened tie with an expensive gold stickpin. He'd at least replaced his work shoes with moccasins. Some kind of smelly pomade kept his long black hair glossy.

Whiteheart didn't look surprised at his visitors but had no

doubt checked them out through the window before opening the door. "What do you want?" he asked.

Roberto tried his smile. It didn't have any effect. "We're wondering," Echabarri said, "about someone you and I may have known back in high school."

"Oh? Given it's a small Rez and a small town, that could be any of a thousand people."

"Agustina Cardenas," Concho said.

Whiteheart's gaze shifted briefly to Concho before returning to Echabarri. Ten-Wolves began to wonder why neither Manuel Night-Run nor Pete Whiteheart seemed to want to acknowledge him. He wasn't friends with either of them but he wouldn't have assumed they were enemies either.

"Hardly remember her," Pete said. "Homely little thing, as I recall."

"You know where she lived?"

Whiteheart offered them a smug smile. "On the Rez."

Echabarri made a face. "Not what I meant."

Whiteheart shrugged. "No idea. So, you asking around of every Indian who knew Cardenas, or you rating me special in some way?"

"She disappeared about eight years ago. We're asking people who rode the school bus with her. I was one of those. You too. We were in the same grade if you recall."

"Right. Don't guess I ever spoke to her on the bus. Some people you just don't really notice."

Echabarri's lips thinned angrily. He definitely seemed to be taking this case personally.

"As I remember, you *did* speak to her," Echabarri said to Whiteheart. "Used to bully her some. Say mean things."

"Don't remember it. But I was a kid. Kids do that sort of thing."

"Not all kids."

Whiteheart smirked. He gave Echabarri a once-over. Pete Whiteheart was a big young man, a little over six feet and well over two hundred pounds, with an ego and confidence to match. He looked small beside Concho but was certainly bigger than the police chief.

"Sure. I guess some people bullied her. But I don't remember you standing up for her. You feeling guilty about that... Chief."

Echabarri flushed; his fingers clenched. The two Kickapoo stared at each other for a long moment.

"One last question," Concho said, interrupting the tableau. "Did you ever see Agustina hanging out with Daniel Alvarado?"

Whiteheart responded with an insolent glare. "How should I know?"

"You and Alvarado were friends," Concho returned.

"Not particularly," Whiteheart said.

Concho smiled, without nearly as much warmth as Echabarri could muster. "You can't rewrite your history when the people you're talking to remember the truth."

Whiteheart flushed. "I ran with him some," he said. "Not as best friends. And as for whether Alvarado ever had anything to do with Aggie, who could keep up with all the bucks that scut serviced."

Echabarri, who was fairly light skinned, flushed a bright red. "What the hell are you saying?" he demanded.

A smirk built and lingered on Pete Whiteheart's face. "I'm saying Aggie Cardenas, or whatever her name was, went with just about everything that walked. Not that I would have had anything to do with her, of course. I've got some self-respect. But I'm surprised you didn't get a piece."

Roberto's hands clenched into fists. He took a step toward Whiteheart. Concho dropped a big hand on his friend's shoulder. The police chief took a breath, then turned abruptly and stalked away.

Whiteheart glanced at Concho and gave an elaborate shrug. "Didn't know our good Sheriff liked old Aggie. Guess he did cut himself in—"

"Shut up!" Concho said. "Or I'll stomp a hole in you right here in front of your house and your pregnant wife."

The skin around Whiteheart's eyes tightened. "You think you can… *Ranger?* You don't scare me."

"Not trying to scare you. Just telling you what'll happen if you keep spitting bile."

"You need to get off my property. The tribe has had to put up with you long enough. Maybe that'll soon change."

Concho grinned. He lifted a finger and poked Whiteheart in the chest. "If that happens, make sure you deliver the message to me personally!"

"Be sure I will."

Concho gave a nod. He dropped his hand and turned away. He rejoined Echabarri in the pickup and could see his friend still boiled with anger.

"He's as bad as Alvarado," Roberto snapped. "Just as much of a bully.

"He learned at Alvarado's shoulder," Concho replied.

"He did. Do you think he's telling the truth about Aggie Cardenas?"

"That she slept around?"

"Yes. It seems to corroborate what my mom suggested."

"Except for the fact that it gives us more suspects, I don't think it matters. No matter who she slept with or didn't, she didn't deserve to die."

***

By the time Concho and Roberto reached KTTT police headquarters, dusk was falling and the younger man had regained control of his emotions. Concho pulled his Dodge up in front of the building to drop his friend off but left his engine running.

"By the way," he started, "you still have Tamara Redvine's cousin in jail for the attack at the casino?"

"No. His father got him a good lawyer. He's out on bail until the trial. Or the plea deal, or whatever happens."

"I promised Tamara I'd look into it but haven't had time."

"You mean, the 'he was slipped the drug without his knowledge' angle?"

"Yeah."

"We've found no such evidence so far."

Ten-Wolves nodded.

Echabarri opened his door but hesitated before climbing out. "Maybe you should spend the night in jail yourself," he said. "You'll have the place to yourself. We can even leave the cell open if you want."

Concho grinned. "Thanks, but I'll be OK."

"They've tried for you twice. What's to say they won't try again tonight. And you're isolated at your place."

"I appreciate the thought. But there are things I need to do. I'll be cautious. I always am."

"Humph," Echabarri snorted. "When-it-suits-you cautious, you mean."

Concho shrugged.

Echabarri slid out of the Dodge. "If you change your mind, there's a room here with your name on it."

"I'll remember," he said, giving a wave.

A hundred yards down the road from the police station, his phone rang. He plucked up his cell and noticed the caller ID. A big smile curved his face and he pulled over to the side to take the call.

"Hello beautiful one," he said.

Maria Morales chuckled. "That's the first time in days I've been called beautiful. I've missed it."

"You must be dealing with a lot of blind people," Concho replied. "But I can't say I'm upset about that."

"You needn't worry. I've only been able to think about you."

"Likewise. Well, except for the skeleton I told you about finding."

"No breakthrough on that yet?"

"No. We've got a few leads but a lot more questions, too."

"Sorry to hear that."

"It'll get done. Are you still coming home tomorrow?"

Maria sighed. "No, actually. I've been invited to observe a series of scheduled events here at a mall in Dallas over the first of the week. Supposed to be some ideas about revitalizing today's malls. I thought I'd better check it out."

"I understand. Sounds like a good opportunity."

"It is, but are you terribly disappointed? I'm terribly disappointed."

"I'm disappointed, certainly. But…well, there's some unusual heat coming down on this case and I don't mind knowing you're safe in Dallas instead of here. It might not be a good time to be around me."

For just an instant there came a pause. Then, "When is it ever a good time?" Maria asked, chopping her words off abruptly.

Concho didn't know what to say so he said nothing.

Maria sighed. "I'm sorry. That was unfair. Please forget it. I just called to tell you I miss you. And even if it's a little while longer before we can see each other, the time will pass."

"Not fast enough."

"Agreed." Her voice deepened a little and grew husky. "I want you!"

"Believe me, I won't be playing hard to get."

Maria chuckled. "Take care of yourself."

"You, too. I'm…going to put in for some vacation time after this case is over. Maybe we can get away."

"Or just stay at home and not leave the bedroom!"

"Sounds even better."

"Good night, baby."

"Good night, Maria."

The end call chime on his phone left Ten-Wolves feeling lonely.

CHAPTER 24

Concho made one stop before heading home, to get more salt to continue curing the boar hide he'd stashed in his bathroom. As he pulled down the dirt road leading to his trailer, he noticed much more light coming from the scene than expected.

A big spotlight stood on a pole next to the damaged side of his house. At first, he thought it must be the FBI back to further examine the site of his attack but, as he pulled cautiously into the driveway, he noticed a gold van parked in his yard with Lucky Eagle Casino spray-painted on the side of it.

Ten-Wolves slid out of his truck with his right hand close to a weapon in case this was some kind of trick. He saw a man walking toward him with one hand raised. It was his friend, John Gray-Dove, wearing a thick coat against the chill in the air. Concho strode to meet him. They shook hands.

"What's going on?" Concho asked, gesturing toward the spotlight.

"Heard what happened this morning," Gray-Dove said. "Thought I'd see what could be done. Brought some help."

"Help?"

A second man came around the corner of the house and walked toward the two friends. He wore no coat, only a short-sleeved gray cotton work shirt with his name over the pocket. Concho recognized him without the name, though he didn't know him well. Finn Hansson was in charge of maintenance and repair at the Kickapoo Lucky Eagle Casino. Rumors claimed he could fix anything that could break.

Finn was a big man, as tall as Concho but not so broad through the shoulders and chest. With blond hair and blue eyes, he looked like a Swede and was, indeed, of Swedish descent, though he'd been born and raised in the United States. His large hands belied the delicate touch he was said to bring to his work.

"Ranger Ten-Wolves," Hansson said, "Glad I am to see you well."

"Call me Concho. And thanks for coming all the way out here to help."

Hansson nodded. He gestured toward the back end of the trailer. "Some of the holes were too big to adequately patch but Mister Gray-Dove and I belted a tarp down over the entire side. Should keep you taken care of for a few weeks. You will need new siding over that whole section. I'll be happy to price some out for you. And can get a crew out to work as soon as we agree on the type you want."

"I appreciate it, Finn," Concho said. "You'll save me a lot of time and effort."

"Happy to do it."

"We also puttied up the bullet holes around your front door," Gray-Dove added. "I see you're as rough on houses as you are on trucks. Do you like being shot at?"

Concho grinned. "It's my magnetic personality. Especially attracts lead."

Finn Hansson looked a little shocked at the casual tone. "I would not be so sanguine about being a target," the man said.

"It's either laugh or cry," Concho replied.

Finn nodded. "Well," he said, "Your house is as sealed as it's going to get. I'll take the light and we can be on our way."

"Thanks again," Concho said. "But how about I give John a ride home?" He glanced over at Gray-Dove. "You mind? I've got something I'd like to talk to you about."

"Don't mind," Gray-Dove said.

Concho and Gray-Dove helped Finn load his van, then waved at him as he pulled out of Ten-Wolves' driveway.

Gray-Dove turned to Concho. "You've got me curious," he said.

"Let's go in," the Ranger replied. "It's still pretty cold out here."

Gray-Dove lifted his hands to signal agreement and followed Ten-Wolves into his trailer. A few moments later, the two sat around the dining room table with bottles of Shiner Bock in their hands. The heater ran in the background.

"What I wanted to ask you," Concho said, "is if you knew Juana Cardenas and her daughter, Agustina?"

Gray-Dove looked surprised. "Names I haven't heard in a long time. Of course, I knew them. Though not well. The mother better than the daughter."

"Any details you can give me?"

"What kind of details?"

"General impressions at first."

"Juana was a troubled woman," Gray-Dove said. "She drank. More a symptom than a cause. You don't know anything of her history?"

"Very little."

"She was a few years older than me. Grew up on the Rez. She wasn't much liked. Those were harder times. Before the casino. Surprised folks when she found a husband. Not Kickapoo. Half Cherokee, I heard. A salesman passing through. She left with him. Came back about a year later with a baby and no husband. Folks said she'd grown crazier than she had been. I don't know about that.

"The daughter was Agustina. She grew up strange, too, but I don't see she had much choice with that mother. I felt badly for both of them. The girl disappeared while you were off at college and in the army. Most said she ran to Mexico with a big fellow she met who worked here for her mama. He had a little Kickapoo in him, I believe. Not full-blood."

"*Most* said she ran off?" Concho asked.

"There were other stories. Some claimed the working man killed her when she wouldn't go with him. Others said her mother killed her because she'd started going around with many men."

"Had she?"

Gray-Dove shrugged. "It is not well to speak badly of the dead. Or those who might be. Why do you want to know these things?"

"I'll tell you something I need you to keep confidential," Concho said by way of an answer.

"Certainly."

"Roberto Echabarri and I are investigating a skeleton I found on the Rez a few days ago. The coroner identified it as a young woman of eighteen or so. Kickapoo. The bones are years old, maybe as much as a decade. Agustina Cardenas was about eighteen when she disappeared and that was eight years ago. The mother filed a missing persons report on her with Ben Deer-Run, back when he was sheriff."

Gray-Dove stared. "You think this skeleton was Agustina Cardenas?"

"We're both pretty sure it is. There's more, though. We also found the skeleton of an infant with her. The coroner says it was still a fetus actually, and the female's child."

Gray-Dove's eyes glittered with quick anger. He bit his lip, then turned to spit and realized there was no ground to spit on. He washed it down with a sip of beer.

"Eyah!" he said. "An evil thing."

"Yes!"

"So you investigate."

"We do."

"Perhaps the mother killed the daughter when she learned of the pregnancy. It must have reminded her of what she herself experienced."

"It's possible. But we think there's a more likely scenario. Daniel Alvarado is rumored to be one of those who slept with the girl. Had you heard anything like that?"

Gray-Dove sat silently for a moment. He scratched his head. "I have not told anyone this," he said, "but something occurred with Agustina Cardenas not long before she disappeared. I always knew her as a shy girl. Not considered attractive or popular. But suddenly she changed. She began to dress provocatively. She wore makeup. She became flirtatious with men. Especially older men. Turned out she was pretty and that made her popular with some men on the reservation. Daniel Alvarado was one such."

"Thank you. That's something we needed to know. I'll tell Roberto but no one else."

Concho didn't mention that Echabarri's mother had said much the same thing, or how Pete Whiteheart had seconded it. Gossip being what it was, any single report of promiscuous behavior in a small community like the Rez could generally be counted as exaggeration. But to have three people corroborate the same information became more compelling. And he'd never known John Gray-Dove to exaggerate. If anything, the man did the reverse.

Gray-Dove sighed and looked down. An appearance of shame crossed his face.

"The girl even," he said, "flirted with me. This was before my wife died. When she was long sick. I must admit I felt tempted. To my shame."

"Shame does not lie in being tempted," Concho said. "Only in actions."

Gray-Dove shook his head as if disagreeing. "I managed to control myself. Others did not. And, of course, the girl's mother could not control *her*. Juana's drinking worsened at that time. It eventually killed her. Though several years after Agustina was gone."

Gray-Dove glanced up to meet the law officer's gaze. "I should have done more to help them. The girl and her mother. But I had many concerns with my own wife then. I did nothing."

Concho reached across the table with his long arms and placed his hands on Gray-Dove's shoulders. "You and Roberto Echabarri both punish yourself too much for things you had no real ability to change. But it does you honor to feel so strongly."

Gray-Dove shrugged.

"Did you ever seriously think Agustina's disappearance might have been foul play?"

Gray-Dove shook his head. "Not really. I only wondered a little about Juana. She was not clear in her head. During one of her drinking bouts, perhaps she could have hurt Agustina. Accidentally. I didn't know about the child, though. That could change many things for whoever was the father. If it were found out."

"Yes. And Daniel Alvarado was married by then. Or close to it. And trying to become a tribal police officer. Reason enough, perhaps, to make a girl disappear whom no one would much miss."

"Alvarado was not a good man," Gray-Dove said. "I cannot say otherwise, even though it is to speak ill of the dead."

"No," Concho said. "He wasn't a good man and we're still discovering how far his evil spread even after his death."

CHAPTER 25

After dropping John Gray-Dove off at his place, Concho called Echabarri with what he'd learned, then returned home and washed and resalted the boar hide. He grabbed himself something to eat and bedded down in the hallway again with his weapons around him. His precautions weren't needed this night; he slept soundly without being interrupted.

The Ranger's first thought upon awakening was that it was Sunday and he wished Maria Morales *was* coming home. He wished he had nothing to do but to wait for her, to take her out to dinner, to make love to her at the end of the evening.

Shaking off the wishful thinking, he started cleaning up the debris left from the attack by the three mercenaries Saturday morning. There was quite a lot of it, partly from the grenade that had blown holes in the wall of his home office, and some from the bullets which had slammed through the front of his house near his bedroom.

He'd filled several trash bags already when a vehicle pulled up in his front yard. He dropped the broom and dustpan he held and drew one of his Double Eagles. After a glance out the window of his front door, he reholstered the gun and stepped out on his small porch to await his visitor.

The vehicle parked beside his Dodge was an even bigger truck, a Ford F-250 Super Duty, built for heavy farm work. Painted on its sides were the words: Whiteheart Farms: Fresh Produce. Sam Whiteheart not only sold his vegetables to Kickapoo on the reservation but also to stores in Eagle Pass. In certain seasons, he even kept a roadside stand just outside the Rez where he did a brisk business.

Samuel Whiteheart disembarked ponderously from his truck. He wore the bib overalls, checked cotton shirt, and work boots that were almost a uniform for local farmers, whether Indian, white or Hispanic. Sam was even taller than his son, Pete, and at age fifty-plus carried a substantial gut. He was one of the wealthiest men on the reservation and one of the most powerful. A lot of people tended to be a little scared of Sam Whiteheart. Concho had always been indifferent to the man. Until now.

"Sam," Concho said, as the man approached and put one foot up on the lowest step of his porch.

Whiteheart made a snicking sound with his mouth as he worked some potential words around over his tongue. Finally, he said, "Ten-Wolves."

"What can I do for you?"

Whiteheart chewed a few more words around in his mouth. "My boy, Pete, says you and our Chief of Police came around to hassle him yesterday."

"We asked him a few questions about a case we're looking into. He got belligerent. With no reason, I could see."

"So you threatened to 'stomp a hole in him'?"

"You know your son, Sam. He's a hothead. He was being deliberately insulting and I called him on it."

Whiteheart reached up and scratched an ear with a big, work-hardened finger. "My boy ain't the most tactful of men," he agreed. "But that don't give you the right to hide behind your badge and threaten him."

"Wasn't any hiding. Anytime Pete wants to make it personal,

I'll take off my badge."

"You! With your army training?"

"I happen to know your son has been training for years in the martial arts. I imagine he's a black belt by now. So the training shouldn't be an issue."

Sam Whiteheart had specks of green threaded through his brown irises. Those specks glittered as he chewed over a response. But when he spoke, he'd changed the topic.

"What case were you questioning my son about anyway?"

"I imagine he told you. The disappearance, eight years ago, of Agustina Cardenas. We're just gathering information, not suspects."

Whiteheart scoffed. "That's no case. Ben Deer-Run knew that eight years ago." He waved his hands around. "It's why Ben never investigated. The girl ran off with her buck. No doubt she's down in Mexico eating tamales right now."

"That doesn't appear to be true."

"Then you and our chief of police aren't much in the way of detectives. Maybe the Tribal Council better look into Echabarri's work. See if maybe we need new leadership over there."

"Roberto Echabarri is a superb police officer. And you know it. Your beef here is with me."

Whiteheart gave a faint nod as he worked his mouth around his thoughts. "You never did fit in here," the man finally said. "Was a relief to everyone when you went off to the army. But when you came back, people made some room, decided to give you a chance. You've done nothing but walk all over their generosity ever since. Like now, when you take the side of some runaway slut over decent, hardworking Kickapoo. I'm getting pretty tired of it, for one. Maybe I'm going to see what I can do to put an end to it."

Concho smiled his shark smile. "Sam, you were gaslighting people before that was even a term. Plenty of people on the Rez don't like me. For various reasons. Others get along with me just fine. Why, I've even got friends. And the Whitehearts and the

Alvarados never did a generous thing for anyone who couldn't or wouldn't help them in turn.

"Talk about getting tired," Concho continued. "Yeah, I'm getting tired. I'm tired of walking softly around men who think it's all right to bully and browbeat and insult those who don't have their money or their position. Those who think it's all right to call a young woman a foul name just because she wasn't their type of Kickapoo. So, you go ahead and do what you want to do about me. Or try it. We'll see who's standing at the end."

Whiteheart's eyes glittered dangerously. "You leave my son out of your investigation."

"I'll follow wherever the evidence leads."

It seemed like Whiteheart wanted to say more but, instead, he leaned over slightly and spat on the trailer's steps. He turned and warped his way back to his truck. In another moment, he'd gone, leaving only a faint dust cloud behind.

Concho waited until Whiteheart's truck disappeared before going to his own truck and taking out a DNA evidence kit. He went quickly back to his front steps and swabbed up a generous portion of Sam Whiteheart's spittle. He transferred this to a collection tube, scratched the name and date on it, then tucked the whole thing in an evidence bag.

In ten minutes, he was on his way into Eagle Pass, heading for the office of Coroner Earl Blake.

***

The tall figure watched Concho Ten-Wolves drive away from his home. He was not seen, even though he cast a large shadow through the mesquite trees where he stood. Ten-Wolves was a trained warrior and excellent woodsman but he had not been living for years at one with the wild. The figure had done so, for longer than he could remember.

As the truck disappeared into the distance, the figure stepped out into the yard. He inspected the scenes of violence, where the bomb had blown up the scarecrow near the fire pit, and where three mercenaries had died, and where damage to the trailer had been caused and repaired.

Drifting around to the rear of the trailer, the figure climbed the wooden steps to the back door. He took hold of the doorknob and twisted until it broke and opened. He stepped inside.

CHAPTER 26

After dropping off the saliva sample to Earl Blake for DNA analysis and calling Echabarri with the news, Concho returned to the reservation. He stopped by John Gray-Dove's shop to pick up the base for his drum and a few tools, then took a spin by the Redvine residence to talk to Tamara Redvine. It was fall break at the local schools this week so she might be home.

While the Whitehearts were the wealthiest family on the reservation, the Redvines were one of the poorest. They lived in an old cinder block house on the edge of Kickapoo Village. The father, Joe, worked as a custodian at one of the Eagle Pass high schools. The mother, Carmina, had a part-time job cooking at the reservation's daycare center.

Concho arrived at the Redvine house to find Tamara watching over her thirteen-year-old sister, Rozene, and her eight-year-old brother, Colt. Colt rode a stick horse around their front yard and paid no attention to the visitor. Rozene came running up with a smile and gave him a hug. She did so every time she saw him but she did the same to just about everyone else. Rozene had Trisomy 21 which most locals called Down Syndrome.

After the hug, Rozene went back to her corn-husk dolls. Concho walked over to Tamara, who sat swinging back and forth in a lawn swing hung between two oak trees. The sixteen-year-old had a book in her hand but didn't appear to be reading it. She stopped swinging as the lawman approached.

"Tamara," Concho said.

"Officer Ten-Wolves."

"I talked to Chief Echabarri. He says your cousin, Randall Wilford, has been bailed out of jail. I was surprised it happened so quickly."

Tamara sighed softly. "His dad came to get him. He's rich. He brought along a big-shot lawyer."

"Well, I'm glad he's out, anyway. He's not still staying here?"

"He's at a hotel in Eagle Pass with his dad."

"I see. Your parents at work?"

"Yeah."

"I wanted to talk to you some more about your cousin and his situation."

Tamara shrugged. "No need. Everything's OK. I shouldn't have bothered you with it anyway."

Concho felt a stab of surprise. Just two days before, Tamara had asked him to look into her cousin's problems and had been very adamant and disturbed about what had happened.

"That's a…sudden change. You were very upset the other day."

Tamara shrugged again. Her gaze drifted down, away from his. "I…overreacted. Randall's lawyer says it's all under control."

"I don't know about that. He could still be in serious trouble because of the knife."

"It was only the first time he's ever been in trouble. And, you know, with it happening here, the lawyer says he'll likely get something called," her brow furrowed, "deferment. Something like that."

"Probably a diversion program," Concho said.

"Yeah, that's it. Diversion."

Concho scratched his head. "So, you no longer think Randall was deliberately targeted and given the drug without his knowledge?"

Tamara glanced at him briefly and smiled. "That was just some silly idea I had." She held up her book, with the title *Black Dragon.* "Mama says I read too much of this kind of thing. Randall wasn't targeted. I think it was just an accident. Just some mix-up."

"And what about the NATV Bloods? Were they involved?"

Tamara shook her head. "That was silly, too. There isn't any NATV Blood activity on the Rez. But you know that. It's just... fables."

"I see."

"So, thank you for coming by to ask but everything is fine. I was just being a silly teenager. I'm sorry I wasted your time." She flashed him a brilliant, if somewhat brittle, smile.

Taking a deep breath, Concho returned the smile, then headed back to his truck after a quick goodbye. Rozene ran over and hugged him again and he climbed into his vehicle and drove off.

He wondered what had terrified Tamara Redvine enough to make her lie to his face. He could guess. The NATV Bloods had gotten to her, threatened her family most likely. Tough as she was, she wouldn't have been able to stand up against that.

Something similar had happened to him at age fifteen. The difference was, his grandmother had already been killed and he'd had no one to worry about except himself and revenge.

***

Concho remembered mornings in the scrublands of the Rez. He especially remembered one particular morning. At fifteen, he'd spent a lot of time alone. He was Kickapoo, like the grandmother he lived with, like the mother he barely remembered and whom many called a "whore."

He was Kickapoo but he didn't look much like it. He had the long, straight dark hair of his mother, but his skin was black like the father he'd never met. And he was big and getting bigger. At fifteen, he already stood over six feet tall, with shoulders broad as the steel front fenders of a tank.

The differences did not endear him to his compatriots on the Rez. Some tolerated him, grudgingly. Others ignored him completely. He could handle either of those. It was the ones who actively hated him that kept him alone. When he was younger, the hate had personified itself in kicks and cuffs and biting laughter, in snide and covert jokes from those his age, and not so covert comments made to his face by older kids and adults about his mother and his "lack" of heritage.

No one said such things to his face anymore. Even adult men hesitated because of his size and the fighting skills he'd developed out of both natural talent and necessity. But Concho could usually tell what people thought. It was a protective skill he'd had to develop at a young age. He'd also found, to his dismay, that he *liked* to fight. He didn't want to be that way and, as long as he stayed alone, it wasn't an issue.

Most of his free time he spent running the rocky fields and mesquite-spotted hills of his reservation home. He'd located every trickling stream, every stand of trees. He knew the deer and coyote trails, the rabbit holes, and where the birds fed and nested. On this particular day, he'd been collecting bird feathers.

At school, which he attended in nearby Eagle Pass, Texas, he'd learned about the work of John James Audubon and his famous illustrated book called *Birds of America*. The gorgeous paintings—some of the birds he recognized and others of strange exotics he hoped one day to see—entranced him.

For a while, he'd thought to continue along the artistic trail blazed by Audubon, who had once claimed he wanted to paint every bird in North America. But, while he could draw adequately, he soon realized he wasn't going to be an outstanding artist on Audubon's level.

He decided, instead, to become an ornithologist, also like Audubon, and he determined to start by sketching and documenting the appearance and habits of birds on the reservation and by collecting their feathers. He found most of his feathers in the places where the creatures nested. But sometimes, he actually caught the birds and plucked a single feather that he knew wouldn't harm them. On this particular day, his dreams of ornithology ended.

A distant boom rumbled his morning. The vibrations flowed through the earth beneath him. He straightened, gazing north toward the sound. Terror seized him. In the brilliant sky above the home he shared with his grandmother, a spiral of inky smoke rose and stained the blue.

Dropping the notebook he'd been writing and sketching in, he took off running. He was fast, with good wind from spending so much time hiking in the wild. He ran, with the cutting wind beating against his face. The smoke grew taller in the sky and closer. It arose right at his house, he realized. His thoughts spun to his grandmother, the only real human touchstone he had in the world.

"No, no, no," he murmured, as he ran harder.

The arroyo behind his grandmother's trailer was narrower in those days, at least at one end. He jumped it on the run, landed hard and stumbled into his front yard. His lungs felt ripped as they screamed for air. Flames crackled in front of him. He smelled gasoline and oil and seared metal and plastic—and something else both stinking and strangely sweet.

His grandmother's yellow and white 1990 Chevrolet Impala stood in the yard, with the paint scorched on one side. A dozen feet away rested what remained of another vehicle, the brown, two-toned 1987 El Camino that Concho normally drove. The Camino's hood had been torn completely off, the grill caved in. Blue-yellow flames ate hungrily across the oil-stained engine and along torn rubber hoses.

Twisted metal parts lay everywhere in the yard. Some had been blown through the glass of the windshield, which hung in spiderweb tatters. The driver's window was somehow still intact and through its smoked exterior showed streamers of fire dancing in glee over the cloth seats. A shape sat in the middle of the flames that shouldn't be there.

"Grandmother!" Concho shouted.

He raced to the car, grabbed the door handle. The heat of the metal seared brutally into his palm. He cried out, but held on, jerking violently on the handle. The door was jammed but with all the power in his shoulders, he wrenched it open. It screeched like a damned soul.

His grandmother sat in the driver's seat, far too still and silent. Fire plucked at her hair, at her clothing. A splinter of metal as long as a football had embedded itself in her chest. There were other wounds too, and blood. Concho grabbed for her, knowing the car's gas tank might explode at any instant.

Grandma never wore a seat belt. He pulled her from the embrace of the flames. She barely weighed a hundred pounds and he barely felt *that* weight as he rushed her across the yard to the front steps of their porch. He sat down with her in his lap. His hands beat out the last flames flickering over her clothing.

"Grandma," he called. "Grandma!"

Of course, she did not answer. He knew she wouldn't. Only coagulated blood dribbled from her mouth. He stroked the gray braid of hair over her left shoulder. That side of her face looked untouched, while the right side was terribly burned and the braid there had been crisped to a nub, like a used smudge of sage.

"Esadowa," Concho whispered.

He almost never used his grandmother's actual name but he used it now, seeking for some way to hold on to her essence. His eyes burned as if fire ants were building nests under his lids.

"Esadowa," he said again, his voice breaking. "Why did you pick my car today? You never drive it. You said you never wanted to."

In the distance came the sound of sirens. Someone must have seen the smoke and called it in. He waited, holding his grandmother. And he wondered who had planted the bomb that killed her.

CHAPTER 27

It was barely 11:00 A.M. when Concho reached home. Wiping memories of the past from his eyes with the back of his hand, he let them fade away into concern for the present. The sky hung a clear blue overhead as he stepped out of his truck. The day had warmed back to the Texas norm for this time of year. He felt grateful for that but he wondered as he surveyed the front of his trailer if the day would ever come again when he could do what most people did when they got home—just walk in the front door with a relaxed sigh.

Seeing no signs of disturbance at the front of his trailer, he walked around to check the back. Instantly, he came to intense alertness and drew a Colt into his right hand. Someone had been here. The knob on the back door had been broken off and the door stood ajar.

He studied his surroundings carefully, looking for any sign of an ambush. When no such signs revealed themselves, he strode cautiously to his back door and eased it open. Even though he kept the hinges oiled, a faint creak brought him to stillness.

He listened. He sniffed. No sound came from within but he smelled something resembling a wild animal more than it did a human. He eased through the door, outwardly calm but with his heart throbbing fast.

The strange scent came wafting from the back of the house. He crept in that direction, took a peek into his laundry room. Nothing there, and nowhere to hide for something the size of a person. Across from the laundry room stood the bathroom. The door was partially closed. Not how he'd left it. He couldn't see anything to suggest a booby trap, however.

Readying his Colt in a two-handed grip, he used his right boot to shove open the bathroom door. His finger tightened on the Colt's trigger as he prepared to fire. The small room was empty. The shower curtain was pulled back to reveal the tub. In the tub rested the wooden frame holding the boar hide he was tanning. That wasn't what smelled, though. Someone had been in this room.

He saw, then, what had been left for him. A floppy, broad-brimmed hat hung by its chin strap from the shower nozzle. The hat must have once been gray but now was badly discolored by stains of various kinds, ranging from paint to berry juice. One particular stain on the crown looked like mustard.

Concho's heart lurched. *The hat of many stains.* This was Meskwaa's favorite hat, the one he almost always wore. But why was it here? By itself? Where was the old medicine man?

Forcing himself to ignore the hat for the moment, Concho systematically searched the rest of the house. He found no other sign of disturbance. The wild animal smell lay heavy in the bathroom but thin everywhere else. Whoever had broken in had gone.

Returning to the bathroom, Concho pulled the hat off the showerhead. He sniffed it. He could smell his old friend on the hat, smell cigarette smoke and the grease Meskwaa used on his hair. A thousand memories surged into his mind.

Carrying the hat to his den, he placed it on the table. His emotions ran raw. Meskwaa was the closest thing he'd ever had to an actual father. The old man had also known his grand-mother, making him the last connection Concho had to the woman who'd raised him.

His thoughts twisted and turned. *Now what? If he's alive, I have to find him. If he's dead, someone will pay! But please, let him be alive!*

***

Concho's cell phone held almost no charge and he didn't want it dying while he searched for Meskwaa. He plugged it in and, while he waited, wolfed down an early lunch of tuna fish and microwavable hash browns. He hardly tasted them.

He brought out the backpack he'd put together the last time he'd followed someone across the Rez. That time, he'd uncovered a skeleton. He hoped the same or worse would not happen again.

At a little past noon, he took up the trail, with his .30-06 in his arms and his bow over his shoulder. The ground had dried considerably in the past few days but he found tracks to follow, starting in his backyard and weaving around the house before crossing the arroyo and heading into the wild. Again, the tracks were smeared rather than distinct, as if whoever had left them wore something over their shoes to keep from leaving identifiable footprints.

As he'd half expected, the trail led directly back to the rocky hilltop where he'd lost it the last time. On this day, though, no obscuring rain had come along to ruin his search for a new trail. Again, he found signs on both sides of the hill, some leading deeper into the reservation while other tracks led away.

Working on the assumption that the trail leading off the reservation was a decoy, he followed the one leading in. He kept to it, though it became increasingly hard to puzzle out. Clearly, the person he tracked had made efforts to hide the last portion of his trail. Soon, dusk arrived to make any further progress impossible.

To avoid warning whomever he pursued of his presence, Concho made a cold camp. In fact, he made two. He built the first right beside the trail, where he made his evening meal of jerky, trail mix, and water. He left a blanket and bedroll there, mounded carefully to make it look like a person sleeping.

Afterward, he slipped on his night-vision goggles and worked his way back from the trail about a hundred yards to a cluster of small boulders where he set up his second camp. It was rockier and less comfortable but a lot more defensible. After clearing his sleeping site of bigger rocks, he spread another blanket and lay back, using his pack for a pillow.

It was early. Not feeling terribly sleepy, he watched the rising of the stars and named the constellations—Pisces, Andromeda, Cassiopeia, Pegasus. These names he'd learned in college. As a kid he'd called the shapes in the stars by different names, some he'd been taught by his grandmother and by Meskwaa, and others he named himself: the bear, tall woman, the canoe, arrow, deer, crow. He'd almost forgotten those old names; it had been too long since he'd spent time camping underneath the night's canopy.

The sounds of evening birds and insects accompanied his star-gazing. A dove called mournfully, though you seldom heard them after dusk. The chirruping of crickets and frogs comforted him. Even though a cold spell had passed through recently, a few mosquitoes buzzed him. They'd never seemed to bite him very much, though, and before long he dozed.

His time sense told him it was near midnight when he awoke. Clouds had moved in, hiding most of the crescent moon's light. The frogs and crickets had ceased their music; darkness hung close on a still, still night. He turned his head slowly toward his fake encampment near the trail.

Something nosed through that camp but even with night goggles on he couldn't make out much more than a shaggy shape. Probably, it was a coyote smelling the food he'd eaten there earlier and looking for scraps.

Then, for a third time in his life, the feeling of being watched by something eerie and sinister washed over him. The first time it happened had been in Afghanistan. The second had been in his own yard here on the reservation—just a few nights ago.

The feeling did not come from whatever sniffed through his false camp, however. It came straight from the heart of the darkness to his west.

He hefted his .30-06 as a sudden chilling sweat covered him. His eyes strained behind the goggles to pick out anything to explain this feeling. They found something. Several hundred yards to his west, perhaps farther since it was difficult to tell distance in the dark, a pair of bright, unblinking eyes stared directly toward him.

Since the goggles distorted the visual experience, he pushed them up to get a look with his naked gaze. A wave of goosebumps swept up his arms and around the back of his neck. Even at a distance, the eyes loomed as big as coffee cups. Their most striking feature was their deep purple color.

CHAPTER 28

Concho had not quite believed in the creature with purple eyes. Maria Morales had seen it, and he knew she wouldn't lie to him about such a thing, but he'd convinced himself she'd been mistaken about what she'd seen. He couldn't deny the facts now.

Sighting through the scope of his .30-06 at whatever it was, he hoped for a clearer view. The scope intensified the color but nothing else. Even slipping the goggles back into place and using the scope with them didn't improve things significantly. He could detect a bulky body behind the eyes but the pale and wispy form remained indeterminate in shape.

He tried to estimate the height of the creature and guessed about six feet. However, many small dips and rises existed in the landscape here and it could be standing down in a depression or up on a mound. It could easily be taller or shorter than his estimate. What in the world could it be?

George Night-Run had seen this thing. He'd claimed it was a Chupacabra. For a good part of his life, Concho had heard of the Chupacabras. The term meant "goat-sucker," and the creature was supposed to be a vampire that fed mostly on the blood of domesticated animals like goats and cattle. It was described as being the size of a small bear with spines along its back.

The first report of the creature hadn't actually occurred until 1995, in Puerto Rico, though sightings had spread rapidly after that. Many sightings had occurred in Mexico. Raul Molina, Concho's closest friend in the Texas Rangers, claimed the Chupacabra was probably an alien who'd crash-landed his spaceship on earth and was just trying to survive. Concho had never been able to determine exactly how seriously Raul meant his words to be taken. The man was an inveterate jokester.

As far as the Ranger knew, most scientists claimed the sightings were actually of dogs or coyotes with the mange, which left the animals looking strange and elongated. He'd generally accepted the "mangy" animal explanation but, judging from the size of the eyes, this thing bulked far larger than any coyote or dog. It was quite possibly bear-sized but he couldn't see any sign of spines on the back.

Concho lowered his rifle. He'd never shoot anything he couldn't get a good, identifying look at. It could be human, though that seemed unlikely. It was probably some animal, though not one familiar to him. Maybe Chupacabra was as good a name as any for such a creature. It surely *wasn't* supernatural, though the eerie power of its presence still encased him and he couldn't explain it.

The creature continued to stare directly at him. Finally, it blinked and turned its head. The eyes disappeared and did not reappear. The lawman's inner chill increased. Where was it? Did it know he was here? Could it be stalking him?

He leaned his rifle against some rocks and drew both his Colts. If anything came after him, it would require close-up shooting. A few minutes later, though, the frogs and crickets started singing again. The feeling of being watched and measured faded. Pressing his back against a boulder, he tried to relax. As his adrenaline surge dissipated, a heavy tiredness flowed over him. It wasn't long before he dozed.

***

As the sun began to gray the sky and seep through his closed eyelids, Concho snapped awake. He studied his surroundings carefully for a few minutes before rising and stretching. A check of his phone to see if he'd missed any messages revealed him to be out of service. The same thing had happened last time he'd been in this area of the Rez.

As he walked down to the fake camp he'd set up, he got a surprise. The bedroll and blanket he'd left here last night were gone. He'd suspected a coyote of nosing through his things but no coyote would have carried them off. He'd had another visitor, a human one. He wondered about the color of their eyes.

Picking up the trail again took every bit of the Kickapoo lawman's experience. The ground grew rockier and efforts had been made to hide any sign. It took him almost an hour to work a few hundred yards but a general direction became clear.

He took a drink from his canteen. The lukewarm water tasted like iron but washed down the dry jerky he chewed for breakfast. A realization struck him, from out of a memory. Half a mile ahead stood a limestone bluff. An overhang at its base created a comfortable, sand-floored nook for anyone seeking shelter in the area. He'd camped there himself a few times, as a teen, when he'd visited looking for fossils.

If it hadn't eroded away and collapsed, the overhang might just be the operational base for whomever he followed. It offered protection from the weather and stood on a rise where you could see anyone coming from three directions. As soon as he thought of it, Concho became convinced he was right.

After working out another fifty yards of trail but finding it increasingly difficult as the ground continued to rise and grow stonier, he decided to gamble. He left the trail and circled so he could come up on the bluff and its overhang from the rear.

Twenty minutes saw Concho on his belly, crawling along the bottom edge of the bluff toward the cliff overhang. He carried the .30-06 across the crook of his arms as he worked forward. The shadowy opening of the overhang showed clearly, with no sights or sounds of life behind it.

Anyone watching would see him as he crossed open ground with nothing but dirt and rock to hide behind. But the only other choice was to wait for night and his worry over Meskwaa prevented him from wasting so much time.

He reached a spot some fifteen yards from the overhang. The stone face of the bluff curved slightly inward here and he rose to his feet behind the curve where no one in the shallow cavern could see him.

He listened. He sniffed. A rank, wild animal smell found his nostrils, the same smell he'd detected in his house. His guess must have been right about the overhang. He darted forward, right to the edge of the cavern-like opening. The rifle hung ready in his hands.

The sun stabbed into the first few feet of the overhang area, revealing only rock and sand. Beyond lay gray shadows, and darkness farther in toward the back wall. A rumbling growl purled up from the shadows. A scurry of movement brought Concho's rifle up.

A black wolf stepped into the light, its body low to the ground, its shoulders hunched. No, not a wolf. This was the same animal he'd seen at the oak where the sacred deer were born—some kind of wolf-dog hybrid. The ears lay flat against the sleek head; the short muzzle curved upward in a vicious snarl.

The last time they'd faced off, the animal had slipped away rather than fight. This time was different. The beast's body language telegraphed attack. Maybe it had something to protect deeper in the overhang. Concho wasn't going to back away either, though. Meskwaa might be here. Alive. Or dead.

"I don't want to kill you, wolf," Concho said. "But I will!"

From back in the blackness a sudden grunt sounded—"Umf."

The wolf-dog startled. It turned its head for an instant, then swung back to face the Ranger. But its posture had changed. It looked unsure.

"Umfff!" came again from deep within the overhang. It sounded like no known animal; it sounded human.

The wolf-dog gave a whine. Its body shook. It looked into the shadows again before slowly backing away. Concho eased forward, his finger holding tight to the rifle's trigger but not firing.

His eyes strained to pierce the darkness but were sun-blind from the bright shine of the day outside. The overhang made a big space, with a roof high enough to allow even a man of his height to stand upright. He took another step; the wolf-dog backed up farther. From the deepest shadows came another sound, a kind of moan mated with a restrained grunt.

Now, Concho's eyes detected a dim, bulky shape almost hidden in the deepest part of the overhang. It wriggled like a caterpillar in a pupa. His eyes began to adjust. He made out a human shape lying supine. The wolf-dog crouched protectively beside it.

CHAPTER 29

"Meskwaa!" Concho exclaimed.

The Ranger's friend, the old Kickapoo shaman, lay against the back wall of the overhang. His feet were bound at the ankles, his hands tied behind him. A bandana gag filled his mouth. The wolf-dog licked his face.

Meskwaa forced an "ahggg" out around the edges of the gag.

Concho slung his rifle over a shoulder and quickly stepped forward to drop to his knees next to Meskwaa's feet. The wolf-dog snarled but made no move to attack, even when the Ranger drew his Bowie knife and sliced through the deer hide thongs binding Meskwaa's ankles.

Concho grasped the newly freed legs above the knees and gently rolled Meskwaa over onto his side. The old man moaned around his gag. His wrists were trussed behind him with more thongs. Concho hooked the blade of his knife beneath the thongs and sliced them away.

Meskwaa pulled his hands around in front of him. The wolf hybrid had risen to its feet and Meskwaa patted it on the neck before grasping the edges of his gag and pulling it down to free his mouth.

"Glad…you're here," the old man murmured. He started to

push himself up with his hands but gave a fresh groan of pain.

Concho grasped his shoulder and pressed him back. He started to knead the old man's legs. "Not yet!" he said. "Let your circulation come back a little."

Meskwaa shook his head but did what he was told. "Watch out. He is still around. I don't know what he might do."

Concho twisted his head to check the opening of the overhang. It was clear, with the sun searingly bright outside. "Who's still here?" he asked.

"I call him Whirlwind."

"Why?"

Meskwaa's light brown eyes focused on the Ranger's face. Despite his situation, a small moue of humor played around his mouth. "It might be better to explain another time."

Concho snorted. "Yeah, probably. Let's get you out of here."

He stood, offered his hand to his old friend. Meskwaa took it and the Ranger pulled him to his feet, slipping an arm around him to take his weight as the old man struggled for balance.

Meskwaa groaned and rubbed at his legs, no doubt trying to ease the pins and needles he felt. The wolf-dog came close enough to nuzzle the old man's knee. He smiled down at it.

"One second," Concho said as he noticed his missing bedroll spread across a pile of dried grasses to one side of the cavern. He leaned Meskwaa against the back wall of the overhang and let go once the old man could stand steady. Next, he knelt beside the bedroll.

So, it had been this "Whirlwind" who'd visited his camp last night and gotten away again without being observed. Not an easy feat. Beside the makeshift bed lay a seemingly random display of items—an empty plastic water bottle with the cap on, a chewed-up toy, a few plastic forks and spoons, a broken comb, a chipped plate someone must have discarded. He picked up the water bottle and glanced at Meskwaa.

"He drink from this?"

Meskwaa nodded.

"Good," Concho said.

He opened a pocket of his backpack and took out a large plastic sandwich bag, into which he inserted the bottle. After sealing it and storing it away, he climbed back to his feet and began to guide his old friend out of the overhang area, drawing his left-hand Colt in case they ran into Whirlwind outside.

As they stepped into the open, Meskwaa's eyes teared and he blinked furiously from the stinging light. A small fall of pebbles trickled down the face of the bluff. Concho spun, looking up. For just an instant, he glimpsed a big shadow ducking back from the cliff's edge above.

"Whirlwind?" he asked.

"Yes," Meskwaa said. "But I think maybe he'll let me go."

"I'll kill him if he doesn't," Concho said.

Meskwaa chuckled. "I do not know if even the great hero Ten-Wolves can kill the Whirlwind. But let us hope we do not have to find out."

"Agreed," Concho said.

***

Scout leaned back in his patrol car with his eyes closed and his mouth twisted in concentration. His breathing was rough and jagged. But he couldn't get there.

"Dammit!" he cursed. "Enough!"

The woman who lay with her head in his lap didn't move fast enough for him. He slapped her on the bottom and pushed her away. She sat up, her face flushed, her eyes darting back and forth in fear.

"Get out!" Scout ordered.

The woman twitched in her seat. She tugged down on the silver tank top she wore. "I'm...I'm sorry. You feeling OK? You seem different."

Scout zipped up his uniform trousers before looking at the

woman. Most of the time he found her thin body and fake blonde hair relatively attractive. But right now he was too aware of the padded bra and pancake makeup she wore, and of how the meth had aged her well beyond her twenty-two years.

"I thought I told you to get out!"

She opened the door immediately and slid out of the police car. "I'm sorry," she said again. Although the weather was warming, it was still a little cool for the outfit she wore, the tank top and a short jean skirt. She rubbed her own arms for warmth.

Scout leaned across the seat toward her.

"Thanks...for not arresting me," she said.

He grasped the passenger side door and slammed it shut without responding, then started his car and drove off, leaving her standing next to the garbage cans in the alley. As he pulled out onto the highway, he cursed the woman but finally admitted to himself that it wasn't her fault.

He'd been given five days to kill Ten-Wolves. A day and a half had already ticked away and he still had no clear plan on how to achieve his goal and live to tell the tale.

***

Concho and Meskwaa started across the rough landscape away from the overhang and toward the Ranger's distant trailer. They moved slowly, with Meskwaa barely able to hobble because of stiff muscles from being bound. Concho constantly checked his surroundings but they were out in the open and he saw no sign of Whirlwind following. On the other hand, the wolf-dog trailed along to their rear.

"What's the story with the dog?" Concho asked.

Meskwaa smiled. "He and I have reached an understanding. He's a good Kickapoo."

"Is it Whirlwind's dog?"

"They...lived together. Perhaps only for mutual convenience. Neither one seemed to own the other. He soon became a closer friend to me than to any other."

"You treated him well."

Meskwaa shrugged. "Maybe so."

"How did this guy take you anyway?"

Meskwaa began to move a little easier as his muscles loosened. He straightened and began to walk on his own, though still moving slowly. "My own fault," he said.

"Explain."

"I had a vision. Of the bluff. Of a secret there. I came seeking it. I found the overhang. Empty at the time. I was looking through his things when the Whirlwind appeared. He is…very strong and fast. He didn't hurt me but would not let me leave. Anytime *he* left, he first tied me up."

"What did he say?"

"Whirlwind does not talk. Perhaps he cannot. But how did *you* find me?"

"Weird as it sounds, I think maybe this guy wanted me to. He left your hat in my house when I was gone. I found some tracks after that. It took me a while to work them out. But I remembered the overhang from when I was a kid."

Meskwaa nodded. "I wondered why he took my hat. I do not think he is a bad man. But he is not quite a typical one."

A thought burst into Concho's awareness. "You say the guy doesn't talk? And he's a big fellow?"

"Very big," Meskwaa agreed. "Almost a mountain. Even taller than you. But not so heavy. Thin as a dollar. I don't imagine he eats four pounds of bacon a day."

Concho made a face. "You shouldn't exaggerate. I seldom have more than a pound."

Meskwaa flashed a sly grin. His ordeal may have affected him physically, but it hadn't altered his personality or sense of humor. But now he put away his grin.

"You know something of the man?" he asked.

"Maybe. A lot has happened you don't know about. I found a

murdered woman's skeleton on the Rez. And the bones of a fetus with her. We don't know for sure but we think it might be a woman named Agustina Cardenas who disappeared about eight years ago. Whoever it was, the fetus was definitely hers. Earl Blake over at the coroner's office confirmed that with a DNA test."

"Ahh," Meskwaa said. "I remember Agustina. And her mother, Juana. Yes, eight years ago the daughter disappeared." He snapped his fingers. "And there was a man. Perhaps involved. A big man. People thought him a mute."

"Whirlwind," Concho said. "Could be."

"I should have put those things together. Spirit forbid but perhaps I am starting to get old."

"Hmph," Concho snorted. "To hear you tell it, you're barely a hundred."

Meskwaa nodded vigorously. "Yes. Still quite young for such as me. But, alas, I did not remember the man they said took away Agustina Cardenas eight years ago."

"Roberto Echabarri found mention of her while going through Ben Deer-Run's old files. That's how we came up with the possible identification for the bones. We've been trying to figure out who killed her."

"And you suspect Whirlwind?"

"Actually, we suspected Daniel Alvarado. That was before I knew about Whirlwind. Surely he hasn't been hiding out on the Rez for eight years with no one seeing him!"

Meskwaa shrugged. "I do not think he has been on the Rez all that time. But I cannot tell you why I think so. And I do not know where else he might have been."

Concho was considering something else. "An interesting thing," he said. "Lately, there have been some...disturbances on the Rez. Animals disappearing. Fences knocked down. Crops being torn up. Someone butchered a feral hog in George Night-Run's barn."

"You suspect Whirlwind again?"

"Maybe. And the interesting thing about that is the problems mostly targeted three families. The Night-Runs, Whitehearts, and Selena Garcia."

"Selena is Daniel Alvarado's niece, of course."

"Yeah."

"Why are these three families of interest in the case?"

"Like I said, we had been suspecting Daniel Alvarado in Agustina's disappearance. We believe he had something going with her. At the same time, he was running with Manuel Night-Run and Pete Whiteheart. Both of them knew Agustina. And when Roberto and I talked to them, they both seemed to be hiding something."

"Maybe their knowledge of the girl's fate?"

"Exactly where my mind went. But now there's Whirlwind. If he's the same guy who Agustina supposedly ran off with, he's suddenly a prime suspect." He shrugged. "Anyway, I took his drinking bottle which hopefully will provide us his DNA. That'll tell us if the baby was his. And maybe give us a motive."

Meskwaa paused to stretch. Concho stopped beside him.

"I don't believe," Meskwaa said, "Whirlwind would be capable of killing a woman. Nor most men. Though he might take vengeance on someone who murdered or hurt a love. Daniel Alvarado, on the other hand. He was capable of murder. And so is Pete Whiteheart. I would be surprised at Manuel Night-Run. But in many ways, he has always been and will always be a child. Easily led."

"I don't know Whirlwind," Concho said. "But I feel the same about the other three. Could be they just harassed Agustina. But if they're guilty of more than that. Of hurting her. I'll find out. Alvarado has already escaped justice. The other two won't."

"And Whirlwind?"

"It sounds as if you rather like him. Even after he held you prisoner."

Meskwaa shrugged. "Perhaps I have a fondness for the big men who are not always so bright."

"Yeah, maybe. But bright or not, if I have to, I'll bring him in. Dead or alive."

CHAPTER 30

Another hour passed before Meskwaa and Concho reached the trailer. As Concho opened the door to lead his friend inside, the dog, which had been trailing them, whined. Meskwaa turned back to pet it and told it to lie down. It did so, at the foot of the wooden steps.

"Your dog now," Concho said.

Meskwaa shrugged. "Perhaps he and I will travel together for a bit."

While Concho heated some chunky soup for Meskwaa, the medicine man buttered some bread and took it out to the dog. By the time his old friend returned, Concho was sitting at his dining room table with a cold glass of tea while a bowl of soup steamed in front of a second chair. On the table in front of the soup rested another item.

Meskwaa sat down by the soup. He reached out and picked up his hat of many stains and placed it almost reverently on his head. "Thank you," he said as he began to spoon soup into his mouth.

The Ranger gazed at his friend with fondness. Meskwaa needed a bath. His face was dirty; his hair hung greasy. He smelled of sweat and wood smoke and other, less pleasant things. Concho didn't care. He was glad, very glad, to have the medicine man back.

"So tell me," he said, as Meskwaa slurped up the last juices of his soup and pushed the bowl away, "why did you name the big man 'Whirlwind'?"

Meskwaa took a long swallow of cool water from a glass Concho had poured for him. He held the glass with both hands, seeming to enjoy the coolness and smoothness of it.

"Do you know the Cherokee story of the bear man?" Meskwaa asked finally.

"Guess not."

"A Cherokee named Whirlwind left his home one day to hunt. He shot a bear with an arrow and wounded it but it didn't die. The bear spoke to him. It led him into the mountains, to a cave where he dwelt with the great beast for many moons. Until he began to grow the fur of the bear, and learned the ways of the bear. Soon, the only thing marking him as human was that he walked upright.

"A Cherokee hunting party came into the mountains. They surrounded the cave and killed the bear. Or thought they did. They recognized the bear-man, though, and took him back to his village where his wife still lived and longed for her husband.

"The bear had told the man how he could become fully human again. He had to remain in a lodge alone for seven days, with no food or drink, and to be seen by no one. But the man's wife came and begged the lodge guardians to let her visit her husband. They resisted. But she came every day and each day her pleas became louder.

On the fifth day, the man himself heard his wife's pleading and came out to see her. He went home with her, though his time alone had not been completed and he'd not fully returned to his human nature. A few days later, he died in his sleep. And now, the man named Whirlwind haunts the land as the ghost of a bear who walks on two legs."

"I see," Concho said. And he did.

***

While Meskwaa napped on his couch, the Ranger called Echabarri to let him know everything that had happened, from the recovery of Meskwaa to the existence of Whirlwind and the details surrounding the man.

"Should I put together some officers to arrest this guy?" Echabarri asked.

"Not yet. He wouldn't be easy to arrest anyway, I suspect. If we go after him, we'll have to do it just right. I've got what I hope is a DNA sample on him. I want to get it to Earl Blake. Find out if *he* could be the father of the fetus.

"I'm pretty sure, however," Concho continued, "that your Whirlwind is responsible for some of the animal disappearances on the Rez. He might have killed some of them for food. Or maybe to protect himself. It's interesting, though, from the problems you've relayed to me, he seems to be targeting the same three families we've been looking at, the Night-Runs, White-hearts, and Alvarados."

"Sounds almost like he's taking some kind of revenge."

"To me, too. And Meskwaa said the same thing. Maybe for what they did to Agustina. Or what he thinks they did. If he was in love with her."

"Could be time to hit up Manuel Night-Run again. He seems most likely to crack."

"Good idea. But I want to get this sample to Blake first. And check on the Sam Whiteheart sample we already gave him. I'm also not sure about leaving Meskwaa alone with Whirlwind still out there."

"Drop him by the office here," Echabarri said. "I can keep an eye on him."

"I was hoping you'd say that," Concho replied.

***

Concho let Meskwaa sleep another fifteen minutes, then awakened the old shaman for the drive into Kickapoo Village. The dog was gone when they went outside but Meskwaa only shrugged and said, "He'll be around."

Concho had expected the medicine man to argue about going to the police station and demand to go directly home instead. Surprisingly, he didn't. Maybe the old man's ordeal had shaken him more than he wanted to admit.

After dropping Meskwaa off at KTTT headquarters, the Ranger drove straight to the coroner's office in Eagle Pass. The building felt empty when he entered but as soon as he called out, "Blake," the coroner appeared out of his office and came to meet him.

"Ten-Wolves," Blake said. "I haven't finished the sample you sent me. If that's what you're here for."

"I hoped, but that's not the main reason I came." He held up the plastic bag containing the water bottle belonging to the man called Whirlwind. "I've got another possible sample I wanted you to look at. A suspect supposedly drank from this. I can see a little something in the bottom. Maybe spit."

Blake took the bag with a frown, held it up to the fluorescent light overhead. "Maybe," he said. "I'll check it."

"Any idea when you might have something on the other sample?"

Blake shrugged. "We had a car wreck. Two dead. Alcohol involved. So I'm doing the autopsies. I'll get to the other thing as soon as I can."

"Thanks. I appreciate it."

"That it?"

"Yeah," Concho said.

Blake gave him a thumbs up and walked away without saying anything else. Concho went back outside to his truck. He was reaching for his door handle when his cell phone rang. The caller ID said, "Della Rice."

"Concho here," he said as he answered.

"Ten-Wolves," Rice said. "You want in on a bust?"

"What kind of bust?"

"Drugs."

"Why invite *me* along?"

"It's at the casino," Rice said. "Might be handy to have you there."

"You call Roberto Echabarri?"

"Done. I also told him I was contacting you."

"All right," Concho said.

"The parking lot," Rice said. "North side of the building."

"Be right there." He hung up.

***

Concho took the road home at speed and, in less than fifteen minutes, he pulled into the parking lot of the Kickapoo Lucky Eagle Hotel and Casino. His truck carried no law enforcement decals or identification so he wasn't worried about being recognized by any criminals. He parked in the relatively small northern lot which lay around the corner from the main entrance.

A white, Dodge Durango with tinted windows had already parked a few spaces away. It had no identifying decals either but Concho had seen this Durango before and knew it for an FBI vehicle. As he approached the SUV, the rear door on the driver's side opened and Della Rice slid out. She wore black pants and a black shirt with body armor over it, and a blue windbreaker marked FBI over the armor. A Glock .40 semi-automatic hung at her right hip. She nodded to the Ranger.

Three others climbed out of the Dodge. All men. Concho knew two of them. He and Roberto had confronted them both a few days earlier for tailing him—Special Agents Brian Duke and Cameron Voight. He wasn't a fan of either man and the sentiment seemed to go both ways.

Duke wasn't wearing his Hawaiian shirt this day. He had on new jeans and a pale blue dress shirt, with body armor and an agency windbreaker over that. Voight had dressed similarly. Both carried Glocks. Voight's facial expression turned bland when he caught sight of Concho. Duke looked pissed. He glared at Della

Rice, his superior. She didn't deign to show notice but she probably had and would not forget.

A fourth man came around the back of the Durango to join his compatriots. He was of Asian descent. Concho thought he might be Vietnamese but couldn't be sure. He was the only one wearing a shirt with a tie under his body armor and FBI windbreaker. Della Rice introduced him as:

"Special Agent Binh Bui."

Definitely a Vietnamese name. Bui carried a Sig Sauer P365 9-millimeter, and a shotgun. Concho offered him a nod and got one in return.

"I'm sure Officer Ten-Wolves knows," Della Rice said, "that there are several trailers behind the casino where various business gets done. We got a tip of a drug deal going down in one of those trailers. One with red trim around the door."

Concho nodded. "I know it.

"Then you can show the rest of us," Rice said. "Duke and Voight! You'll take the back of the trailer. The rest of us will take the front and initiate the raid. We clear?"

Nods came from all around. Rice took the lead; Concho strode beside her. The others followed. Ten-Wolves began to feel the familiar excitement of impending action. The next few moments would determine life and death for him and others. He had no misconceptions that he was bound to survive. His right hand found the butt of his Colt and held tight.

CHAPTER 31

As they turned the corner of the casino into the closed back lot, Concho identified the three trailers he knew would be there. One was a construction office, where Finn Hansson, the head of casino maintenance and repairs, kept his desk. He spent most of his time in the casino itself and seldom went in his office. The second trailer mostly served for storage. The third and closest to them had red trim around the front door. Their target. Concho pointed it out to the others.

"The walls and doors of these trailers are thin," Concho said. "Just remember, bullets will go through them both ways."

"Don't tell us our jobs," Duke said as he drew his Glock.

The redheaded agent peeled away from the rest of them before his superior, Della Rice, could reprimand him for his words. Voight followed his colleague toward the back side of the target.

Concho, Rice, and Bui moved to the front. If anyone inside the trailer were watching for the police, they didn't call out. As the three approached the door, raised voices came from inside, as if an argument were taking place. All noise ceased as Agent Rice rapped sharply on the front door and called out:

"FBI! Open immediately!"

All three law officers stepped back and crouched as soon as

Rice finished her demand. Concho drew his right-hand Colt. What he hoped wouldn't happen, happened. Running footsteps pounded inside the trailer; the front window next to the door shattered outward. A rifle barrel poked through.

Concho fired into the shadowy shape behind the gun barrel. Binh Bui cut loose an instant later with his shotgun. A man's voice screamed as more window glass shattered—inward this time.

A shout came from behind the trailer: "Drop your weapons!"

More shots sounded. Concho recognized the FBI men's Glocks, and the higher-pitched *pop pop* of a different weapon. Della Rice leaped to her feet, started toward the trailer's front door. Concho beat her there. He lunged up the four front steps and smashed his left shoulder into the door.

The flimsy barrier exploded inward. Ten-Wolves went through, throwing himself to the floor just inside in case anyone awaited such a move. To his left, the man who'd tried to shoot through the front window lay on his back with blood painting his upper body. There'd be no more fight from this one; he was dead.

To Concho's front, a woman sat quietly on a couch facing him, with a table in front of her littered with drugs and money. Della Rice entered. Bui followed. More shooting came from another room toward the back of the house. Concho pushed to his feet but Rice stepped in front of him.

"Watch her!" she ordered, pointing at the woman. Rice turned and ran toward the back of the house. Bui followed her. Concho growled in irritation but did as he was told. This wasn't his operation.

"Freeze!" Rice yelled at someone unseen.

A single shot sounded, and then silence.

"You all right?" Concho called.

"Fine," Rice's voice came back.

Concho took a few steps toward the young woman on the couch. She had shoulder-length black hair and light brown eyes. He recognized the Kickapoo in her. He also knew her name, though it escaped him at the moment.

"You're…" he said, "the one…from the knife attack. Bella…" He lifted a finger. "Bella Mora."

She shrugged.

"So, did you slip that man PCP?"

A tiny smile tugged at the corner of Bella's mouth. "Why don't you tell me? You know as much about it as I do."

The Ranger frowned. "You seem awfully calm for someone who's about to lose her job and experience some jail time."

The woman shrugged. "The job sucks anyway." She arched an eyebrow, almost flirtatiously. "Maybe I could work for you."

"Afraid I'm not hiring."

"That's not what I heard."

Concho frowned again. "I feel like we're having two different conversations. And your side isn't making any sense. Maybe you should lay off your own product."

Bella shrugged and glanced away.

Della Rice strode back into the room. Bui came in next, pushing a handcuffed prisoner in front of him. The man was white and walking with a limp. Blood spotted the left leg of his jeans but the wound looked like no more than a graze. He had long, stringy hair of a dirty blond color. Bella's gaze shifted toward the man and then away. A hint of what might have been relief showed in her face. So, the two were connected.

"Another one dead in the back room," Rice said. "Duke and Voight took him out. African American. Well dressed. Looks like he was the buyer and these two," she gestured with her chin toward Bella Mora and the long-haired man, "were the sellers."

Concho walked up to the drug table. He used the barrel of his Double Eagle to brush through a dozen baggies of junk, ranging from marijuana to meth to what he felt sure was PCP.

"Not a lot here," he said. "Maybe we're looking at a 'get to know you' buy."

Rice glanced at the handcuffed man. "What about it?" she

demanded. "If that's all there was to it, no one needed to die."

The man smirked, though the pain from his leg wound turned it into more of a grimace. Voight came into the room on the radio to someone. Rice shifted her gaze back and forth between Concho and Bella Mora.

Concho glanced at the agent. He felt like the lightbulb that suddenly flashed on over his head should have blinded everyone in the room. Rage twisted his stomach and knotted his muscles. He stomped out of the trailer, holstering his pistol.

Della Rice came rushing after him. He was already down the steps and heading toward his truck when she caught him. Her hand grabbed his arm. He spun toward her, throwing her grip away.

"Let me explain," the Special Agent said.

"Explain why you tried to entrap me? The girl tipped you about the drugs. And she's wired, isn't she?"

"Yes, on both counts."

"And if the shooting hadn't given you an excuse, you'd have found some other way to put me together with her alone for a few minutes in hopes I'd give something away."

"Yes."

"Did you think I was working with her?"

"We talked to her. After the event on the casino floor the other night. The knife attack you foiled. Duke found something on her. We turned her. Found out she was involved in the drugs flowing onto the reservation."

"Did she name me as her contact?"

"No. She's clearly lower echelon. She said she didn't know who ran things behind the scenes. But, she thought it was someone with…influence. I believed her."

"And since the person with influence had to be me, a plan immediately popped into your mind." Concho shook his head. "I didn't see it at all. Walked right into it. A good illustration of my own naivety."

"The fact that you didn't see it...," Rice said. "Well, that... maybe more than anything, makes me believe you."

The smile that twisted Concho's lips held no humor. "Surely you don't expect me to believe that."

Rice sighed. "I wouldn't. If I were you. But it *is* true.

Concho stared at her. "We're done here," he said.

He stalked off. This time she didn't follow.

CHAPTER 32

Still fuming at being tricked and feeling the need to get away, Concho drove over to the Wagon Wheel restaurant on US 277 for a late lunch. He ordered their giant steak sandwich with fries and paired it with sweet iced tea. He tried to convince himself that Della Rice was just doing her job as best she could but he didn't have much luck. It all felt personal to him, almost a persecution. It was one thing as a law officer to have criminals after you, another entirely to have people on your own side taking potshots in your direction.

He thought of Maria Morales and wished she was coming home today. It would help to see her, to hold her. It might have helped to talk to Meskwaa but the old Kickapoo medicine man had enough to deal with from his own recent ordeal. There wasn't anyone else he felt comfortable confiding in.

Everything together left a hole that food couldn't fill. He pushed away his sandwich half eaten. For the first time since he'd joined the Texas Rangers, he thought about leaving the job. He had an education. He had skills. He was good with languages. He could do other things besides law enforcement.

After paying his bill, Concho drove back to the Rez in a melancholy mood and stopped at John Gray-Dove's automotive shop.

He'd almost forgotten it was Monday and the mechanic had promised him his own truck back today. As he climbed out of his loaner Dodge Ram, he caught sight of his big silver Ford F-150 parked next to Gray-Dove's shop. It sparkled clean and looked brand new. That improved his mood a little.

After paying Gray-Dove for his hard work and completing the familiar task of transferring all his gear from one truck to another, Concho climbed in his Ford and wheeled down the road a piece to the Kickapoo sheriff's office. Meskwaa sat on a bench in front of the building smoking one of his ubiquitous unfiltered cigarettes. He didn't look happy.

"You all right?" Concho asked.

The old man put down his cigarette and stared at Ten-Wolves. "I understand you and our good chief of police are concerned for my wellbeing. Out of deference for those feelings, I have remained here. But now I wish to go home."

Concho swallowed the sigh he felt coming on. "Of course," he said. "I need to talk to Roberto a few minutes and then I'll take you."

"I'll be happy to walk."

"I wanted to ask you a few questions so do you mind if I take you? It'll only be a few minutes."

Meskwaa nodded and returned to his cigarette.

***

After checking in with Echabarri, Concho drove Mesk-waa home. The two normally gregarious friends did not speak. Neither seemed to be in a good mood. Only after they reached Meskwaa's place and Concho killed the big Ford's engine did the old medicine man turn and say,

"You had questions for me. What are they?"

"The questions don't matter much right now," Concho said quietly, "but there is something I need to tell you."

Meskwaa steepled his hands in front of him. "You have no

need to worry about me," he said sternly. "Whirlwind will not come for me. He did not before. As I told you, I went to him. And I won't do that again."

"I know. Guess I'm being a little silly."

Meskwaa's expression softened. "Sometimes I am a little foolish myself," he replied. "We are quite a pair. What do you need to tell me?"

"While you were gone, someone broke into your house and stole some of your clothes. I don't know if they took anything else."

Meskwaa frowned. "How do you know this?"

Concho told Meskwaa the truth, though he didn't get to the part where Meskwaa's clothes and hat had been used to distract him for a bomb attempt on his life.

"I came to see you. Last Thursday. You weren't around but your front door was unlocked. I went inside to check on you. I caught someone running out your back door with a package under their arm. He wore a ski mask but had the hair of an Indian. He seemed young. When I pursued him, someone shot at me from the woods. Not sure who but I believe it was a woman. Or a girl."

Meskwaa took a moment to process the information. He took a small pouch of red-dyed doeskin out of his pocket and fished through it to finger out a fresh cigarette. This, he stuck in the corner of his mouth but did not yet light it.

"Selena Garcia," he said. "And likely her brother, Francisco."

Now it was Concho's turn to frown, though he'd had the same thought. "Why do you suspect them?"

Meskwaa sighed. "Selena has come to me several times. She has asked me to train her in the ways of the Naataineniiha. I would not."

"I see. She wants to be a shaman. But for power. Not to do good."

Meskwaa nodded.

"So, you think they broke into your house to steal magic?"

"To search for those things that have power. She does not realize. Magic cannot be stolen. It has to be earned. At a cost."

"Does she have any talent?"

"Considerable. But wild. It may destroy her. But I don't see her stepping from this path. Not by choice."

"That ties some things together. Truth is, I had my suspicions about Selena and Cisco myself."

Meskwaa opened his door and slid out of the truck. Pulling a match from a pocket, he snapped it to life on a thumbnail and lit his cigarette. A faint breeze pushed the acrid smoke away from his face, revealing unreadable brown eyes.

"Concho Ten-Wolves," the old man said in a strangely formal tone. "Your own path continues as it was. It is not time for you to leave the work you're doing. Many have need of what only you can give."

A wry smile crossed Concho's broad face. "I think I needed to hear that," he said.

Meskwaa chuckled. "Of course, you did. Why do you think I said it?"

He waved a hand and shoved the door shut, then walked away from the Ford, toward his wickiup rather than his trailer.

Concho twisted the key in the Ford; the engine roared to life. He made a U-turn in Meskwaa's dirt yard and headed back toward Kickapoo Village. His doubts about staying in the Texas Rangers were gone. His focus came back. He had to solve the mystery and the murder of the skeleton he'd found. He knew just where to start.

***

At almost five in the afternoon, Concho pulled into the parking lot of the Kickapoo police station. He'd called ahead and Roberto Echabarri awaited him just outside the door. The young police chief joined him in the Ford.

"Let's go," he said.

Concho merely nodded and pulled out for George Night-

Run's farm. They hoped to exert a little pressure on Manuel Night-Run. Maybe they could create a break in the Agustina Cardenas case.

Long, shadowy fingers of dusk reached across the landscape as the two lawmen pulled into the Night-Run's yard. Lights were on in the house. The three dogs came to greet them and Concho let his hands trail over their heads as they started toward the house.

The screen door opened and Manuel Night-Run stepped out. He saw them. Concho held up his hand in a wave. Manuel took off running.

CHAPTER 33

Concho tore off in pursuit of Manuel Night-Run. The young man headed toward a barn at a dead run, not the barn where he'd been feeding cattle the last time they'd seen him, but a long shed to the left that stood open in the early evening.

"Watch for George!" Concho yelled over his shoulder at Echabarri.

Ten-Wolves' long legs churned. He gained but Manuel should reach the shed before the Ranger could catch him. What could the young man have in there? A weapon? Some means of escape?

Manuel darted through the opening into the shed. Concho was still twenty feet away. He heard Roberto yelling something at George Night-Run, Manuel's father. He heard an engine start. Not an automobile engine. Something smaller. Maybe a motor-bike. He kicked in every bit of speed he could muster.

Manuel roared out of the shed aboard a green four-wheeler. He swung to the left as he glimpsed his pursuer coming for him. The wheels churned up dirt, sent it flying. The engine throbbed at full power.

Concho made a diving leap. His right arm swept across Manuel's body and ripped him off the back of the ATV. They hit and rolled in the dirt. Concho came up on top, holding the younger man down.

Without Manuel's thumb on the accelerator, the four-wheeler rolled to a stop, the engine noise dropping to a low thrum. Concho pulled Manuel to his feet and gave him a shake.

"That was stupid," he said.

Manuel made no effort to fight. His shoulders slumped. He stared down at the ground. Concho gripped his left arm tight and started pulling the young man back toward the house. As he passed the four-wheeler, he shut it off.

Chief Echabarri stood on the porch next to George Night-Run. He held an old shotgun he must have taken from the farmer. Behind George and to the right, Delores Night-Run peered anxiously through the screen door of the house. Concho pulled Manuel up to the porch's steps.

"What are you doing to my son?" George demanded. His face shifted back and forth between fear and anger.

"All we wanted was to talk to him," Concho said. "By running, he just made it clear he knows something we need to find out."

George considered that. He stared at his son. "Boy! Why you run? What's going on?"

Manuel finally looked up. Sweat beaded at the ends of his short hair and dripped down his face. "I thought they were going to arrest me," he said.

"Arrest you for what?" Concho demanded. "What are you feeling guilty about?"

Delores pushed through the screen door. She was a tall woman, an inch or so taller than her husband, who stood 5'8". She'd been an athlete at school, in both track and swimming, and still had the strong but lean build despite the gray dappling her short dark hair.

"I want my son to have a lawyer!" she said.

Concho started to respond but George interrupted. "If the boy has nothing to hide, he doesn't need a lawyer." George glared sternly at Manuel, whose gaze dropped. "You will tell me, Manuel. What did you think these officers would arrest you for?"

The young man scuffed his feet in the dirt. He pulled against the hold on his arm but the Ranger would not be moved. Manuel's voice made barely a murmur when it came:

"Aggie," he said.

Delores Night-Run gasped.

George demanded: "Aggie! Who is Aggie?"

"Aggie Cardenas," Manuel said, louder.

George's face changed. It fell. He expelled a long slow breath and his shoulders slumped.

"Let's talk inside," Concho said.

***

The man called Whirlwind stared down at the George Night-Run farm as he stood in evening shadows beneath a large oak. He noted the presence of the big man with the Kickapoo face and hair and the color of an African American. He was quite familiar with Concho Ten-Wolves by now. He'd even learned the fellow's name from listening to the old medicine man who he'd kept by his side for a while.

Now, the Concho chased the young man of the Night-Run family. The chase ended with a brief scuffle. A few minutes passed before everyone below moved into the family house. Whirlwind felt tension grow in him, rising toward a peak.

Behind him in a field of dried grasses, shapes rustled as they foraged for green stems, tasty tubers, and acorns. He did not turn. He knew the shapes. After all, he'd drawn them here. For a purpose. It was almost time for that purpose to be realized.

***

George Night-Run and his wife, Delores, sat on the couch in their living room. Their son, Manuel, slumped in an easy chair across from them. It was near supper time for the Night-Runs. The house smelled of savory tamales. Concho's mouth watered for a moment, until more pressing thoughts pushed away the delicious scent. He stood where he could see Manuel's face and be seen in return.

A fuming Delores Night-Run spoke first. "Everyone knows Aggie Cardenas ran off to Mexico eight years ago with a man who had only a touch of Kickapoo in him."

"We don't think so," Concho replied. He flicked a thumb toward Roberto, who stood just inside the farmhouse door. "Chief Echabarri there has called every village in Mexico with a known population of Kickapoo. No one has seen or heard of Agustina Cardenas, nor of the man she supposedly fled with."

The young chief of police nodded at the words. He'd shucked the shells from George Night-Run's shotgun and pocketed them, then leaned the gun itself against the wall.

"So, what happened to her?" George asked.

"We're afraid she's dead," Concho replied.

Delores's shoulders gave a little jerk; Manuel slumped deeper into his chair.

"You think she was murdered," George said.

"We do."

George's gaze shifted to his son, scanned back to focus on Concho. "My son is no murderer."

"He was only sixteen when the girl disappeared," Delores protested.

Concho raised his right hand, palm out. "We're not suspecting Manuel of murder," he said although he'd not ruled out that possibility to himself. "We wanted to ask him some questions about Daniel Alvarado."

Manuel looked up suddenly as if surprised.

"Alvarado is dead, for sure," George said. "What does this have to do with him?"

"He wasn't dead eight years ago," Concho replied. "And we believe he had a relationship with Aggie, with Agustina Cardenas." He focused on Manuel. "That true, Manuel?" he asked.

"People claimed she wasn't pretty," Manuel said in a low monotone. "But she was. When she was eighteen. She'd…gotten some magazines. And she learned how to…do stuff with her hair. And use makeup. She was…very pretty."

"And what about Alvarado?" Concho prompted.

"He liked pretty. He went…after her. He was good at that sort of thing." The words had taken on an edge of anger now.

"So, they did have a relationship?"

Manuel scratched his nose with a thumb. "Yes. It only lasted a few weeks."

"How did it end?"

Manuel shrugged.

"That's no answer," Concho said forcefully.

Manuel took a couple of quick, panting breathes. He looked down at his hands in his lap. "He broke her," he finally said.

"They broke up?" Delores Night-Run asked. Or maybe it was a statement.

Manuel's quick glance at his mother came almost as a glare. "He broke her!"

"What does that mean exactly?" Concho asked.

Manuel glanced at the Ranger. His eyes gleamed with red. He seemed on the verge of tears. "He broke her heart. Her spirit. Everything about her. She thought he loved her. She was never the same after. She started…running around." His voice rose. "He destroyed her!"

Concho was surprised by the vehemence in Manuel's voice and by the underlying emotion triggering it. It sounded as if Manuel had been in love with Agustina Cardenas himself. He was about to say something to that effect when a wild squealing erupted from outside. Something banged against the house. A wave of sound rushed into the yard as if a sudden hard wind had risen. The dogs went crazy.

Roberto Echabarri gave a yelp of surprise. He spun toward the front door and flung it open. George Night-Run was on his feet, his face filled with confusion. Delores stood, too, with her hands on her son's shoulders and her eyes frightened. The house seemed to shudder. The world filled with barking, squealing, grunting.

"Stay inside!" Concho snapped quickly.

But Echabarri was already pushing open the screen and stepping out onto the front porch. Concho leaped after his friend, to back him up in case of danger. The normally proper-mouthed police chief revealed his shock with a curse. Concho saw Roberto draw his gun; he drew one of his own as he followed onto the porch.

Night had fallen but the outside light was on, revealing a surging mass of beasts swarming past the house. Ten-Wolves gaped in surprise. The yard was full of feral hogs. They rushed this way and that, creating cacophony and chaos as they collided with each other and defecated everywhere. The musky stench of animal bodies and manure was overwhelming. Concho cupped his free hand over his mouth and nose.

The Night-Run dogs barked wildly, snapping at the smaller pigs rushing by. They had no luck in stemming the tide and all three scattered with yelps of terror as a big boar charged and hooked at them with its tusks.

A massive sow rammed into the side of Concho's newly refurbished Ford, leaving a dent. Two more pushed through the wooden fence protecting the Night-Run's garden. As the fence folded, more pigs rushed into the garden and began tearing up the ground and whatever plants still grew there this late in the season.

Concho fired twice over the heads of the herd. A few animals squealed in fear and pushed away from the source of the sound. They were shoved right back by the mass of others pulsing into the yard. Domesticated hogs sometimes joined these wild groups and they weren't much afraid of gunfire. Many of the others seemed to have taken their cue from that.

George Night-Run shouted in outrage at what was happening to his garden. He grabbed the shotgun from where it leaned against the wall just inside the door. He pointed directly at the milling pigs and pulled the trigger but Roberto had removed the shells.

Concho pushed George back into the house. "It's no use!" he shouted. "There are too many!"

A young boar was forced up on the porch by the pressure of its neighbors. Its small angry eyes glared at the men in front of it as if to blame them for its predicament. With a high-pitched squeal, it charged. Echabarri swung his pistol around to shoot the attacking animal. Concho grabbed him by the shirt collar and jerked him back into the house just as the boar rushed past and tore the open screen door off its hinges.

Concho slammed the main door behind them. "It's no normal sounder," he snapped to the others. "Must be more than two hundred pigs out there. They're moving through. We stay inside until they're gone."

The Ranger stalked back into the living room. He cursed. Manuel and Delores Night-Run were both gone.

CHAPTER 34

"Search the house," Concho said to Roberto.

George Night-Run stood nearby but Ten-Wolves didn't ask for permission. George seemed too far gone in shock to give it anyway.

"I'll take the upstairs," Echabarri said.

Concho nodded. He headed down the hallway leading away from the living room to search the downstairs. He found Delores Night-Run calmly dishing up two plates of tamales in the kitchen. The tools of her trade, rolling pin, flour sifter, and cooking pans lay dirty next to the sink beside her. She turned when Ten-Wolves entered the room.

"Where is he?" Concho demanded. "Did you hide him? Or tell him to run?"

"He's gone," the woman said calmly. "That's all you need to know. So you can go too."

"It's not that easy. You've committed a crime now. Aiding a fugitive."

The woman's calm demeanor dissolved. "My son is no fugitive!" she shouted. "He has done nothing to deserve what you are accusing him of."

"We haven't accused him of anything yet but he did something. Or knows something. Otherwise, he wouldn't have run when we

first got here. And he'd be far safer in our custody than out there."
He gestured toward the back door and the night beyond.

"I doubt that."

"Then you're wrong."

As Delores continued to glare at him, Concho sighed and
rubbed his face with a hand. "Manuel was in love with Agustina
Cardenas, wasn't he?" he asked.

Delores's shoulders slumped. She set down the plate of tamales
she held. A dirty towel lay on the counter near her and she used it
to dab her eyes before looking up to meet the lawman's gaze.

"She was not a good girl," she said. "She was not for him.
But he was only sixteen. And she was the first girl he…kissed. He
thought he loved her."

"But *she* was in love with Daniel Alvarado!"

"She wasn't in love with my son. That's all I know." Her voice
turned bitter. "She only wanted to use him. She would come to
him when everyone else failed her."

Concho took a breath. He leaned against the counter. "Why
don't you tell me everything you know? Maybe it'll help me understand. And that'll help Manuel."

Delores considered his words. "Let me give George his supper
first," she said. "He is not well. He needs to eat."

"All right."

As Delores left the room with a big plate of tamales for her
husband, Concho called Roberto on his cell phone and told
him to give up the search and come to the kitchen. He swiped
his phone off and walked over to look out the curtainless back
window. Feral hogs rooted here too, but the horde had mostly
passed. He could still see a few animals nosing through the yard.
If the dogs ever regained their courage, they'd quickly run the
remnants of the pig flood away.

Something drew the Ranger's attention to a low ridge about
seventy yards off. A pair of purple eyes appeared on the ridge,
then almost immediately disappeared again. A chill washed

over him. It felt almost as if the thing were following him. But what was it?

He jumped when Roberto said, "What's up?" from behind him.

***

Concho, Roberto, and Delores sat around a small Formica table in the kitchen. George Night-Run remained in the other room eating. He'd clicked on the TV. *Wheel of Fortune* played.

Delores had dished out plates of tamales to both lawmen. Roberto only toyed with his. Despite the strangeness of the eve, Concho was hungry and happy to eat. The tamales were both fragrant and savory. He found them delicious.

"Anyone ever tell you that you have the stomach of an iron grizzly?" Roberto asked dryly.

"Meskwaa has a thousand times. Or something to the same effect." Concho tapped his temple. "But I gotta keep the old noodle working."

Delores had dished herself some tamales, too, but had not touched hers. Instead, she toyed with a dishrag in her hands, twisting and knotting the stained white cloth as she stared down at the table. She had big hands for a woman, strong hands callused with hard work.

"So what do you know about what happened to Agustina Cardenas?" Concho asked the woman. He took a sip of the cold sweet tea she'd poured for them.

Delores's gaze flicked toward Concho and back down at the table. "She was always a quiet girl," the woman said. "Until she wasn't. She began to wear makeup and…clothes that weren't half decent. She flirted with every man around. Even my George. Though, of course, he had nothing to do with her. She flirted with Manuel and he thought he loved her and she loved him."

"Did George know about Manuel's feelings?" Concho asked.

Delores shook her head. "Men do not know such things. Only women. I saw. I knew. I told Manuel she did not feel the same way about him."

"But he didn't believe you," Concho said.

Delores shook her head. "No. Men are fools. Even my son."

"What about Daniel Alvarado?" Roberto asked.

Delores's mouth pursed in disapproval. "Daniel Alvarado is the cause of all this. When Agustina began to…blossom, Alvarado came around. Like a dog with the scent of female in his nostrils. He flirted with her. He teased her. He took her."

"How do you know?" Concho asked.

"Manuel told me much. He was friends with Alvarado at that time. Some I had to figure out for myself. It wasn't difficult for anyone with eyes."

"Manuel said Alvarado 'broke' Agustina. What do you think he meant?"

"Broke her heart."

"It sounded like more," Concho said. "Manuel used the term 'destroyed.'"

Delores shrugged. "I do not know of anything else. Only, it was after Daniel Alvarado broke up with Agustina that she truly went wild. Now she did more than flirting. With any man who would have her."

"What about the big guy she supposedly ran off with?" Roberto asked. "Where did he come in?"

"I don't know much of him. He came to work for Juana, Agustina's mother. She had an idea to make her place a working farm. To compete with us and with the Whitehearts. It did not last long but she hired the man for that. He came from Mexico is all I really know. He had some Kickapoo in him but not much. He was mostly something else." She shrugged again. "Maybe just Mexican."

Roberto's phone rang and he pulled it out of his pocket. He nodded to Concho, then rose and left the room to take the call.

The Ranger finished his tamales and took a long sip of tea before asking, "Why does everyone think this hired man and Agustina ran off together?"

"They both disappeared at the same time. They were seen often together in the few weeks prior to their disappearance. No one thought anyone would harm the girl. I still do not believe you that anyone did."

Concho ignored Delores's expression of doubt. "If Agustina's mother thought she'd run off with the help, she would have mentioned it in her missing person's report. She didn't."

Delores shrugged. "I cannot say what that crazy woman might do."

Roberto leaned back into the kitchen. "I've got some news you might want to hear," he told Concho.

Concho finished his tea and stood. "Thank you very much for the tamales," he said to Delores. "I really hope you tell Manuel to turn himself in to us. You've got to know we'll treat him fairly."

Delores made no response in word or gesture. Concho joined Roberto in the hallway and they headed for the door. The chief's expression held about equal parts excitement and concern.

"Sounds like something big," Concho said.

"You got it," Roberto replied.

CHAPTER 35

George Night-Run didn't even look at Concho and Rober-
to as they left. He stared into the TV and did not respond when they
told him good night. Outside, the moon glimmered on the horizon
and most of the feral pigs were gone. The few still rooting through
the garden couldn't do much more damage. Concho shook his head
at the dent in the side of his truck. He climbed in and started the
engine and Roberto got in beside him.

"So, what did you get from the phone call?" Concho asked
his friend.

"It was Earl Blake from the coroner's office. He DNA typed
the spit you brought in from Sam Whiteheart!"

"And?"

"He found some of the same genetic markers in both Sam and
the fetus. Said it didn't mean *Sam* was the father but that someone
related to Sam was."

Concho felt a fierce elation sweep through him. "Pete Whiteheart!"

Roberto nodded. "Almost certainly. We've got him. We can require a DNA sample from him now, and conclusively prove he
fathered the child."

"Doesn't mean we can get him for murder."

Roberto sighed. "No. But it's our first big break in the case."

"Agreed. But what do we do? Confront him? We can't arrest him."

"We could put the fear of the law into him. Take him in and question him. See if that would crack him."

"I doubt it would," Concho said. "And you know, the minute you take him into the office, his father is gonna call a session of the Tribal Council and probably try to have you kicked off the force."

"And have you kicked off the Rez."

"I'm not worried about that. He doesn't have any control over me. He has some over your job."

"Guess we start by questioning Pete at his house?"

"Agreed. Let me take the lead. I've got an idea."

"Sure," Roberto said.

They arrived at Pete Whiteheart's home fifteen minutes later. Full dark had fallen but the moon spread some light. Whiteheart also had an outside light that smeared a purplish fog over everything. From the corner of the house, the same tomcat they'd seen last time watched them with glowing eyes.

No one came out of the house at the sound of the truck pulling into the yard. The two officers walked up and rang the doorbell. Pete Whiteheart opened the door a few moments later and pushed the screen back six inches.

"You two," Whiteheart said. He smirked. "Thought I ran you both off a few days ago."

Concho laughed. "If you were a quarter as tough as you talked, I'd be scared."

Whiteheart's smirk faded. "What do you want? And make it quick. My show is about to start."

"Just wanted to tell you," Concho said, "we know you fathered the child."

Shock swept across Whiteheart's features, more than expected. But the shock quickly shifted to anger.

"That's a lie!" he snapped. "I told you that slut slept with everything she could get her hands on. Alvarado was probably the father. Or that farmhand she ran off with. Or even naïve little Manuel Night-Run. He sniffed around her like a hound."

"Interesting," Concho said. "I didn't mention *what* child. But you went right to Aggie Cardenas."

A different kind of shock crossed Whiteheart's face now, the shock of being tricked. "You... That's...who we were talking about." His anger started to flow back. "Of course I knew you meant her. That's why you're here. It's why you came here before."

"You assumed," Concho said. "But the weird part is, almost no one seems to have had any idea Agustina was pregnant. I certainly never mentioned it to *you*." The Ranger glanced at his partner. "Roberto, you ever mention it to ol' Pete here?"

"Never did," Roberto said. "So how did he know?"

"Yeah," Concho said. "How did he know?"

"One of you said it," Whiteheart sputtered. "I heard you. Talking about it."

"No," Concho said. "You already knew. Like you were there." He leaned toward Whiteheart, gave him a little 'wink, wink, nudge, nudge.' "That why you killed her, Pete? Didn't want that kind of news to get out? Pretty embarrassing for you, I guess."

Whiteheart shoved Concho away. It looked for an instant as if he'd take a swing. Concho hoped he would. Even if this man hadn't killed Agustina, he'd bullied her. He'd taken advantage of her. He'd used her. The Ranger wanted an excuse to dispense some justice.

Whiteheart was too smart for that. He straightened and closed the screen door, though he remained visible behind it. "This is harassment," he said. He glanced at Roberto. "I'm going to report this to the Council. We'll see if they'll tolerate it. Now both of you better get off my property!"

"Why don't you try throwing me off!" Concho snapped, his anger surging. He stepped toward the screen door and White-heart recoiled.

Roberto grasped the Ranger's shoulder, stopping him cold. "Not yet," he said.

Concho took a deep breath and stepped back.

Roberto looked through the screen at Pete Whiteheart. "We're going," he said. "When we come back, we'll be bringing a warrant for your arrest. Bank on it!"

Without waiting for a response, the two lawmen strode away.

***

Fifteen minutes after the officers left, Pete Whiteheart came out of his house and climbed into his blue Chevy pickup. He'd told his wife he wanted to make a quick run to the store for some smokes. That was a lie. Instead, he turned off on a road leading into an unfrequented region of the reservation.

A mile or so out of town, he pulled to the side. In a field, to his right, stood a muddy pond used to water cattle. Pete reached under his front seat to bring out a plastic bag holding half a dozen cheap cell phones. He pulled one out and quickly punched in a number from memory. It rang only once before someone answered; he was pleased.

"It's me," he said to the person on the other end of the phone. "We've got an issue."

The answering voice must have said something Pete didn't like. He frowned, then snapped, "Just listen and don't talk. It was supposed to already be handled but someone messed up. Concho Ten-Wolves is close to finding out something that could ruin us. It can't happen. I want him stopped."

The voice said something.

"Nothing fancy this time," Pete responded. "Just shoot him at a distance. But make sure you kill him. And don't leave any clues behind."

The voice on the other end of the phone must have asked a question.

"I know," Pete responded. "Echabarri is a problem, too. But I'll take care of that. I've got a feeling the Tribal Council is going to reevaluate Echabarri's service. He'll either be out soon or under control. As long as Ten-Wolves isn't around to encourage him."

The phone voice asked another question.

"As quick as you can," Pete said. "Every minute that passes, they're closing in. And…you handle this and I'll see you get your feather. Your dues will have been paid and you'll be in all the way."

Pete swiped the call dead and slid out of his truck. He broke the burner phone in half and threw the pieces into the nearby pond. Heading back home, he had a smile on his face. He'd solve the problem of Ten-Wolves without his father's help.

CHAPTER 36

After dropping Echabarri off, Concho drove home. It was after 10:00 PM but a copper-colored Lexus ES sat parked in his yard. He pulled in cautiously beside it. The driver of the vehicle flipped on the inside light to show herself. Della Rice.

The Ranger frowned as he climbed out of his truck. Rice joined him. She wore a tailored black suit over an ivory blouse. She didn't have her Glock strapped on but carried a large purse over her shoulder that probably held the weapon.

"New truck?" she questioned, gesturing at his Ford.

"My actual truck," Concho replied. "The other was a loaner from the Maverick County Sheriff's Office while this one was being repaired."

Rice nodded, then smiled as she pointed at the dent in the Ford's door. "Looks like the repairers missed a spot."

"That happened after."

Rice was still smiling as she added, "Seems you're pretty hard on vehicles."

"John Gray-Dove tells me the same thing. Of course, he's a good friend."

Rice's smile faded. "Also seems like you harbor grudges."

"Fresh ones, maybe," Concho acknowledged.

"I'd like to talk to you."

"Not sure what we have to talk about."

"Well, maybe I can talk and you can listen," Rice said.

Concho rubbed his chin which was rough with whiskers. He normally shaved every day when he got up but he'd broken that routine more than once recently.

"All right," he said. "But you better take out your gun and get it ready. I had a break-in yesterday. I bolted the back door from inside when I left earlier but I don't want to walk in cold."

"All right," Rice said. She unslung and unzipped her purse, pulled out her Glock .40. "I'm with you."

Concho merely pulled one of his own Colts and led the way to his front porch. He paused there, looking for any sign of forced entry or a potential bomb. He'd left the outside light on when he'd left for just this reason but he saw nothing out of the ordinary.

The front door opened under his hand and he stepped inside with Della Rice right behind him. Both crouched slightly in a shooter's stance. Concho hadn't left any lights on inside but his eyes were already adapted to the dark.

He studied the living room for a minute, then flipped on the light. He smelled mint faintly but knew it was only Della Rice's perfume. After checking the main bedroom and the rest of the house, he finally straightened and holstered his Colt. Agent Rice did the same as they returned to the kitchen.

"Any idea who broke in?" Rice asked.

Concho debated whether or not to tell her but finally said, "A man we're calling Whirlwind. Don't know much more about him but he's been living wild on the reservation and I'm trying to find out why."

"OK," Rice said. "I appreciate you inviting me in."

"Normally, I'd have asked you to wait outside while I checked the house. But I figured you'd think I was flushing drugs or something."

Rice vented a long breath. "Frankly, a few days ago I might

have thought just that. But not now."

"So, you've decided I'm innocent of corruption? Am I sup-posed to believe that?"

She shrugged. "I can't control what you believe."

Concho walked over to his refrigerator and opened the freezer compartment. He pulled out a TV dinner, broccoli and beef tips.

"Hope you don't mind," he said, "but I'm hungry."

"No problem."

"You want anything? I've got more TV dinners. For emer-gencies."

"I'm good," Rice said.

Concho opened the fridge itself next and pulled out a Shiner Bock beer. He offered this to Rice and she held out her hand. He passed her the beer and took a second one for himself.

Shiners had twist-off caps and Rice sat down at the kitchen bar and opened hers while Concho stuck his dinner in the microwave and punched buttons.

"What convinced you of my innocence?" the Ranger asked.

"Everything I've seen since I started this investigation. Good people all like you. Criminals don't. You wear your emotions on your sleeve but they do you credit rather than condemn you. Your explanations of the anomalies that seemed to provide ev-idence against you have checked out as we've examined them. And...one more thing..."

"What's that?" Concho asked, as the microwave beeped and he took his beef and broccoli out and carried it to his dining room table.

Della Rice joined him, sitting and sipping before she spoke: "I got another call from our informant. He's getting desperate. He stinks of it even through the phone. He wants you taken down and it feels like a personal vendetta."

Concho took a bite and chewed before responding. "I've made enemies."

Rice gave a little half nod to the comment. "There's something else, though. Something that makes this informant less believable now."

"Oh?"

"I think he's a police officer."

Concho jerked in surprise. "What makes you say that?"

"Little things he let slip. Words he used. His voice was different this time. Hurried. I told you he sounded desperate. And maybe not so guarded and careful as before. At the Academy, in Quantico, I took several behavioral science classes. I didn't make an 'A' in any of them but I learned some things. He's either an active officer or he's been in the profession.

"And if he *is* a cop, and legit, this isn't how he'd play it. The secretive informer thing. He might not want *you* to know about him but he'd work through the system. It makes him sound like a corrupt cop with a grudge. You know any officers or ex-officers who have it in for you?"

"Can't think of any. There are a few people who don't want me to succeed. Because of what I represent. I don't see any of them going so far as to inform on me, though. Cops are generally pretty close-mouthed about their own."

Rice pulled her purse toward her and took out a pen and a small notepad. She clicked the pen. "Can you give me those names?"

Concho considered, then shook his head. "I won't spread rumors. That's how this whole thing got started against me. But I'll consider the issue. See if I can make any connections worth investigating."

Rice sighed but seemed to accept the decision. She tossed her pen and pad back in her purse.

Concho finished his TV dinner and pushed the empty plastic tray away. "So, what's the purpose in telling me all this now?"

"The drug situation here is worse than I thought. After I turned over my initial report to my supervisor, he decided I should relocate for the duration. As of today, I'm officially assigned to Maverick County and the Eagle Pass area. I'm your new neighbor."

"What does 'for the duration' mean?"

Rice shrugged. "As long as it takes to see improvement. Maybe six months. Maybe a year. Or longer. The two of us. We'll almost certainly be crossing paths. Since we got off on the wrong foot, I thought it best to make peace. Or try to."

"So you're buttering me up in case you need my cooperation down the line?"

Rice offered him a wry grin. "Not precisely what I meant but there is an aspect of that. Look, I've never been known for tact. My mama used to say I was hiding behind the door when God gave it out. But I'm trying to make some amends here. I misjudged you. I handled things wrong. I'm hoping we can get past it."

"I'll give it some thought. That's the best I can do at the moment."

"Fair enough," Rice said. "Tell me what you decide."

"You'll be the second to know. Right after I do."

CHAPTER 37

The man known as Scout lay on his couch with his eyes
wide open. The TV was on. A *Space 1999* marathon ran but he
wasn't paying attention. He'd actually been hoping he'd fall asleep.
He often did while watching old TV just like this.

But no such luck tonight. He was acutely aware of the date—
Tuesday now. He had two days left to take out Concho Ten-Wolves
or suffer the consequences. Those could be a lot worse than merely being dead. And he had no idea how to complete his task without putting himself at risk.

His phone rang; he welcomed the distraction. He didn't recognize the number but answered anyway.

A woman's voice spoke on the other end. A young woman.
"Can I talk to Kenneth?"

"You have a wrong number," he said.

"Oh, sorry."

The phone disconnected. Scout got up and went to his bedroom. He opened a drawer and took out a cheap plastic cell
phone, still in its packaging. He used his pocketknife to saw the
package open and took out the burner phone. He quickly dialed
the "wrong number" he'd just gotten a call from.

A young woman's voice answered. "Yes."

"It's me."

The woman took a deep breath of relief and Scout felt a sense of pleasure in hearing it. It was good to be needed. "What's up?" he asked.

"It's…Ten-Wolves. Why won't he die?"

"I know what you mean."

"I don't know how he escaped the bomb you gave us. We set it up just like you suggested."

"The army trained him well," Scout said. "And he has a certain animal cunning."

"We need him dead. He's causing trouble for…well, for someone I need to stay on the good side of. I'm supposed to shoot him."

Scout was pretty sure he knew who the young woman referred to but didn't say the name. "I need the man dead, too. Maybe we can work together on it."

"Again?"

"Again. You have a rifle to shoot him with?"

"Only a .22. I don't think it would even kill him unless we hit him in the head. Maybe not then. And it doesn't have a scope. We need a hunting rifle."

Scout knew who the "we" referred to as well. "You know how to *use* a rifle like that?" he asked.

The woman scoffed. "I'm sure I've killed more deer than you have."

Scout was surprised by his own chuckle. "I bet you have. But look, I've got a rifle you could use. Untraceable. And," an idea popped into his head, "I've got a plan."

"I'm listening."

"Where he lives. On the reservation. There's only one road into town, right?"

"Yeah."

"Then an ambush. I've got a set of spike strips you can use to blow out all his tires. You find a place with some cover-up close to that road. You know any place like that?"

"A couple."

"Good. You'll bury the spike strip so he doesn't see it. He'll lose control. If we're lucky, he'll run off the road. But either way it should give you a close-up shot at a still target. What do you think?"

A long pause came before, "I like it. It oughta work."

"Good, good," Scout said. "I'm leaving here in fifteen minutes. It'll take me another twenty, twenty-five to get to the casino. You meet me in the usual place and I'll give you the gun and the spike strip."

"All right."

They disconnected and, for the first time in days, Scout felt his spirit lift. Maybe, just maybe, Ten-Wolves was about to become a footnote in local history. And Scout wouldn't have to lift a finger directly.

***

After Della Rice left, Concho lay down but couldn't sleep. He felt exhausted; his eyes burned. But rest wouldn't come. He got up again and wandered through his house. Soon, he found himself in the bathroom studying the boar hide staked out in his tub. The hide wasn't completely cured but he decided he could work with it. Maybe he *needed* to work with it.

Unstrapping the hide from its rack, he cleaned it carefully of salt and massaged it between his hands until its stiffness relaxed. He carried it to his dining room table and spread it out. After bringing in his tools and the wooden base he'd already made for the medicine shield, he selected a pencil and marked out the shape on the hide that he wanted for the round face of the piece.

He'd found from experience that you couldn't cut hide well with scissors, no matter how sharp. He used an Exacto knife to make the slices. Once he'd removed the shield piece from the rest of the hide, he used an awl to punch several small holes around the edges.

Concho's tool chest contained a variety of leather piggin strings. He threaded a few of the smaller ones through the holes. Next, he smeared the underside of the hide with leather glue. He fitted this to the shield base and pressed it tight, then tied off the piggin strings to hold everything steady.

The glue had to dry before he could trim the edges of the hide and paint the surface, so he tried again for bed. This time he did sleep, though restlessly and with a mind full of dreams.

***

Concho woke a few minutes after six in the morning. He'd slept barely four hours and still felt groggy but he climbed out of bed anyway and dressed. After a quick shave, he went into the kitchen to make breakfast. The dining room table caught his eye. He walked over with a frown.

The medicine shield lay on the table. But it was different than how he'd left it. It had been trimmed of excess leather for one thing. But, more importantly, it had been marked with symbols of power. A boar's head glared from the center of the shield, painted in black and red. Around the edges were other symbols, all in black. They stood at the four cardinal points of the shield—eagle at top, wolf at bottom, feather to the left, and arrow to the right.

His gaze lifted, darted to his surroundings. The back door was still locked from the inside. He certainly would have heard the front door open next to his bedroom. No one could have come into his house and done these sketches.

He glanced back at the shield, picked it up. The drawings! He could see now. They were his, in his style. But he didn't remember making them. He recalled only…dreams. Odd and disjointed.

He'd never sleepwalked in his life. Much less sleep-painted. But he must have done this in some dazed, semi-conscious state. It scared him a little. He was not used to being out of control.

He strapped the medicine shield to his left forearm, as it was meant to be carried. It fit perfectly. Such a shield would not stop a bullet, or even a hard-shot arrow, but it felt right. It felt powerful.

Energy flowed into him. His fatigue dissipated. He told himself it was his imagination but he wasn't completely convinced. It was still early. He had things to do, but as soon as it grew light, he intended to drive over to Meskwaa's and show the old medicine man his handiwork. He thought Meskwaa would be proud and maybe would tell him why making this shield had been so important to him.

CHAPTER 38

"You ready?" Selena Garcia asked her big brother.

Cisco Garcia sat in the crotch of a big mesquite tree about fifteen yards from the dirt road leading to Concho Ten-Wolves' home on the reservation. It was just after seven in the morning and Ten-Wolves himself should be driving along that road soon. A few birds sang to the dawn. An armadillo crossed the road on its way home. All the animals were blissfully unaware of any pending violence.

Cisco held a Winchester .243 bolt action deer rifle in his hands. The gun had been supplied by the man they both knew as "Scout." It had a scope on it and Cisco had taken several targeting shots with it earlier this morning. He'd hit what he shot at and soon he'd be shooting at a Texas Ranger.

In answer to his sister's question, Cisco first nodded, then spoke anyway, "Yeah." His voice cracked a little.

Selena knew her brother was afraid. Despite his assumed posture of cold-blooded toughness, Cisco had never actually hurt anyone seriously, much less killed a person. Selena would have taken the shot herself but she had to admit Cisco was better with a rifle. A small astigmatism in her right eye often caused her problems shooting.

She glanced away from her brother toward the ambush site. They'd selected the spot carefully. Ten-Wolves would come from the south along the road. Several juniper trees and other mesquite bushes growing there would screen Cisco and Selena until the last moment. By that time, Ten-Wolves would have already hit the spike strip they'd buried in the dust of the road. This would bring him to a stop right in front of them.

It was a warm morning too, and Selena knew Ten-Wolves' habits. In nice weather, he always drove the reservation with his windows down. He was a big man, a big target behind the wheel. One shot from the .243 and it would be over. Ten-Wolves wouldn't be bothering Pete Whiteheart or anyone else again.

And...she and Cisco would become full-fledged members of the local NATV Bloods. Pete Whiteheart had promised. It was something she'd worked hard for over the last couple of years, ever since she'd been recruited to help her uncle, Daniel Alvarado, move drugs through the Rez. Too bad Uncle Daniel was dead. He would have been proud of how both Selena and Cisco had grown.

An engine sound caught Selena's attention. Her heart began to hammer. She felt sweat beading on her upper lip. Quickly, she slid behind the mesquite tree and crouched, her hands wet on the black nylon stock of the .22 Savage rifle she held. If she got a shot at Ten-Wolves, she'd take it. But she had no scope on the .22 and Cisco would have to get the first shot.

The early morning sun flashed off the windshield of a truck coming fast along the road. Ten-Wolves in his Ford pickup. Cisco mumbled a curse as he swung the deer rifle into position. Selena said a brief prayer to the powers she'd tried to invoke for this moment.

At the last instant, Concho must have seen the spike strip. He slammed on his brakes, tried to cut the wheel to the left. The front tires hit the strip one after another and exploded like dynamite.

The Ranger lost control of the pickup. It thundered toward the ditch. The right-back tire slid over the spike strip. It blew out with the sound of a gunshot. Concho steered away from the skid now, trying to keep to the road. His speed had dropped almost to zero.

Through the open window of the driver's side, Selena could see the Ranger's big head and the long black hair. She could see the man's mouth twisted in concentration.

"Now!" Selena begged as she waited for Cisco to fire. He did.

The high-pitched crack of the .243 ripped the morning air. The bullet crossed the ditch in an instant. Selena watched Concho thrown sideways. He disappeared below the level of the window. The truck slid to a stop, then lurched forward and died.

Selena leaped to her feet; Cisco piled out of the tree and raced toward the pickup. He worked the bolt on his rifle, chambering a second round. Selena followed, carrying her own rifle. Some combination of fear and exhilaration filled her mouth with brass.

The morning appeared to have frozen. Birds had fallen silent. No sound came from the truck. Cisco leaped the ditch, reached the driver's side of the pickup. He crouched and grabbed the door handle.

"No!" Selena shouted. But Cisco started to jerk the truck open. Instead, the door seemed to leap toward him. The heavy metal frame of the Ford's door slammed Cisco brutally in the face and upper body. His rifle went flying; he twisted to one side and fell. Dust spurted up in the road when he hit.

Selena bit her lower lip in terror as Ten-Wolves sat up suddenly inside the truck. A blue-steel Colt .45 gleamed in his right hand as he lunged out onto the road. His black eyes loomed huge in his squared-off face. Blood covered his left cheek from just below the eye all the way to his neck. It glistened like wet wax. Sprayed droplets of crimson flecked his white shirt.

Selena started to throw her .22 rifle to her shoulder. Concho fired over her head. She jumped and froze; her legs went weak. Concho pointed his pistol at Cisco lying hurt or unconscious on the ground.

"Drop it or I kill your brother," the lawman snarled. His voice sounded like he'd gargled with razor blades.

Selena hurled her .22 away as if it were a snake.

"Smart," Concho said, as he leaned over and grasped the collar of Cisco's shirt and pulled him to his feet.

Spattered blood from Cisco's flattened nose painted a Rorschach image on the boy's face. His mouth hung open, with drool at the corner. He was clearly only half conscious, trying to stand but unable to without Concho's grip holding him up.

"All right," Concho snapped to Selena. "Who ordered you to kill me?" He pressed the barrel of the pistol up against Cisco's temple. "Tell me or I empty your brother's brains all over the road."

***

Some combination of physical exhaustion and mental stimulation kept Concho from seeing the buried spike strip until the last second. He slammed his brakes but knew he wasn't going to be able to avoid it. As the front tires blew, dropping the front end of the truck, he fought to steer against the skid to keep from winding up in the ditch.

Next, one of the back tires blew and the Ford slewed back toward the center of the road. In the instant that his mind shouted, *Ambush*, something wicked struck Concho along the left cheekbone. Had the shot struck squarely, it would have killed him. But his head was turned as he fought the wheel; the slug dug a bloody channel across his cheek and went tumbling out through the passenger side window.

The impact was numbing, though. Close to losing consciousness, he fell sideways across the truck's front seat. Some part of his mind shrieked at him to *Get up!* His right hand fumbled at his holster. The Colt Double Eagle came loose into his hand.

Footsteps pounded on the road outside. Concho twisted onto his back. The side window of the F-150 sat up high. He couldn't see anyone through it but he heard a hand fumble at the outside door latch; the door started to open. He kicked out with both boots, punching into the inside of the door. It smashed open, taking down whoever had approached the other side.

In an adrenaline-fueled rage, Concho hurled himself out of the truck, his pistol rising. He could smell his own blood, taste it. He saw a body at his feet, and across the ditch in the nearby field, a young woman with long hair holding a small rifle. Selena Garcia.

Selena started to lift her gun and Concho fired over her head. He realized almost as quickly that it was Selena's brother, Francisco, who lay in the dirt by his boots. He knew Selena cared for her brother. A threat to Cisco made Selena throw away her gun.

Concho leaned over and grasped the injured and barely conscious young man by his collar and hauled him to his feet. He pointed the barrel of his Colt at Cisco's head, and under threat of death to her brother, ordered Selena to tell him who had sent the two young Kickapoo to kill him.

The threat was empty; he wouldn't kill either of them. But he put every bit of savagery into his voice he could muster. Selena trembled. Her tough girl act shattered. Her shoulders slumped. Tears wicked into her eyes. She told him: "Pete Whiteheart!"

"Selena, no!" Cisco cried out.

Concho shook the young man like a wet dog. "Shut up if you wanna live," he ordered. He had not looked away from Selena. His eyes burned.

"Why?" he demanded.

"You— I don't know. You were causing him trouble."

Concho turned his head toward Cisco. Blood starred his left eye and he tried to blink it away. "It's the NATV Bloods, isn't it?" he demanded of Cisco. "Pete took over the leadership once Daniel Alvarado died." He shook Cisco again. "Isn't that true?"

"Yes!" Cisco shouted. "Yes. Please!"

An emptiness swept through Concho as the adrenaline surge began to subside. His belly hurt. These two were so young. Hardly more than children. But shaped to hate by their uncle, Daniel Alvarado, and by Pete Whiteheart, and even by their own mother.

The Ranger spat coppery blood into the dirt, then holstered his Colt and pulled out his handcuffs. He slapped these on Cisco's wrists and pushed him against the truck. He gestured to Selena.

"Come here."

The girl shook her head. She looked around for some miracle.

"If you run, you know I'll catch you. Come here!"

Selena shivered. She barely looked her fifteen years now. A child indeed. Yet, he was pretty sure she'd been the one who took a shot at him outside Meskwaa's house when her brother had broken into the place. Even a child can be dangerous if they're taught how.

Selena stumbled across the ditch toward him, nearly limp with fear. She held out her hands for cuffs as she reached him, but he grasped her arm and turned her to face away from him.

Holding her still, he opened the toolbox in the bed of his pick-up and took out a set of zip ties. He strapped her wrists together behind her before using another zip tie to link her and Cisco back-to-back so they couldn't run.

After stepping away from the kids, he fished his cell phone out of his pocket and called KTTT police headquarters to request backup. He told them to bring a tow truck too.

CHAPTER 39

Blue lights and sirens fractured the morning, coming fast down the road toward Concho with a pillar of dust rising behind. Roberto Echabarri's white police SUV slid to a stop a dozen feet from the Ranger's dead pickup. Roberto bailed out one side; Nila Willow bailed out the other. They had their hands on their guns but found no need to draw them.

Concho faced them. Selena and Cisco stood next to him, bound back-to-back. Roberto winced as he saw his friend's face. The whole left side was bloody and swollen. The left eye was half closed.

"You OK?" Roberto asked.

"Been better, been worse," Concho said. He winced as if it hurt to talk.

Roberto shook his head. Nila Willow moved to examine the two kids.

"Cisco's got a broken nose to treat," Concho said.

Nila nodded. She pulled a knife from her belt and cut the zip tie binding the two kids together. Taking each by an elbow, she led them toward the SUV. She soon had them tucked safely behind the wire partition in the back of the vehicle.

Roberto walked up to Concho and stood studying his wound.

"Rifle slug?" he asked.

"Yeah. Mostly just a graze." He pointed out the .243 lying in the dirt by the truck. "Across the ditch in the field, you'll find Selena's .22."

"They ambushed you?"

"Yeah. Buried a spike strip in the road. I hit it. You contact the tow truck?"

"I did. John Gray-Dove is on the way."

Concho glanced at his damaged pickup with a forlorn look. "I'm gonna get teased about this."

Roberto couldn't help a small smile. "Well, you are pretty hard on your machinery."

"Seems like it."

"Did the kids say anything about why?" Roberto asked.

"They said Pete Whiteheart ordered it. And admitted he's the leader of the local NATV Bloods."

"Wow! Pete must be running scared. Looks like he's digging himself a hole."

"Maybe," Concho said. "They told me because *they* were scared. Getting them to testify to it in court is a different matter."

Roberto sighed. "True. But it's enough to arrest him on."

"You might end up with a riot on your hands. His father will stir up trouble and Letty Garcia will help him."

"I've already been notified that I'm expected to appear in front of the full Tribal Council tomorrow at noon," Roberto said.

Concho shook his head. "Ridiculous!"

"But inevitable."

"I suppose. You want me to go along?"

"No. It's not a trial. All they can do is censure me. At this point at least."

"If you need me, call."

"Will do. Now, we need to get you sewed up. That's going to require stitches."

"If we're going to move on Pete Whiteheart, it should be

done as quickly as possible."

"I can make that arrest. I'll bring backup. You need your wound tended."

"Fortunately, I clot fast. I'll ride along. We can drop Nila and the kids at the jail."

"The kids, yes. I need Nila here to examine the scene and get some photos. She can ride back into town with Gray-Dove."

"All right," Concho said. "Let's go."

***

Pete Whiteheart worked in Eagle Pass as the assistant manager of a Chevrolet dealership. Concho and Roberto figured it would be safer arresting him at work on this Tuesday morning than at home later where he'd have access to guns and friends. They went in quietly, hoping to avoid any violence, but garnered some surprised looks as they passed through the display area on their way to Whiteheart's office.

Whiteheart heard them as they stepped through his open door without knocking. He glanced up. His whole body twitched when he saw Concho's face but he quickly controlled his reaction and offered an, "Ouch, looks like that hurt."

"Not as bad as it was intended to," Concho said.

Whiteheart lifted an eyebrow. "I don't understand," he said. "And, I don't understand why the two of you are here? If you needed to harass me again, you could have seen me at home."

"It couldn't wait," Concho said.

"Why not just say why you're here," Whiteheart snapped.

Roberto spoke. "Remember what I told you at the end of our last conversation? That when we came back it would be to arrest you. Well, surprise!"

Whiteheart stiffened in his seat. His glance toward one drawer of his desk was telling.

"I wouldn't," Concho said. "You'd never reach the gun in your drawer before I shot you."

Whiteheart's pretense of friendliness faded into a scowl. "I'll add that threat to the list of complaints I'll file against you," he said.

"Do whatever makes your little heart go pitty-pat," Concho said. "But stand up now."

"And if I don't?"

Ten-Wolves grinned with the right side of his face but wasn't sure Whiteheart caught it because of all the swelling. He explained. "That'll just make it more fun for me."

Whiteheart shrugged. "Doesn't matter. I'll be out again before you two finish patting each other on the back."

He rose to his feet. Roberto took a set of handcuffs off his belt and stepped toward him.

"Couldn't we walk out of here without the cuffs?" Whiteheart asked. "This is my work. I've got friends here."

"That's not how it goes," Roberto said. "Turn around."

Whiteheart did as ordered. Roberto reached for his wrists. Whiteheart snapped an elbow back into the police chief's face, knocking him sideways and making him trip over the desk. Files of papers crashed to the floor as the chief toppled.

Whiteheart spun and snapped a kick at Concho. Concho stepped into the blow as the other man's leg whipped around. The kick connected against the Ranger's hip. But he was too close for it to do anything more than jar him. His hand snapped down and locked around Whiteheart's leg. He gave a jerk, upending the other man, who crashed down on his back and hit his head against the floor.

While Whiteheart lay stunned, Roberto lunged at him, twisted him over onto his belly and snapped on the cuffs. He jerked the man to his feet. Someone who'd heard the scuffle appeared at Whiteheart's door to ask if everything was all right.

"We're good," Concho said.

The man backed away as he saw the Ranger's face. But all eyes watched them as they led a handcuffed Pete Whiteheart through the dealership's display floor and out to Roberto's SUV. With Whiteheart locked in the back, they headed for the Rez.

***

Half a dozen people milled around the parking lot of tribal police headquarters when Concho and Roberto pulled in with Pete Whiteheart in the back. One held up a sign reading, "Children Do Not Belong In Jail!"

Of more immediate concern was Tessa Teshigahara. Tessa was a woman of mixed Kickapoo and Japanese descent who'd recently moved to the Rez from out of state. Her stated purpose was to document the plight of the Texas Kickapoo and she had just recently started a reservation newspaper. It ran to only one page at present but Tessa didn't seem the type to think small.

Concho slid out of Echabarri's SUV and waited for the chief. Voices shouted his name, yelling questions and statements. He heard, "Let the children out! Let the children out!"

Roberto stepped free of the SUV and pulled Pete Whiteheart out of the cage in the back. The shouts of the onlookers grew louder. Two more people ran down the street to join the party.

"Chief Echabarri!" Tessa Teshigahara shouted. "What's going on? Why have you arrested the Garcia children and Pete Whiteheart?"

"No comment!" Roberto said loudly. He pulled Whiteheart toward the front door of the station.

"The tribe has a right to know!" Tessa shouted. She strode toward Roberto with her phone held up and recording.

Concho stepped in between the police chief and Tessa. She stuck her phone in *his* face. "Why are the Texas Rangers involved? What have your prisoners done? Why are you hurt?"

"You'll all get the full story in time," Concho said to the crowd as a whole. "But we can't comment on an active investigation."

"Bullshit!" Tessa shouted.

Concho shook his head and followed Echabarri into the building. Inside swarmed a small beehive of confused activity. Arturo Ramon held the door open for them and then shut and locked it. A second deputy, Timbo Corbett, who was only one-quarter Kickapoo and could easily pass for white with his light skin and sandy brown hair, kept scratching at his chin as he shifted from one foot to the other.

Araceli Espaderos, who everyone called Ara and who was the second woman to serve on the Kickapoo tribal police force, sat fidgeting at the dispatcher's desk. She kept biting her lip in shock.

"Arturo," Echabarri said. "Take this gentleman back to a cell." He pushed Pete Whiteheart toward him. "Put him as far away from our other two guests as possible. And stay with them. I don't want them communicating."

Arturo nodded as he grabbed Whiteheart's arm and led him away.

"Ara," Roberto continued. "You heard anything from Letty Garcia?"

"No, sir. Not yet."

"All right. Let me know if you see any sign. And call any of our units in the field and tell them to stay away from the office for the moment."

"Yes, sir," Ara responded as she reached for her radio. She seemed happy to have something to do to take her mind off what was going on outside, where more people had joined the crowd and the shouts had grown louder.

Concho followed Roberto into his office. "When Leticia comes she'll be bringing the big guns," he said to his friend.

"I hope you're talking about her lawyers," Roberto replied in a wry tone.

"Maybe."

Someone threw a rock that banged off the roof.

CHAPTER 40

"Sorry to abandon you," Concho said to Roberto, **"but I** need to get this thing sewed up." He pointed to the bullet gash on the left side of his face which continued to seep a little blood.

"Understood," Roberto said. "But wait." He went around the desk in his office and opened a drawer to pull out a set of automobile keys. "Good thing we haven't had a chance to send your loaner pickup back to the county," he said, tossing the keys to Ten-Wolves. "It's parked out back by the jail."

Concho caught them. "Yeah, good thing. I'm hoping Gray-Dove won't have to do anything but replace the tires on the Ford. But I guess we'll see."

The gathering crowd of protestors had not made their way around the back of the police station yet. Concho slipped out the rear door and climbed in the white Dodge Ram pickup which, it seemed, he drove about as much as or more than his own Ford.

The casino stood only a few blocks away and he parked there and made his way to the second-floor clinic maintained for patrons by the casino/hotel. He was relieved to see Samuel Reyes on duty. Samuel was a young Kickapoo tribesman in his mid-twenties, in training to be a nurse practitioner. He'd stitched Concho up before and the Ranger trusted him.

Reyes winced when he saw his new patient's face. "What happened to you?"

"Someone mistook me for a rabid dog and tried to put me down."

Reyes seemed momentarily taken aback. "Well," he finally said as he ushered Concho to a seat, "I'm glad they failed."

Concho was the only patient in the clinic. For the next ten minutes, he tried not to move his face while Reyes anesthetized, cleaned, sterilized, and sewed up his left cheek. Samuel kept up a near-constant patter while doing so which was just part of his bedside manner. After Reyes had finished, he pointed Concho toward a mirror.

The Ranger studied himself. The left side of his face was still badly swollen but the puffiness around his left eye had begun to go down. Six black stitches laced his cheek. Most of the blood on his face had been cleaned away though plenty of it splotched the collar of his shirt.

"My head looks like a lopsided football with these stitches," he said.

"You want me to take them out and try again?" Reyes asked, grinning.

"Not on a bet."

Reyes went to one of the many glass cabinets in the clinic and took out a small orange plastic vial of pills. He handed these to Concho, who pocketed them.

"Pain killers," he said. "They should help. The cheekbone is cracked but not shattered. Not much I can do about it. I don't know if you're lucky or tougher than whalebone. Either way, you'll heal. But you ought to take it easy for a while."

"I will as I can."

A knock sounded on the clinic door. Both men glanced up as Melissa Nolan peeked into the room. Nolan ran the casino. She also sat on the Tribal Council although no one outside the council knew how much power she wielded there.

"Ten-Wolves," Nolan said. "Heard you were here. Let's talk."

***

Melissa Nolan's office stood down the hall from the ca-
sino clinic. She led Concho through her reception area which
was staffed by a young man who studiously avoided making eye
contact with the Ranger, and into her inner office. She motioned
him to a seat. He sat.

Nolan walked around behind her desk. She was in her forties,
a beautiful woman with long, platinum blonde hair and a willowy
build. She had hazel eyes and no one who saw her would have
suspected her of having any Kickapoo blood. She did, though, or
else she couldn't have sat on the Tribal Council.

"After your past run-ins with him, my assistant has developed a
bit of a phobia about you, Ten-Wolves," Nolan said.

"You can tell him I don't eat children," Concho replied.

A tiny smile flickered briefly over Nolan's features. She
smoothed down her long, yellow pencil skirt and sat. Today, she
wore a conservative, long-sleeved white blouse with a bow. Her
perfume smelled clean and fresh. As always, she appeared cool,
neat, and in control. Concho felt grubby sitting across from her.

"If I'd known I was going to be summoned before the Queen, I
would have taken a spa day and gotten a manicure," Concho said.

"I'm used to your lack of personal hygiene," Nolan said.
"But...I'll never get used to how you like to smash through things
that might better be handled with some decorum."

"You're referring to the arrest of Pete Whiteheart and the
Garcia kids?"

"I am."

"Cisco and Selena Garcia tried to kill me with a rifle this
morning," Concho said, pointing at his stitched cheek. "Pete
Whiteheart ordered it."

Nolan raised an eyebrow. It seemed like everyone could except for Concho. He managed to keep his jealousy to a mini-
mum as he added, "But I don't suppose that's much of a crime

in some folks' eyes."

"I guess the question is, Why?" Nolan said.

"I can't really comment on an ongoing investigation."

Nolan's lips curved into a smirk. "Convenient. But you've put me in a delicate position. You probably know the Tribal Council has scheduled a meeting for noon tomorrow?"

"Terribly sorry for your inconvenience."

Nolan's mouth tightened into a line. "Cut the crap! I'm not your enemy. I'm especially not the enemy of Roberto Echabarri. But his position is in a great deal of danger right now because of what you've done."

Concho leaned forward a little across Nolan's desk. To her credit, she didn't draw back.

"All I've done is my job," Concho said. "And the same is true of Roberto. He's an excellent chief of police. It would be absolutely stupid to get rid of him. Pete Whiteheart is as corrupt as they come. And you probably know that. But to protect him, his father will try to break Echabarri. If you care anything about justice, or about the future of the reservation, you won't let that happen."

"I wish I had your simplistic view of life," Nolan said as she leaned back in her cushioned leather chair.

Concho leaned back as well and offered her a grin, a small one because of his injured cheek. "Simple, not simplistic," he said. "And it makes your choices a lot easier. I hope you'll do the right thing at tomorrow's meeting."

Nolan sighed. "I hope so, too."

***

As Concho left the casino, his cell phone rang. He didn't recognize the number but it was local—a reservation number. His heart sped a bit as he hit accept.

"Hello?"

"It's…it's…"

"Manuel?"

"Yes."

"Glad you called."

The young man's voice managed to sound scared and exhausted at the same time as he added, "I want to meet. But just you."

"When and where?"

"I don't really…know where. I think it's still on the Rez. There's a bluff and an overhang. You know where I'm talking about?"

Concho's heart had been slowing down; it sped up again. "I do. And I take it you're not alone."

"No. There's a man. A big man."

"I know him."

"He…caught me. After I left the house. Like he was waiting. Brought me here. He's the one who wants the meeting. I don't know…what he'll do to me."

"I think if you just take it easy, he won't hurt you. But, he doesn't talk much. How did you figure out what he wanted?"

"He wrote 'Ten-Wolves' in the sand. Then pointed to my cell phone. We had to climb up on the bluff to get a signal. He's also made it clear the meeting has to be tonight. After dark. I don't think we'll be here if you come too early."

"Gotcha."

"He's signaling me to get off. I—"

The phone disconnected. Concho released a pent-up breath, then called Roberto and explained what had happened.

"What does this guy want?" Roberto asked. "Sounds like it could be a trap."

"I don't think so. He could have done something when I was out there rescuing Meskwaa. I've got this weird feeling he's trying to help us with our investigation. Not sure why I think that."

"All right. It's your call. Don't come back to the office here or you could get caught. The crowd is still growing. We've seen nothing of Leticia Garcia or Sam Whiteheart. It's got me worried. What are they planning?"

"You know anyone with any law experience?"

"A couple of people, I guess. Maybe I'll call them."

"Hang in there. If we're lucky, Manuel will give us some information to help us hold onto Pete Whiteheart. I'll be in touch as soon as I can."

"All right. And be careful."

"It may not seem like it but I do try." He swiped the phone off.

CHAPTER 41

To avoid the crowd outside Kickapoo police headquar-
ters, Concho took a roundabout way to John Gray-Dove's shop.
His Ford still sat on the bed of the tow truck but John promised
he'd get to it today and that all it required was new tires and a little
cosmetic work. That was a relief.

Concho began to move weapons and gear out of the Ford into
the Dodge with practiced ease. The last thing he took from the
Ford was the new medicine shield he'd constructed. He decided to
run by Meskwaa's place to show him the shield and pick his brain
about Whirlwind's possible motives for taking Manuel prisoner. It
wasn't even noon yet, and he had to wait until tonight anyway to
meet Whirlwind and Manuel.

Gray-Dove also had several four-wheelers around his shop and
Concho asked if he could borrow one. It would make getting to and
from the overhang a lot faster. Gray-Dove offered him a red Honda
Fourtrax Recon with a 250-class engine already loaded on a trailer.
Concho hooked the trailer to the Dodge and headed on his way.

He arrived at Meskwaa's to find the old medicine man seated
comfortably on the ramada of his wickiup with a cigarette burning between his lips. It was a good sight to see and the smell of
the tobacco was a good smell to rediscover.

As Concho stepped out of his truck holding a package wrapped in a blanket, the black wolf-dog lying at the old man's feet rose and gave a warning growl. Meskwaa dropped a hand on the dog's back and the animal immediately quietened and lay down again.

"I see he found you," Concho said as he approached.

"A friend finds his friends," Meskwaa replied as he gestured for the Ranger to sit.

Concho sat on the other end of the same bench as Meskwaa. The old man picked up the water bucket beside him and passed it to Concho, who used the dipper to take a sip of fresh, cold water.

"Thank you," he said, returning the bucket.

"No es nada."

"I brought something to show you," Concho said.

He pulled the blanket away from the medicine shield and held it up for Meskwaa to look at. The old man opened his hands and the Ranger passed the shield to him. He took it and let it rest on his bony lap. It covered his legs from waist to knees. The dog, suddenly restless, climbed to its feet and walked away. Concho frowned after it.

"Do not concern yourself about him," Meskwaa said. "He is still much of the wild. And this…" Meskwaa turned the shield back and forth as he examined it, nodding repeatedly to himself, "…this is very fine. Your workmanship has improved."

"I don't know if I can take full credit for it. Apparently, I put the finishing touches on it while sleepwalking. At least, I don't remember doing the final trimming or painting the symbols. But I can see the work is by my hand."

Meskwaa bobbed his head in acknowledgment. "Magic came to visit you, my old friend."

Concho did not argue. He had no better explanation.

"I need to ask you something," Concho said. "Whirlwind has captured Manuel Night-Run. And he wants to meet with me tonight. At the overhang where he kept you. I'm very curious as to why. Would you have any idea?"

Meskwaa handed the shield back to Concho, who rewrapped it in the blanket and set it aside. The wolf-dog immediately returned to the old man's feet and lay down. Meskwaa did not seem to notice as he contemplated the question he'd been asked.

"I suspect," he finally said, "that Whirlwind is a left hand to your right."

"What?"

"It is hard to put into words," Meskwaa said. "This man is neither a shadow of you nor a reflection. But you are connected. He has a purpose that parallels yours."

"You're saying he's a kind of detective. Working the same case as I am but from the opposite side."

"Yes. The secret of what happened to Agustina Cardenas."

"Hmmm. I can see the possibility. He harasses the Whitehearts and Night-Runs because he thinks they were involved with what happened to Aggie. It would explain why he took Manuel hostage."

"You are most likely correct."

"But why involve me?"

"If he loved Agustina…" Meskwaa started.

"He'd want her killers punished," Concho finished.

"Thus, Ten-Wolves," Meskwaa said.

"You think he figures I can uncover the murderer?"

"Will you not?"

"I'll do everything I can. We know, by the way, Whirlwind wasn't the father of the fetus. That was Pete Whiteheart."

"Ah," Meskwaa said. "Do you think Whiteheart killed her?"

"I'm hoping Manuel can shed some light on everything this evening." He pointed to the blanket-wrapped shield and added, "There's something else. I'm pretty sure Whirlwind is the one who first stole the white boar I shot, then skinned it and returned the hide, which I used to make the shield."

Meskwaa nodded. "It sounds right. Be sure to take the shield with you."

"Why?"

Meskwaa finished his cigarette, pinched out the ember at the tip with his fingers and tucked the butt into his shirt pocket. "I don't know."

***

Evening shadows stretched long as Concho powered his borrowed four-wheeler through the drylands toward his evening rendezvous. As the world darkened, he switched on the lights of the Honda Recon. The yellowish beams of light seemed to drain the world of life rather than bestow it.

The Ranger pushed the melancholy thought away. He was well rested and well fed. With nothing else to do in the afternoon, he'd napped and later fixed himself a steak and potato dinner. He didn't know how long this night might run but he was prepared for the duration.

Strapped across the back of the Recon were his range weapons, his .30-06 and hunting bow, as well as the medicine shield Meskwaa had urged him to bring along. His night-vision goggles were also there. Both his Colt Double Eagles hung holstered on the belt around his waist, along with a Bowie knife with an eight-inch blade. He was ready for war, though he hoped it wouldn't come.

Concho pulled to a stop as he came within sight of the limestone bluff where the overhang lay. He was still half a mile away. He'd been told to arrive after dark and some daylight still clung to the sky and haloed the top of the bluff. So he waited, sipping water from his canteen.

A slight ringing lingered in Concho's ears from the recent explosions he'd been exposed to. Now, in the quiet, the ringing took on the rhythm of a low, distant murmur of voices.

Along with the sound and the darkness, an eeriness gathered around the Ranger. The temperature dropped or so it felt to him. The night suddenly had weight and it pressed on his shoulders and chest. His neck prickled but when he twisted to look behind him, nothing was there. He'd almost expected to see purple eyes.

A sense of malaise crept over him. Why was he here? Truly? What did he hope to accomplish? To find the killer of a woman who'd been dead eight years? Of a fetus who had never drawn breath? Two skeletons with no family left to mourn them?

Concho shook his head to scatter the thoughts. He recognized what Meskwaa would call a spiritual attack. Ridiculous, of course. It was no more than human nature to have doubts, to sometimes let those doubts build to the point where they took on flesh.

But, he reached behind him on the ATV. He unhooked the medicine shield and brought it into his lap. Sliding his left forearm through the straps, he seated the shield in position for defense. His thoughts calmed.

Judging the world as dark enough, Concho restarted the Recon. He was reaching for his night goggles when the gleam of a campfire sparked up in the direction of the overhang. Leaving the goggles off, he used the fire as a guide as he committed to his final approach.

He had no clear idea what to expect. His nerves thrummed with tension; his muscles held the familiar ache of potential vio-lence. Yet, the shield on his arm gave him some comfort.

Rolling to a stop about fifteen feet from the fire, Concho studied the scene. A man sat on the ground behind the firepit. He stood up as Concho killed the four-wheeler's engine and climbed off. The figure was Manuel, limned by crackling red-orange flames. His hands were bound by ropes in front of him.

"Where's Whirlwind?" Concho asked with his right hand on the butt of a Colt.

"Who?" Manuel asked.

"The man who tied your hands."

"Oh! He's…around…somewhere."

Concho's gaze roamed over the desert and bluff. He could see nothing other than rock, prickly pear, and a few withered bushes. He lifted his voice to say, "Nothing gets discussed until *everyone* is present. I need to see Whirlwind."

Though Whirlwind didn't seem to talk, Concho was sure

he understood language and he'd understand what the Ranger wanted. That appeared to be the case as the shadows behind Manuel flickered and a man appeared from within the overhang.

In his description, Meskwaa had captured the essence of Whirlwind. The man was tall, at least 6'7", but gaunt to the point of emaciation. His face was huge and almost flat except for an abnormally wide jaw covered in thin bristles, and high cheekbones jutting against the skin like ax-heads. He was an Indian, though not Kickapoo—at least not much. Concho thought he might be Apache or from some other southwestern tribe.

Whirlwind was older than Concho had imagined—his face deeply creased. His dirty and haphazardly braided hair held as much gray in it as black. The faded cotton trousers he wore were torn at the knees and held up by a rope belt. He didn't wear shoes. Instead, his feet were wrapped in canvas cut from a tarp, which would explain the scuffed tracks left wherever he'd traveled.

A stained gray t-shirt, mostly a collar, two sleeves, and some dangling threads, revealed as much of Whirlwind's upper body as it concealed. Gray fuzz covered half his gaunt chest. Ribs showed through the skin beneath. The only thing about him that looked dangerous was an unsheathed knife stuck through his rope belt. It had been sharpened so often the blade was no wider than the business end of a screwdriver.

Whirlwind's gaze found the shield on Concho's arm. The man opened his mouth as if he wanted to speak. The lips worked. The teeth were stained and cracked. A yellowish film covered the tongue. But if the man said anything, Concho didn't hear it.

Whirlwind stepped up behind Manuel and placed a large hand on the young man's shoulder. Manuel winced and seemed to shrink into himself. "He…he wants me…to tell you…some things," he said.

The evening had grown steadily colder. Embers whirled off the fire and Concho squatted beside it to feel the heat coming off the flames. "Then I guess you better," he said.

CHAPTER 42

"Aggie... Agustina...Cardenas," Manuel began. **"I rode** the school bus with her a while. She was a couple of years older. About sixteen then. But she...dropped out."

Concho was getting a lesson in things he already knew but he didn't want to interrupt Manuel's flow of words. Eventually, the young man would get to something new. He hoped.

"Even after she dropped out, I sometimes saw her," Manuel continued. "She used to walk by our farm. Don't know why. Sometimes, when I walked down her way, I'd see her. She...changed when she was about seventeen. She started...making herself pretty. I thought she was really pretty.

"One day I was...well, sort of watching her. On the road. Daniel Alvarado pulled up beside her. He had a convertible then. A blue Mustang. He must have offered her a ride. Anyway, she...got in. She was smiling. I didn't see her smile very often.

"I knew Daniel a little bit. He was friends with Pete Whiteheart. I knew Pete because his family's farm is just down from ours. We were sorta friends, though he was like a year older. We fished together sometimes. One day, I was over at Pete's. Alvarado pulled in and wanted Pete to go with him for something. Pete asked him about me and Alvarado just laughed and said, 'Bring him along.'

"We drove…over to Aggie's place. Daniel and Pete were drinking beer. Aggie's mother wasn't home which was really unusual. It seemed Aggie expected Daniel. She invited us all in, though I don't think she liked that Pete was along. Or especially that I was. After a while, she and Daniel went…upstairs together."

Manuel stopped talking. His face blushed from more than the heat of the fire. Clearly, the young man had understood what was going on between Alvarado and Aggie and he hadn't liked it. Manuel had obviously developed a crush on Aggie.

"Go on," Concho said.

Manuel took a breath. "When Alvarado came down, he had this ugly look on his face. Like you see on a cat that's gotten into the cream. All smug. Like he'd gotten away with something.

"The three of us left after that. We drove around. Alvarado and Pete got more beer. Alvarado started telling things about Aggie. Bad things." Manuel blushed harder. "It made me mad to hear him talk about her that way. But I didn't say anything. I just sat there in the back seat.

"They gave me a beer and I drank it. Then another one. I remember we stopped somewhere and built a little fire." He gestured. "Like this one. I guess I was pretty drunk by then. I'd never had beer before. I remember what Pete said. At first it made me mad, but finally I just…laughed."

"What did Pete say?"

Manuel took a very deep breath. "He said, 'I wouldn't mind cutting off a piece of that myself.' I knew exactly what he meant. I wanted to scream at him but I…couldn't. I laughed. I hate that I laughed. And then I threw up. They thought it was just the beer and *they* laughed."

Manuel stopped talking. Concho let him sit quietly for a minute.

"There's more to the story," the lawman finally said.

"Yeah. I decided I didn't want to be Pete's friend anymore. But a couple of weeks later, the two of them came by the house in Alvarado's car. They were drunk and getting drunker. They said they were going over to see Aggie again. Said I should come along. I didn't want to. I couldn't bear not to. I went.

"Aggie had waited for us along the road away from her house. So her mom wouldn't see. We drove off the Rez. Aggie sat in the front seat between Daniel and Pete. She was drinking beer and laughing. I kept getting madder and madder, but I couldn't say anything.

"We stopped at some…" Manuel shook his head, "out of the way spot along the Rio Grande. It was summer. Dry. There'd been a fish kill. I remember how it stank. Though it seemed I was the only one to notice. We built a campfire. They were all drinking and laughing.

"Alvarado… He…slept with…Agg…ie. Right in the back seat of his car. Just a few feet from the fire. I could hear them. When they finished, Alvarado came back to the fire. He looked at Pete and Pete got up. I could tell they'd talked about it before. Pete went over to the car."

Tears began to roll down Manuel's face and he sank to his knees.

"When—" Manuel's voice hitched once before he continued. "When Pete came back to the fire, he pointed at me and said, 'Now it's your turn. You don't even have to thank me.' I was horrified. I thought I was going to be sick. I wanted to be. But I couldn't even do that.

"I just sat there until Alvarado came over and pulled me to my feet. He…shoved me toward the car. He just kept shoving me. And then I could see her. In the backseat. She had…had her legs…open."

In the pause that followed, Concho glanced over Manuel's shoulder to the face of Whirlwind. In the reflected light of the campfire, the big man's features looked like rivered stone. But the hands—the knotted, gnarled hands—were clenched bloodless. And the dirty nails worked against the palms, scratching, scraping.

"Go on!" Concho said, hearing how rough his own voice

was now, how clotted with spit.

Manuel's words grated, then rose abruptly in pitch. The boy was close to cracking. His body trembled; he seemed to shed the glow of the fire as if the light didn't want to touch him.

"She...she...she beckoned me. She was moaning. I tried... tried to do what they all wanted me to do. But I couldn't." His face twisted as he glanced up to meet Concho's gaze. "I couldn't. It was the stink. The dead fish in the river. I tried and tried but... finally, Pete pulled me away. I fell down by the fire and lay there while he went again.

"I don't really remember the drive home. It was like we were... ghosts in the summer night. I sat in front with Alvarado. He sang. Pete and Aggie sat in the back. They dropped me off before they took her home. I don't know what happened after that."

Concho wiped his mouth on the back of his hand. He'd seen horrors in Afghanistan, had imagined he was hardened to just about anything humans might do to each other. But the relentlessness of Manuel's story, the bone-deep sadness. He wished he hadn't come here tonight. He wished Whirlwind would have chosen another to hear this tale. But it wasn't over. More pus had to be squeezed out of this infection. More had to be told.

"Manuel! When did you next see Aggie?"

***

Scout swiped off the burner phone, ending the call from one of his informants on the Kickapoo reservation. The news wasn't good. He stood silently in his apartment for a moment, then hurled the cheap phone into the floor with a savage oath. Plastic shattered and sprayed across the room. He didn't care.

Day four of his five-day deadline to take out Concho Ten-Wolves had passed. And his last hope of getting someone else to do it had fled. The Garcia siblings had failed; they were in jail.

Knowing Ten-Wolves, the connection between the Garcias and himself would soon become known. His career, and probably his life, would be over—just as the man who'd ordered him to make the kill had promised five days ago. The only thing left to do was to face Ten-Wolves himself. He shook when he thought of it but he had no other options left.

He strode toward his bedroom, his boots crunching on pieces of the ruined phone. Pulling out the bottom drawer on his chest of drawers, he drew out a hand-tooled black leather belt and holster. A revolver rested in the holster and he shucked it out to examine.

The pistol made most observers think of something a gunfighter would have carried in the 1870s. But it was no old weapon. It was a working western replica, manufactured by an Italian company called *Uberti*. It had been modeled on the so-called Bisley Colt, first manufactured in 1894.

The Bisley was a shooter's gun, made for accuracy and speed on the draw. The swept-under grip and the enlarged trigger and trigger guard made fast handling of the gun a dream. The hammer spur had been lowered and grooved to make for easy cocking with the thumb and to allow for fanning the weapon if need be.

This Uberti was the spitting image of the Bisley, with a case-hardened frame and a blued barrel. It also had a brass backstrap and trigger guard to go along with the walnut handle, making it a work of art as well as a deadly weapon. The barrel measured only 4¾ inches long, just fine for the close-up ranges these guns were intended for. The only non-traditional aspect of this Uberti was that it was chambered for the .357 round rather than the .45.

As a kid, Scout had often dreamed of living in the Wild West, of riding with the outlaw gang of Jesse James and Cole Younger or of drawing down on the likes of Wild Bill Hickok or Doc Holliday. He'd bought a single action .22 pistol in the western-style when he was fourteen. Single action meant you had to cock the hammer before you could pull the trigger. It was safer than double action, where trigger pull alone could fire the gun and generally allowed for better accuracy. He'd spent hours practicing his draw with that weapon.

In his twenties, Scout had gotten serious about the sport of gunslinging. He'd joined the Cowboy Fast Draw Association, which claimed numerous clubs in Texas. He'd competed in some local tournaments and won a few trophies. Twice, he'd even attended the organization's fast draw championship in Fallon, Nevada, making a respectable showing in the four-tenths of a second range. The winners, however, consistently shot in the three-tenths range.

Half cocking the hammer and opening the loading gate, he spun the cylinder to make sure the pistol was unloaded. A rapid series of clicks sounded as the well-oiled cylinder spun smoothly. Easing the hammer down, he slid the weapon back into the holster and strapped on the gun belt, tying the leather thongs at the bottom of the holster to his right leg.

Standing in front of his bedroom mirror, he positioned his hand close to the walnut grip of the revolver. Without warning, his hand grasped the butt and he drew in a lightning flash as he simultaneously jerked his upper body backward. His thumb cocked the hammer; his index finger pulled the trigger. The snap of a dry firing sounded.

Almost despite himself, a smile creased his lips. He'd lost none of his speed and he doubted Ten-Wolves would be this fast. Tomorrow, he'd face the Ranger. He'd surprise him. As soon as he saw the man, he'd draw and shoot. He'd find some way to explain the killing later. He'd say Ten-Wolves went rogue. Everyone knew the man was wound too tight. In the end, it would be Scout's word against a dead man's.

It was the only chance he had.

CHAPTER 43

"When did you next see Aggie?" Concho asked Manuel.

Young Night-Run sniffed. He wiped his eyes with a hand. He continued to stare into the fire, but he began to talk again.

"A couple of months after…that night. Aggie came to see me. Came to my house. I was in the barn. She told me she was sorry I had to see her with David and Pete. She said she'd been very drunk. And that…I was the one she really wanted to be with. I told her I didn't want to talk to her. I climbed up in the loft to escape. But she followed me. She…kissed me. Touched me. We… made love. In the hay."

Manuel scratched at his right thigh through his jeans. "We saw each other quite a bit after that. One day she told me she was pregnant. She said it was mine. I kind of believed her. I guess I wanted to.

"But I was scared. I told my mother. She told me not to be stupid, that Aggie was using me, that she was a…a…whore. She forbade me from seeing Aggie again. She said if I didn't break it off, she would have Aggie arrested. Aggie was eighteen by then. I was still…sixteen."

Again, Concho glanced at Whirlwind. The man looked as impassive as before. But his fists were still clenched and his hands shook. Concho had to look away from the big man's agony. He turned back to Manuel.

"But you didn't break it off, did you?" he asked.

The youth shook his head. "I...couldn't. I told her I wanted her to run away with me. That we'd get married in Oklahoma. At the Kickapoo reservation there. She said she wanted to. She'd try. But..."

"What?" Concho prodded.

"I was...suspicious of her. Maybe because of what my mother said. One night I snuck out of the house. I went over to Aggie's place. Her mother was gone again. There was...another man there. I didn't know him. He wasn't Kickapoo. He was white. Aggie seemed very...friendly with him.

"I ran home. And when she came the next day to see me, I called her a bad name. I called her what my mother called her. She walked away. A couple of afternoons later she called the house. Mother answered. I refused to take the call.

"I went...out. Walked. Dad was checking on the cows in the south pasture. I joined him. I never saw nor heard from Aggie again. A few days later, they said she'd run away with a workman on their farm. I felt...relieved. I tried not to ever think about her again."

"Who said she'd run away?"

"My mother told me. She'd heard it around."

Concho didn't try to explain to Manuel that Whirlwind was the "workman" Aggie had supposedly run away with. Maybe the boy suspected. Maybe he didn't. The lawman had one other question he did want to ask, though.

"When Chief Echabarri and I came to see you about Aggie, that first time, you lied to us quite a bit about seeing her after she dropped out of school and about knowing where she lived. And the second time we came, you ran. Why? What were you afraid of?"

"If I tell you, he'll hurt me. He'll hurt...others."

"Who'll hurt them?"

Manuel hunched his shoulders and said nothing. Whirlwind took a step toward him. Concho sprung up from his crouch, to protect the boy if he had to. But the wild man stopped as Manuel blurted out, "Pete Whiteheart!"

Everyone went still.

"What about him?" Concho asked.

Manuel looked up. His eyes glistened and pleaded in the firelight. "Don't tell him I said anything."

"I won't. Unless I'm ordered to by a judge in a trial."

"You think there'll be a trial?"

"Can't say."

Manuel sighed but then nodded. "After…after Aggie ran away, Pete and Alvarado came to see me. Alvarado was about to get married. They told me I better not *ever* say anything about what happened with them and Aggie. They said they'd kill me. Kill my parents. Even years later. Pete. He'd see me and…point his finger at me. Like a gun."

Concho wanted to spit but controlled the impulse. "I'll do my best to make sure Pete Whiteheart never finds out what you've told me."

"Thank you. Do you think Pete and Alvarado murdered Aggie?"

"Did *you* think they did?"

"Sometimes I suspected it." He shook his head violently back and forth. "I tried not to think of it."

"Did you tell your mother what you suspected?"

"No. After…Aggie ran away, my mother wouldn't talk about any of it. Like it never happened."

As if he'd completely emptied himself and was deflating, Manuel slid slowly over onto his side and lay down by the fire. Concho straightened to his full height and stretched his back, which still grew stiff on occasion from a knife wound he'd gotten a few months back. He walked over to Whirlwind and stopped a few feet away.

The big man met his gaze, with the red of embers refracting

from his eyes. He turned slowly and moved away from the camp-fire and from Manuel. Concho followed. They stopped again in the darkness, just at the edge of the glow cast by the fire.

Concho heard a sound, a slow drip, drip. He glanced at Whirlwind's hands. Blood droplets ran down the fingers from where the man had scored his palms with his own nails while Manuel told his story. The drops fell, spattering tiny wet craters in the dry desert soil.

"I see you loved her," the Ranger said softly, so Manuel wouldn't hear.

Whirlwind did not respond.

"Are you the one who buried her and the child out here? And took off the flesh?"

Whirlwind nodded.

"To honor them?"

Again, Whirlwind nodded

"Do you know who killed them?"

Whirlwind shook his head.

"Right," Concho said. "But you figured it had something to do with Manuel Nigh-Run. And with Pete Whiteheart. And Daniel Alvarado."

Again came a nod.

"Manuel has to go back," Concho said. "To jail. Though I'm sure he's not the one who killed Agustina Cardenas. We'll find out who did. I promise you. The story we heard tonight lives inside me now. As it lives inside you. It won't be hidden again. If you had any debt in this, it's paid."

Whirlwind stared. He opened his mouth and said one word, perfectly enunciated in a voice that barely sounded human.

"Justice."

He walked back toward the campfire, then disappeared beneath the overhang as if he were a figment of the night's imagination.

***

Concho loaded Manuel on the four-wheeler and hauled him back to his house. He fed the boy there and then put him in his truck. After unhooking the trailer for the ATV and leaving it behind, he drove into Kickapoo Village, to the police station. He came in the back way to avoid the crowd but there was no crowd. The protesters were gone.

Though it was near midnight, the building burned with light. Concho knocked on the back door. Nila Willow admitted him. She smiled and pointed toward the front of the building. He handed Manuel off to her with instructions to keep him separate from the jail inmates. She nodded her understanding.

The Ranger strode toward the front of the building, passing other deputies along the way. It seemed like every member of the Tribal Police was present and all of them animated. Concho knocked on Echabarri's open office door and was waved inside.

"What's going on?" he asked. "I was expecting a very different scene when I got back here."

Roberto grinned. He acted excited and full of energy. He practically squirmed in his chair, though he must have had a long day. "A lot has happened since I saw you last," he said.

"Do tell."

"Well, you saw the protestors who'd gathered outside."

"Yes."

"Just after noon, we started getting counterprotestors, people who supported our actions. And pretty soon they outnumbered the others. It seems like the Whiteheart and the Alvarado clans have made a few enemies over the years with their heavy-handed ways.

"In the afternoon, when Sam Whiteheart and Leticia Garcia arrived with their lawyers in tow, they were met by a considerable uproar. When I stepped out to address the crowd, every deputy we have stood at my back. When I told Sam and Leticia I wouldn't release their kids until a judge had a chance to set bail, most of the crowd cheered. Sam made things worse for himself by shouting at the people. Letty just stormed off."

Roberto practically chortled as he added, "I don't think Sam is going to have everything his way at tomorrow's tribal council meeting. People are getting fed up with the way some things are run around here."

Concho grinned, though it pulled on his stitches. "That's great news. Both parts of it. You've developed a lot of goodwill among the people by your handling of things. I'm glad to see it paying dividends."

Roberto nodded vigorously. "People shouted your name, too. Saying good things. You've got plenty of support among certain factions. Mostly the poorer ones. But it's the same for me and those are the people who most need our services."

"Good to see hard work being rewarded."

"Yes," Roberto agreed. "But, what about your meeting with this Whirlwind? Was Manuel there? How did things go?"

"Well, we can eliminate Whirlwind as a suspect. I got some answers from him. He positively identified the skeletons we found as Agustina Cardenas and her baby. He's the one who buried them and removed all the flesh. But it was a ritual cleansing. He did it because he was in love with Aggie. He also indicated that he didn't know who killed her but was sure it was connected to the White-hearts, the Night-Runs, and the Alvarados and their kin."

Roberto sighed.

"Manuel's story told me the same thing," Concho added. "He watched Alvarado and Pete abuse Aggie. They manipulated her. They used alcohol. We know Pete fathered her child and the story of how that occurred wasn't pretty."

The police chief's mouth became a grim line. His fists clenched. "Guess it explains why Manuel broke with them."

"Yeah. Manuel was younger than them all. His only role in the sordid tale was to be hurt and angry. And scared. First of Alvarado and later of Pete Whiteheart. He's not the one who killed Agustina, but he may have given me the clue I need to settle that question."

"How's that?"

"I've got to check one more thing out first. Then I think I'll be able to give you a name."

"All right. When?"

"I'm going out to the Night-Run farm first thing in the morning. I should be back here by the time you get out of the Tribal Council meeting. In the meantime, I turned Manuel over to Nila. He's not under arrest but don't let him go home until you see me again."

"Keep him away from the others, I imagine?"

"Keep him away from all contact outside your officers. Including his family if they happen to call."

"Will do."

Concho leaned across Roberto's desk and squeezed his friend's shoulder. "Maybe we've got 'em on the run," he said. "Let's keep it that way. See you tomorrow."

CHAPTER 44

Concho went home and slept a few hours. Just after dawn, he drove over to the Night-Run farmhouse. Lights burned in the kitchen and, when he knocked at the front door, he heard soft footsteps coming through the house. Delores Night-Run answered the door. She didn't appear surprised to see him.

"Any news about my son?" she demanded belligerently.

"He's in police custody. He's physically OK."

"Physically?"

"He spent much of the evening crying. Or near to it as he told me his story."

Delores's shoulders slumped. Her eyes looked haunted as she processed what Concho was saying.

"Can I come in?" Concho asked.

Delores seemed to consider refusing but finally held the door open for him, then walked away. "Let's talk in the kitchen," she said over her shoulder. "I've got coffee on."

Concho followed the woman. She wore blue jeans and a checked cotton shirt, with her short hair clipped up even shorter behind her head. Her movements were lithe. He noted again the impression he'd always gotten of strength in her leanly muscled, athletic body.

"Is George home?" Concho asked as they walked down the hallway.

"No. He's already feeding the cows. Without Manuel here, he has to do all the chores himself." She glanced over her shoulder. "But you knew he wouldn't be."

"I figured. I actually wanted to talk to you alone."

Delores shrugged as they entered the kitchen. She walked straight to the coffee pot, which burbled with steam. She unplugged it. A large ceramic mug sat next to the pot and she poured herself a cup. She gestured with the pot toward Concho.

"No thanks," he said.

The woman shrugged again and leaned against the counter next to the pot. "What do you want from me?"

"When I was here before, you kept insisting Aggie Cardenas ran off with a farmhand. We know now that wasn't true. We found her remains. On the Rez. They've been positively identified."

Delores's mouth worked back and forth. She finally shrugged a third time. "So, I was wrong. No doubt the Mexican she ran off with killed her when he found out what kind of girl she was."

Concho let that pass. "You also told me Manuel thought he'd fallen in love with Aggie."

Delores scoffed. "Yes. At first. It was nothing more than infatuation."

"You said 'at first,'" Concho repeated. "Manuel got very angry with Aggie later, didn't he?"

Delores looked instantly wary. She sipped her coffee as she considered her words. "He was…hurt. When he found out what she was. But not angry, not enough to kill her as you believe."

"He was hurt when he found out that what you told him repeatedly about her seemed to be true!"

"What do you mean?"

"You told Manuel she was a whore, didn't you?"

Delores's eyes crackled with sudden flames. "She was!"

Again, Concho let the insult to Aggie pass. "When we spoke

before on this issue," he said, "you left out something important."

"I don't know what you mean."

"Aggie was pregnant. She told Manuel it was his. And Manuel told you."

"She was lying. Obviously. It was Alvarado's baby. Most likely. Or…someone else. It could have been any one of many."

"But Manuel did sleep with her."

"She seduced him," Delores snapped. "And only so she could lie about the child being his. She cared nothing for him. It was only to use him."

"Is that why you killed her?"

Delores stiffened with her coffee cup halfway to her mouth. Her eyes darted left and right. She lowered the cup.

"You are full of nonsense. Next you'll be accusing my George."

"I doubt George knew enough about what was going on to be angry. But you, you knew it all. And you're the one who told Manuel that Aggie ran off with a hired farmhand. Turns out, you're the one who started that rumor. And you had the best reason to do so."

"Said like a man of evil ways," Delores said. "Not a good man!"

"Guess I better watch myself. Seeing the way you treat people whom you don't judge as 'good.'"

Delores set her coffee cup down on the counter with a clink. She picked up the pot as if to refill her cup. Concho watched the pot, knowing the liquid inside would still be boiling hot.

"So, if you know so much," the woman said, "how did I kill the whore?"

Concho took a step toward Delores, holding out his hands, palms up in a kind of shrug.

"She called here on her last day," the Ranger said. "You took the call. Manuel told me, though he has no idea what followed. Manuel didn't want to talk to Aggie. You'd seen to that. He left the house. Running, I imagine. He went to see his father with the cows. With Manuel gone, that left no one to overhear what you said to Aggie. You must have done a good job of acting when you invited her over. Did you tell her you'd help patch things up with your son?"

"You crazy snake," Delores hissed. "Full of poison."

"You hit her first," Concho continued. "With something smooth and hard. Probably right in this kitchen. Maybe a rolling pin like the one you use to roll out your tamales. Then you strangled her. You were an athlete in school. And eight years younger, of course. You had the strength and the rage. It was premeditated. You knew what you were going to do when you invited her over. You probably figured she'd *never* leave Manuel alone. That she'd ruin his life."

"She would have," the woman said.

Concho's next question was the hardest one he'd ever asked anyone. "What I can't figure out is why you cut the fetus out? After!"

For a moment, the woman looked stricken. Then her hard shell returned. "*She* turned her child into a weapon! All of it rested on *her* head!"

"How did you get rid of the bodies?"

Delores twisted toward Concho, still holding the coffee pot. She hurled the pot and its boiling contents at his face. He dodged; the pot hurtled past his head, exploded against the kitchen wall in a spray of black liquid.

Delores grabbed a butcher knife off the counter and threw herself toward the lawman with a shriek. She whipped the knife across at his midsection. It swished past an inch away as Concho dodged a second time.

The woman was quick. She spun, slashed at him again. He caught her wrist with his left hand, bent it backward. Delores grunted but did not release the knife. Her other hand swept across, yanked the knife away. She lifted it to swing. Concho did the only thing he could think to do. He hit her in the chin with the heel of his hand. The jab was short and hard, with only a part of his strength behind it.

Delores grunted again. She wobbled on legs gone suddenly

weak. Concho slapped the knife out of her hand, sending it crashing to the floor. Holding both her wrists, he twisted them behind her and forced her against the massive oaken weight of the kitchen table. It held her still as he pulled his handcuffs and got them locked on her wrists.

She brought her heel up, trying to kick him between the legs but he blocked with a knee. He yanked her around and pushed her down into a chair. He stepped back. She glared up at him with black, hateful eyes. Her hair clip had come loose; the hair looked like a rat's nest around her head.

"It's over!" Concho snapped.

The woman's gaze cooled, then filled with despair. She leaned forward and laid her forehead on the cool oaken surface of the table.

"I'm sorry," she said, her voice muffled. "I shouldn't have attacked you. I just... I *can't* go to jail."

"You murdered someone," Concho said. "You took away Aggie's future. Whether it would have been a good one or a bad one, it wasn't yours to take."

Delores moaned. "I just wanted her to leave my son alone." She looked up. "If you had a child, you'd understand. What will George think? Or Manuel? Or everyone?"

Concho couldn't think of anything to say other than, "Delores Night-Run, you're under arrest for the murder of Agustina Cardenas. I'm going to inform you of your rights."

CHAPTER 45

Concho phoned Echabarri, who answered on the first ring.

"Been waiting to hear from you," Roberto said.

"Delores Night-Run killed Aggie Cardenas," Concho said. "She admitted it."

"Delores!" Echabarri exclaimed. "I…" He sighed.

"She wouldn't tell me what she did with the bodies. Probably put them in the desert. Where Whirlwind found them."

A long silence followed. "I wanted the crime solved. But this…"

"I know. Doesn't feel good.

Roberto sighed again. "So…what's next?"

"I'm taking her to Sheriff Isaac Parkland's office in Eagle Pass for the time being. Better to have her in jail there. You can release Manuel, let him go home. I have no idea what to tell him or George Night-Run."

"I'll…think of something," Echabarri said.

"All right. After I drop her off, I'm coming back to your office. I want to talk to Pete Whiteheart and the Garcia kids."

"Sure. But for what purpose?"

"I'm considering dropping the charges against them."

"What? No! They tried to kill you!"

"Pete ordered it but we'll never make that stick against him.

Cisco and Selena won't testify in court. They won't dare. Particularly now that we know he's the leader of the local NATV Bloods. There'll be other members we haven't identified and Selena is certainly smart enough to know they'll become targets themselves if they say a word against Pete. Plus, we can't hold Pete on suspicion of Aggie's murder anymore."

"He raped her," Echabarri said, spitting the words. "He's got to pay for that."

"He raped her," Concho agreed. "But we'll never be able to prove it eight years down the line without Aggie around to testify. Manuel... Even if he did testify against Pete. And who knows what the arrest of his mother will do to him. Well, it would be Manuel's word against Pete's. And Manuel admits he also had sex with Aggie. We'll never get a conviction."

"So, we just let him get away with it? Even if he didn't actually kill her, he and Alvarado set the whole thing in motion. They're the reason she's dead."

"Agreed. But we know who and what he is now. We'll be watching for a misstep that he can't escape. And, I think you're forgetting something."

"What's that?"

"Whirlwind. He heard Manuel's story just as I did. He knows exactly what Pete Whiteheart did to the girl he loved. Once I tell Pete about him, Pete might just *want* to stay in jail to avoid facing him."

Echabarri snorted mirthlessly. "Yeah, I see what you mean. OK, it's your call. If I'm already gone when you get here, you have your talk with the prisoners. Tell Nila what you want done with them. I'll let her know to follow your orders."

"Thanks. And good luck with the Council today. Sure you don't want me to show up?"

"No. Better not. I'll let you know as soon as I know what happens. Don't feel much like going now."

"I understand. But the world doesn't stop just because a life did."

"I guess not."

"Later," Concho said, swiping off his phone.

***

After depositing Delores Night-Run in the Maverick County jail under the care of Isaac Parkland, the county sheriff, Concho returned to the reservation. Roberto had already left for his meeting with the Tribal Council by the time Concho arrived. The Ranger went directly to the jail and walked in.

Three of the six cells were occupied. He'd never seen it this full before. Pete Whiteheart sat on a narrow cot in the first cell. The jail had no windows but a TV had been installed over the doorway and Pete sat staring at the screen.

Francisco Garcia lay on his bunk with his legs crossed at the ankles. He also stared toward the TV but didn't seem to be watching it. Selena Garcia sat cross-legged on the floor of her cell. She had her eyes closed as if meditating. She was the only one with a privacy screen around the toilet area of her cell.

All three Kickapoo looked up when Concho came in. He muted the TV, then stood staring at the man who'd tried to orchestrate his murder and the two teenagers who'd tried to carry it out. Pete rose to his feet and offered him a smirk; Selena's face was neutral; Cisco looked scared.

"I'm not going to press charges on any of you for trying to kill me," the Ranger said.

"Smart," Pete replied. "For so many reasons."

Concho took a few steps right up to the bars of Pete's cell. He offered the man his shark smile and Pete stepped back. The law officer glanced around to take in the two teenagers. Both had climbed to their own feet and looked like they wanted to flee. If there'd been anywhere for them to go.

"No," Concho said. "I want all three of you out in the open. Where I can find you alone."

Cisco's face blanched. He began to shake. Selena tried to control her expression but the whitening of her lips and a sudden sweat on her forehead made her fear palpable.

Concho focused his cold glance back on Pete Whiteheart. "And, for you, I'll give you an extra, friendly warning. You better keep an eye out for a man named Whirlwind. He's on the Rez and knows what you did to Aggie Cardenas."

"I don't know what or who you're talking about."

"Whirlwind worked for the Cardenas family eight years ago. You probably remember him. Big guy. Really big. Well, he's a lot scarier these days. He was in love with Aggie and he wants justice for what happened to her. He told me himself."

Pete tried to shrug but it came off like a twitch instead. "I still don't know what you're talking about."

Again, Concho smiled. "Hang around and find out," he said. "You'll all be released in a few minutes. I'll be here. On the Rez. I'm sure I'll be seeing you."

He clicked the sound back on the TV and walked out.

***

After telling Nila Willow to release the three prisoners in half an hour, Concho slid back into his truck and drove over to John Gray-Dove's shop. He promised John he'd soon return the four-wheeler he'd borrowed, then picked up his Ford with its three new tires and a little bodywork touch up.

It wasn't yet noon but he took a spin by the casino and saw Echabarri's white police SUV parked out front. The meeting of the Tribal Council would be starting soon. The parking lot was crowded and he figured his friend would have both support and detractors present. He hoped more of the former than the latter.

On the spur of the moment, he drove off the Rez and picked up a big bucket of Kentucky Fried Chicken, original recipe, along with mashed potatoes, gravy, and biscuits. He ate a little as soon as he got home, packed the rest in a small igloo cooler he had and loaded it on the back of the Honda Recon four-wheeler. In a paper sack, he rolled up a t-shirt that was oversized even on him, added sweatpants, a pair of socks, and a six-pack of soda.

By 12:30 PM, he was motoring across the spare landscape toward the bluff and overhang where he'd last seen Whirlwind. The man deserved closure on the story of Aggie Cardenas. And he deserved a decent meal and something to wear besides rags. The place looked quiet as he pulled up in front. Last night's fire had burned out and the ashes were already scattering on the incessant desert wind.

A mélange of tracks brought Concho to a halt as he climbed off the Recon. He noted the footprints of Whirlwind and Manuel, as well as his own. Overlaying these were numerous feral pig prints, including a deep set that were absolutely huge, bigger than any wild pig he'd ever seen. Bigger even than any domesticated one. The beast must have weighed a thousand pounds.

Concho frowned. He called out but got no response. The Honda ATV had a small tool kit and inside was a powerful Maglite flashlight. He pulled this out and approached the overhang with the light in his left hand and a .45 in his right.

Pausing at the entrance to the overhang, Concho called again. He didn't think it a good idea to surprise the big man. No response came, though. He ventured deeper, playing the light of the flashlight over everything. Soon, he came to the rear wall of the cave where he'd once found Meskwaa tied up.

The rocky ground revealed no footprints but something else had changed. Not only was Whirlwind gone but so were the meager possessions the man had collected here—the sleeping bag he'd taken from Concho himself and the few other items the Ranger had noticed his first time here.

It looked like Whirlwind had pulled up stakes and moved on. Concho should probably have guessed that would happen. The question was, had the wild man simply relocated to another site on the Rez? Or had he left the reservation entirely after Concho promised him justice for Aggie Cardenas?

The Ranger searched every corner of the overhang for clues to Whirlwind's whereabouts but only when he shone the light upward did he find something worth noting.

At the center of the overhang's roof, a narrow open chimney extended upward into the bluff. It stretched wide enough to hide someone small, although not anyone of Concho's or Whirlwind's bulk. A hide rope hung down that hole and suspended from it was a skull. It wasn't a human skull but the massive cranium of a wild boar with immense tusks.

The skull refracted the light as it rotated slowly on its rope. A sudden flash of purple sent Concho's heart skittering. He took an involuntary step backward before realizing what he was seeing. Someone had implanted cut and polished purple gemstones into the empty eye sockets of the great beast—amethysts the size of a baby's fist.

Hanging from the same leather strap, stretching across the back of the skull and down, was the hide of a boar—likely from the same animal as the head. It was immense and thick, with white curly hair so spikey as to resemble porcupine spines.

Another albino, Concho thought, maybe the sire of the one whose hide he'd used to make his shield.

Everything else Whirlwind had kept beneath the overhang had been taken. Only the skull and hide remained. Why had they been left? Did the man plan to come back for them? Concho didn't think so. He thought, instead, they'd been left deliberately, either because Whirlwind was through with them, or because he wanted and expected Concho to find them. And know!

Drawing his hunting knife from his belt sheath, he reached up and cut the leather strap, dropping the skull and hide into his arms. He carried them outside the overhang to inspect in the sunlight.

The hide contained leather clasps at one end, meaning it could be worn like a cape. The skull had been hollowed out almost entirely and would fit over the top of a human head so human eyes could peer out through the fully articulated jaws.

Concho chewed his lower lip as he examined his finds. He wondered if Meskwaa had seen these as a captive here. Surely the old shaman would have told him. Unless he'd felt it important not to.

The Ranger decided to take the hide and skull with him. He'd show Meskwaa. He'd ask him about them. He had an idea what his friend, the Naataineniiha, would say. He said it himself: "Skinwalker!"

CHAPTER 46

As Concho drove the four-wheeler toward home, he considered the implications of his find—the boar hide and skull. The Skinwalker was a Navajo legend, not Kickapoo, but many Native American populations held similar concepts, including his own people.

For some Navajos, the "yee naaldlooshii" was a witch who could possess animals or even take on their forms, often by covering themselves with the hide of the animal they wanted to become. Even more power came to a witch who wore the skull of a beast.

Such witches might work evil while in animal form. They might kill. Or they might cause less deadly mischief. Concho could not help but think of the missing animals reported across the Rez recently and of the torn-up fences and gardens. The Night-Runs, Whitehearts, and Garcias had been targeted for much of that. The witch *always* has a target for his or her magic. Had Whirlwind been responsible for the turmoil? Surely he'd caused some of it.

Perhaps it was telling that Whirlwind seemed likely to be from a southwestern tribe. Navajo perhaps. Or some related group such as Hopi, Ute, or Apache. He might well have grown up with the legends of Skinwalkers. And if he'd grown up with such legends, he might be able to imitate them.

Concho's rational mind told him there could be no such beings as true Skinwalkers. Yet, he shivered a little as he remembered such things as a knock on his door late one night with no one there or Bearfoot's fearful report of the "not a person" who'd followed him the same night, or the thing with purple eyes he and others had seen more than once. Such things had often been reported of Skinwalkers, although the eyes were usually said to be red.

As the thoughts worked in him, Concho found himself glad for the sunlight, although afternoon shadows grew long. Soon, he was pleased to see home looming ahead of him. He rode the Honda ATV through the shallow part of the arroyo a hundred yards down from his trailer, then pulled into his yard.

Everything seemed normal here. The breeze whispered through the mesquite and juniper. Birds sang and chirped as they hunted berries and bugs. The susurration of the dry grasses in his yard comforted him. As he climbed off the four-wheeler, his phone rang. When he saw the name of the caller the last of his anxieties and strange thoughts peeled away. He swiped the phone on.

"Hello, Beautiful," he said.

"Lover!" Maria Morales replied, in the voice that sent a very different kind of shiver through the Ranger's body. "I'm a couple of hours from home. I want to see you and you better not make any excuses."

"Not even if the world were ending."

"That's what a girl likes to hear," Maria said. "I'll call again when I'm home."

"I'll be here."

Maria hung up. Concho stared at his phone for a moment before tucking it into his pocket with a smile. He carried the food he'd not been able to give Whirlwind back into the house and took it out of the cooler to place in his refrigerator. Back outside, he loaded the boar skull and hide into his Ford and was about to put his shield back as well when he heard the sound of an approaching vehicle.

He watched, curiously and cautiously, as a state police car pulled into his driveway and parked a dozen feet away. A man wearing the hat of a Texas Highway Patrolman climbed out of the car on the side away from the Ranger. Concho glimpsed blond hair, and as the man turned toward him he recognized him—Gage Herrington.

He'd interacted with Herrington before and found him a competent officer, though strangely off-putting in his ways. Concho couldn't say he really liked the man, though he couldn't name any specific reason.

Herrington had parked where the setting sun lay behind him. The glare shone into the Ranger's eyes. The officer raised his hand in a wave. "Ten-Wolves!" he called. "Glad I caught you."

"What's up?" Concho asked, squinting against the light.

Herrington strode around the front of his car and stopped about ten feet away. The Ranger stared. A frown started to crease his face. Herrington wore a gun belt and tied-down gun in a western-style holster.

Concho realized what was about to happen as his heart suddenly thundered. Herrington drew his pistol in a silver-blue flash. Concho flung his shield toward the police officer and dropped his hand for his own gun a fraction of a second after. Something like a jackhammer struck him in the left side, about halfway between shoulder and waist. He heard the hollow boom of the shot.

The shield hit Herrington's shooting arm just as the man fired again. The bullet hummed past Concho's ear and cut a sharp burning slice along the top of his shoulder. And now Concho fired, double actioning his pistol. The slam of the .45 bucked against his hand.

The first bullet struck Herrington's center of mass, knocked him a step backward. He fired twice more. Both bullets hit Herrington hard in the lower chest. The officer's eyes flared wide. He tried to straighten his arm to aim. His arm and the pistol in his hand shook.

Concho took deliberate aim, fired one more time. A dark hole appeared in Herrington's forehead just under the brim of his hat. The man's head jerked back and he fell, the hat flying off, the pistol rolling from his fingers.

Concho became aware of his own gasps for breath. He couldn't get enough oxygen. His left leg trembled, then failed him. He collapsed to both knees. A groan tore its way out of his throat.

Ten-Wolves tried to holster his Colt and missed. The gun dropped from his fingers. His whole left side felt on fire. He thrust his right hand into the pocket of his jeans and yanked out his cell phone. He swiped it on. His eyes were blurry. His head pulsed with pain. He found the number for the Kickapoo police and hit send.

Nila Willow answered.

"Officer down," Concho said as he fell sideways into the dirt and lost himself to darkness.

CHAPTER 47

Concho knew exactly where he was when he awoke. The off-white walls, the diffuse but somehow antiseptic lighting, the hushed voices mixed with beeping machinery, and the smells—isopropyl alcohol, electronics, powdered milk and eggs, and old, ingrained body odors told him he was in the hospital.

He was grateful for it. Gage Herrington's bullet had hit him hard. He'd been afraid it nicked an artery and he would bleed out. As he'd lost consciousness, he'd wondered if he'd wake at all. It seemed he'd been lucky. Again. This even looked like the same room he'd been in a few months previously after taking a knife in the back.

"Congratulations on your return to the land of the living," a voice said from his right.

The Ranger twisted his head slowly to see the speaker. Roberto Echabarri sat in a multicolored cloth chair against the wall. Next to him sat Special Agent Della Rice. Both got to their feet and walked over to the bed.

"How you feeling?" Roberto asked.

Even to Concho, his voice sounded like his mouth and throat were filled with sand as he said, "Like a stick of gum that's been chewed, spit out, and run over by a tanker truck."

"Colorful as always," Della Rice remarked.

Roberto winced at Ten-Wolves' voice and quickly picked up a plastic cup of ice and water from a nearby tray table. He stuck a plastic straw in it, then raised the head of the bed and held the cup as Concho drank long enough to drain the liquid, leaving only the rattle of ice behind.

"Thanks," he said, with his voice sounding a little more normal. He glanced down at his body to see that most of his chest, especially the left side, was covered with thick bandages. "So, what's the story?" he asked.

"Maybe the doctor—" Roberto started.

"You know wounds," Concho interrupted. "Tell me."

Roberto nodded. "Well, the bullet entered your left side under the sternum. It did a fair amount of damage and triggered some heavy bleeding. But it didn't get an artery. You were in surgery for about four hours as they removed the bullet and repaired the damage. They said you should be OK."

"Should?"

"That's what they said. Knowing your recuperative powers, though, I figure you'll be fine. Agent Rice and I have a bet as to how long it'll be before you climb out of this bed."

"What kind of time frame you looking at?"

Roberto smiled. "Can't tell you. It might bias the outcome."

Concho started to nod, thought better of it. "I'm not hurting too badly but I guess that's the pain meds."

"Probably."

"What happened at the Council meeting?" Concho asked.

"A vote of no confidence. It ended 3 to 2."

"I hope you got the three?"

Roberto gave him a thumbs up. "Melissa Nolan cast the deciding vote."

"Good." Concho turned his gaze toward Della Rice. "Why are you here?"

Rice arched one brow over a dark eye. "Maybe I just came

to check on you."

"And?"

Rice shook her head and made a face. "The man you shot. Gage Herrington. We're pretty sure he was the 'informant' telling us bad things about you. He appears to have gone under the name 'Scout' in local criminal circles. Seems he had an agenda. As you suggested. We're digging into him now but it looks like he had connections to the Aryan Brotherhood, who certainly aren't your biggest fans."

"I think I'm growing on 'em. May take a while."

"You think there'll be any of them left by that time?" Rice asked with a mixed smirk and smile curving her lips.

"Who's counting?"

"Anyway," Rice said, "I did want to check on you. Since you're OK, I'll head out. Call me when you're feeling better. We still may have to work together."

"I appreciate the warning."

As Rice left, Concho glanced at Roberto. "What other news?" he asked.

Roberto shook his head with the twist of a smile on his lips. "I don't know what you said to our three prisoners but you put the fear of Concho into them. The Garcia kids. Selena and Francisco. Their parents announced they're both going to Mexico for a year. Spend some time with their relatives below the border."

"And Whiteheart?"

"Pete Whiteheart and his wife moved back home to his father's place. Sounds like they may be hiring a security force. According to rumors, it's because of the damage someone did to their fields recently."

"Naturally. What about George and Manuel Night-Run?"

Roberto sobered. "George is devastated. I think he's at a complete loss as to what to do without Delores to tell him. Manuel, though, seems actually to have risen to the occasion. Maybe it's the need to take care of his father. He's handling it better than George."

Concho let out a shallow breath. "Two families destroyed," he said. "No winners in the story of Aggie Cardenas."

"Nope."

A knock sounded on the hospital room's door. Earl Blake, the county coroner, poked his head in.

"Hey," Roberto said with surprise. "Come in."

Blake warped his way into the room. He shook hands with Roberto and held up his palm to acknowledge Concho. "Don't get up," he said.

Concho smiled. "Thanks for dropping by."

Blake nodded. "Well, I heard about your...incident, and wanted to check on you. But I had something I wanted to ask you about too. Something that's got me curious."

"Oh?"

Blake frowned. "That last sample you brought me. The plastic water bottle with the spit in the bottom. You wanted me to type the DNA."

"Yeah, what about it?" Concho asked.

"You sure the sample came from a...person?"

Concho frowned while Roberto looked on curiously. "It was in a bottle someone had been drinking from," he replied. "Why?"

Blake worked his mouth around as he sought for words. "Uh... weird. I extracted a sample from the bottle, but when I ran it... Well, it showed some human DNA. And something else. Something...animal like. Then the whole sample just disintegrated as I started to run further tests. I've never seen a sample act like that before. You have any potential explanation?"

A chill pulled at stitches and bandages all over the Ranger's body. He cleared his throat before speaking. Both Roberto and Blake stared at him, Roberto with confused curiosity, Blake with something more.

"It came from a man named Whirlwind," Concho said. "He wasn't in good health so maybe that's part of it. He also had a wolf-dog. Could be he let the dog drink from the bottle? And, maybe the sample was just old."

Blake made a face. He reached up and scratched at a spot below his left eye. His mouth worked as if he were going to protest Concho's statement but then he just shook his head.

"Suppose that could be," he said. "Anyway, you look like you're gonna be all right."

"Seems like it. Could be, I'll be bringing you more strange samples down the line."

"Lord forbid," Blake said. He chuckled.

After a few more minutes of visiting, Earl Blake and Roberto left for other work. Concho remained in the bed, alone. His thoughts bothered him. He thought of Aggie Cardenas. Could there be any meaning to the tragedy surrounding her brief life, and that which had followed after her death? If so, he couldn't find it just now.

He also thought of a man named Whirlwind, and of magic both dark and light. And then Maria Morales walked through the door of his room and everything became light.

A LOOK AT:
AVENGING ANGELS:
VENGEANCE TRAIL

SADDLE UP FOR A HEART-POUNDING, BULLET-BURN-ING, BIBLE-THUMPING WESTERN SERIES LIKE NONE YOU'VE EVER READ BEFORE!

Reno Bass and his sister Sara are young, blond, blue-eyed twins from western Kansas. Raised right in a good Christian family, they're pure as the driven snow. But when their family is massacred, they ride the Vengeance Trail to fulfill their father's dying request—to purge the earth of the Devil's spawn in the name of God.

In the first book of this shocking new series, Reno and Sara's farm is burned and their family murdered by a group of ex-Confederate soldiers known as the Devil's Horde. These ex-Confederates—led by Major Eustace The Bad Old Man Montgomery and Major Black Bob Robert Hobbs—have a chip on their shoulders, and they're burning a broad swath across the Yankee north, murdering, pillaging, and raping their way to the Colorado Territory.

But when they burn the Bass farm, they find out not every follower of God is a sheep. Sworn to vengeance, Reno and Sara become black-winged avenging angels on a mission from God. Hounding the Confederate devils' every step, these black-winged angels begin efficiently and bloodily killing them—one by one and two by two—reading to them from the Good Book while sending them back to Hell.

AVAILABLE NOW

ABOUT THE AUTHOR

Charles Gramlich lives amid the piney woods of southern Louisiana and is the author of the Talera fantasy series, the SF novel Under the Ember Star, and the thriller Cold in the Light. His work has appeared in magazines such as Star*Line, Beat to a Pulp, Night to Dawn, Pedestal Magazine, and others. Many of his stories have been collected in the anthologies, Bitter Steel, (fantasy), Midnight in Rosary (Vampires/Werewolves), and In the Language of Scorpions (Horror). Charles also writes westerns under the name Tyler Boone. Although he writes in many different genres, all of his fiction work is known for its intense action and strong visuals.